THE MIDDLING AFFLICTION

THE MIDDLING AFFLICTION

THE CONRADVERSE CHRONICLES

ALEX SHVARTSMAN

CAEZIK
SF & FANTASY
ARC MANOR
ROCKVILLE, MARYLAND

✳

SHAHID MAHMUD
PUBLISHER

www.CaezikSF.com

Cover art by Túlio Brito.

ISBN: 978-1-64710-054-4

First Edition. 1st Printing, May 2022.
1 2 3 4 5 6 7 8 9 10

An imprint of Arc Manor LLC

www.CaezikSF.com

CHAPTER 1

MY job that morning was to banish a demon, but I was determined to finish my cup of coffee first.

I sipped my java in front of Demetrios's warehouse in Sunset Park, enjoying the panoramic view of the Manhattan skyline and New York harbor. I stared at the Statue of Liberty, which appeared the size and shade of a toy soldier at this distance. A warm breeze caressed my face. Next to me, Demetrios was shaking like a leaf.

"What in the world are you thinking, Conrad?" Demetrios spoke in his typical rapid-fire fashion. "You're just going to go in there, alone, to face this infernal thing? Without any help or backup from others at the Watch? Without even a priest? This is all kinds of crazy."

"I can handle it," I said, projecting casual confidence. "You did ask for this to be resolved quickly, and it's not like I haven't dealt with an occasional demon before."

In fact, I'd never even seen any demons. I was not in any way whatsoever equipped to deal with a supernatural being of that magnitude. That was the bad news. The good news was, in my two decades with the Watch, I'd never once heard of a demon showing up in Brooklyn. Even if one arrived, it wouldn't be slumming it in

1

Demetrios's warehouse. And if, by some miracle, a major baddie from Down Below decided to take up residence there, Demetrios wouldn't have survived the encounter long enough to come crying for my help. Something else was going on, but if the guy with the thick checkbook expected the job to be extremely dangerous, who was I to dissuade him?

"Quickly, yes," said Demetrios. "You wouldn't believe how far this has put us behind on deliveries. My customers are screaming bloody murder. On top of everything, there's a shipment of Sumatran persimmons that is already beginning to rot. I hope you really know what you're doing. I don't relish the thought of having to scrape what's left of you off the container walls."

"That's the Demetrios I know and love. Sentimental to the end. Here, hold this." I handed him the empty foam cup and headed for the entrance.

The warehouse was packed with every kind of package and crate imaginable. The huge metal shipping containers were clustered in the center, with just enough room left to maneuver them in and out. Around the edges, mountains of smaller parcels occupied every available nook and cranny, arranged in an order apparent only to Demetrios and his staff.

I primarily knew Demetrios as a wholesale trader in magical goods, but that was only a fraction of his business. Metal racks in his warehouse were crammed with imports, everything from Ecuadorian melons to Taiwanese vacuum cleaners. The place looked like the world's most overstocked Costco. There were plenty of nooks for whatever was haunting the building to hide in.

I walked past a tower of knockoff toys destined for dollar-store shelves. Boxes labeled *Tackle Me Emo* and *Hangry Hangry Hipsters* stretched toward the warehouse ceiling atop the sturdy foundation of cases of Poke-a-Moon cards. A pungent odor of rotting fruit wafted through the aisles.

Since I hadn't known what sort of trouble to expect, I'd brought as many weapons, charms, and amulets as I could carry without making my reliance on such tools apparent. I've made a lot more enemies than friends over the years, and having any of them learn that I was powerless without my trinkets would be incredibly dangerous.

Only one out of every thirty thousand people is born gifted. Those lucky few can perceive auras, recognize supernatural beings for what they are, cast spells, and imbue their magic into artifacts by enchanting physical items the way batteries store electricity. I could perceive perfectly; casting was another story. I could use stored magic as well as any gifted but could never recharge the metaphysical battery of even the simplest of charms. In a secret world filled with superheroes and supervillains, I was the magical Batman: a grumpy and possibly somewhat unhinged vigilante with no special powers, who relied on his gadgets to keep up with the super-Joneses. Except I didn't have Batman's riches, or a mansion, or even a butler. Them's the breaks.

Not even my superiors at the Watch knew about my disability. They wouldn't have kept me around—possibly with extreme preju-dice—if they'd ever found out. So, I pretended to be a badass wizard and did my job well, giving no one cause to think otherwise. One day I hoped to find a cure for my condition. Or, failing that, a damn good explanation for it.

I worked my way through the labyrinth of packages until I heard faint growling sounds emanating from a few aisles over. I unholstered a revolver that was loaded with silver bullets doused in holy water. Cliché, I know, but in my experience only the most effective solutions get to become clichés in the first place. Weapon drawn, I advanced slowly toward the noise. I turned the corner of a ceiling-high shelving unit stocked with waffle makers and found myself face to face with a Lovecraftian nightmare.

The creature resembled a ten-foot-tall bulldog with several rows of jagged teeth protruding from its oversized mouth. It stared at me with cold fish eyes and emitted a low rumble from deep within its ugly-as-sin belly. I breathed a sigh of relief as I studied the telltale shimmer barely visible around the critter's frame. Definitely not a demon.

"Nice doggie," I told it as I holstered the gun and rummaged through the inner pockets of my trench coat. Moving very slowly so as not to spook it, I withdrew a plastic pill bottle filled with orange powder.

"Cujo wants a treat?" I asked in a soothing voice as I struggled momentarily with the childproof cover.

Visibly annoyed with my apparent lack of desire to run away terrified, the critter let out a thunderous roar that, I hoped, Demetrios could hear outside. While it was busy posturing, I took a pair of quick steps forward and flung the contents of the pill bottle, aiming for its midsection.

The monstrous visage quivered, gradually losing its shape, and blinked out. At my feet lay a furry little animal that looked like an ugly koala bear. It was knocked out cold by the sleeping powder. The Sumatran changeling snoring on the ground before me was a harmless creature. Its species projects images of big, scary monsters in order to repel predators, but they're all bark and no bite. Poor thing must've gotten into the persimmon shipment and munched the long journey away, happy in the container full of its favorite snacks. The potent orange mix would keep the changeling dormant until I could get it to a buddy of mine at the Bronx Zoo who cared for a menagerie of supernatural animals.

I checked the rest of the building to make sure there were no more changelings. Also, just to be nosy. Demetrios's shipping company handled arcane imports from all over the globe, and I was always curious to know what he was up to, even if I had to search past pallets of slow cookers and shelves filled with auto parts to find anything noteworthy. After a sufficient amount of time spent wandering the aisles, I took off my trench coat and wrapped it gently around the changeling. Carrying the bundle under my arm, I exited the warehouse.

"That was one nasty hellspawn." I smiled at Demetrios, who was pacing nervously outside. "See, it even made me break a sweat."

"Is the demon gone now? Did you banish it?" he demanded.

"It will not be bothering you again," I said with utmost confidence.

Magical items don't come cheap, and given my unique situation I burned through them faster than an average teenage girl used up her cell phone battery. Demetrios would pay me handsomely for the morning's work, and all it cost me was a vial of sleeping powder. What's more, he would tell anyone who cared to listen about how I went one-on-one with a demon and won. So grows the legend of Conrad Brent.

I glanced at the check he handed me and frowned. "You seem to have left off a zero."

With the infernal threat gone, Demetrios was quickly recovering his wits. "It's what I've always paid you," he said. Was that a note of annoyance I detected in his voice?

"Some jobs are easier than others," I said. "And while you can't put a price tag on a quality exorcism, you should at least *try*. Because, believe me, you don't want to be calling your exterminator next time you find yourself in this sort of a predicament."

I'm not a greedy man, but money is a useful resource, and you wouldn't believe what some people charge for top-grade arcane artifacts. Haggling over the bill was yet another problem Batman didn't have to deal with.

Demetrios crossed his arms. "You're getting more than most people earn in a month."

Sensing a losing battle, I changed tactics. "I'm just as happy to be paid the balance in information. You hear all sorts of things that might be of interest to the Watch."

His wallet safe for the moment, Demetrios relaxed. He scratched his chin, pretending to think, even though we both knew he could rattle off a dozen factoids about the illicit goings-on around the city if he wanted to.

"The Kwan brothers are back in town," he said. "They're trying to offload a shipment of cursed coins—"

"Yes, my associates in Manhattan are already on it," I said. Inability to tell a demon from a changeling aside, Demetrios was no fool. The Kwans were his competitors—sort of, they weren't really in the same league—and having the Watch take them out would benefit him. "Tell me something I don't already know."

"There's a new high-end fortuneteller in Williamsburg," said Demetrios. "Bilking the mundanes and making waves. I can track down his name and address—"

I waved him off again. "If the only thing getting hurt is their bank account, I don't really care."

The Watch has one very specific mandate: to protect the mundanes. Any conflict between magic users, no matter how bloody, is outside our purview, which is perhaps a good thing given our limited numbers. We focus on defending the most vulnerable. Vampires treating the New York City subway system as their personal cafeteria?

Werewolves in Central Park? Wizards using mind control to entice baseball fans to root for the Mets? We come down on them like a ton of supernatural bricks. But we don't care about tarot readers.

Demetrios thought for a moment before offering up another tidbit. "The Traveling Fair is coming to Queens next Friday."

Now *that* was interesting. The Traveling Fair was an exclusive auction house, sort of a magical Sotheby's. They dealt in upscale arcane items and weren't too particular about how dangerous their wares might be or whose hands they would end up in, so long as the buyer could afford the tab. They set up private pop-up events in places like New York, Paris, London, and Tokyo. Attendance was strictly by invitation, and only the invited bidders knew where and when the auction would take place. That helped with security, and to keep the unwashed masses away. Frankly, I was surprised someone like Demetrios knew about it. He must've been on the lowest rung of the invitees and, even so, doing better financially than I had suspected. And yet he had the temerity to argue over my payment!

"What sort of outrageously overpriced crap is on offer this time?"

Demetrios fished out a folded postcard from his wallet.

The card was printed on fancy, thick stock and embroidered with the logo of the Traveling Fair. It was the crest of a minor Romanian baron, hinting at the Fair's humble origins two centuries ago.

"Let's see." Demetrios squinted at the cursive font. "They've got a da Vinci manuscript outlining his views on arcane weather manipulation, an Etruscan ring of invisibility, and a mudlark."

I was so stunned I nearly dropped the changeling I still held bundled in my trench coat. "A *what*lark?"

"Oh, I'm sorry. That's the term they used, but mudlarks are known by many other names, such as middlings or voids. It's a person who can perceive magic but is impotent to create it."

Of course, I knew what he was talking about. I *was* what he was talking about. A middling. A mudlark. A scavenger. There was a plethora of terms for a person like me—none of them flattering. But I'd never met another, nor knew of another who was alive. As best I could tell, while the gifted appeared roughly once among every thirty thousand humans, the odds of a middling were well north of one in a million. And the smart ones were hiding.

I couldn't express any of those things, so instead I just said, "Jesus, why would anyone want to buy a middling?"

"They're anathema to many of the traditionalist groups," Demetrios said, looking at me like I was an infant who needed really simple things explained to him—slowly. "Some will pay good money for a chance to kill a middling."

No kidding. There were cults and covens and secret societies whose members would be all over something like that. The Salem witch trials had been all about finding and exterminating a single middling who was rumored to be hiding in that insignificant little town. As far as I know, there had been no actual middling. They did manage to hang several real witches, though.

It wasn't just the crazy cultists. Superstition against the middlings ran deep within the gifted society. The Watch wouldn't protect them as they weren't considered mundane, despite their lack of innate ability. Early in my career I had spent sleepless nights trying to figure out who among my colleagues might try to kill me if they ever learned the truth.

I was showing too much interest in the subject and needed to backpedal. "I suppose there are people rich and eccentric enough to throw money away on all kinds of nonsense. The ring of invisibility though, that's something I could actually use."

"You don't seriously think you could afford the winning bid on it, do you, Conrad?"

I looked him in the eye. "Perhaps if you paid me a fair wage for demon slaying I could."

That deflated Demetrios pretty good.

"Tell you what," I said. "Hand over the invitation and we'll call it even. I may not be able to afford the ring, but I'd enjoy window-shopping. And rubbing shoulders with all sorts of interesting people. Could make a load of useful connections, meet clients willing to pay top dollar for my services."

For all its power and influence, the Watch was a volunteer organization. It was more a neighborhood watch, as the name implied, than a police department. Its members had to earn their own living, which meant getting people like Demetrios to pony up the cash for services rendered. But I was also expected—and quite willing—to hunt monsters and bust ghosts pro bono when necessary. As such, my excuse for wanting to attend the Traveling Fair should have sounded reasonable. When Demetrios hesitated I added, "Come on. It's not like *you* are going to bid on any of those things."

He sighed theatrically and handed over the invitation. I said my goodbyes and deposited the changeling onto the back seat of my car. At some point I'd have to drive it to the Bronx, and then figure out how to rescue a fellow middling from a bunch of bloodthirsty fat cats. But all of that would have to wait. I had a packed schedule, and my day was only starting.

I was going to need a lot more coffee.

CHAPTER 2

ONE by one, I set off car alarms.

I walked along the curb and methodically gave each parked car a gentle kick, just hard enough to trigger the siren. Behind me, a dozen violated vehicles blared out of tune. I wanted nothing more than to focus my efforts on figuring out how to help the captive middling, and what revelations into my condition I might glean from them. But I had my job to do, and I was saddled with babysitting a recent recruit, so I did my best to push those thoughts out of my mind for the moment.

The prospect hung back, sullen and quiet. He was having a tough week, and my erratic behavior wasn't helping his mood any. Applicants to the Watch had to work hard as they learned on the job, apprenticed to the guardian assigned to protect a specific area. In New York City, there were five of us, one for each borough. Each prospect had to survive a grueling boot camp of learning magical combat, and I wasn't the kindest or most patient of teachers. Only a few lasted all the way through the training to join the Watch and earn themselves a name.

With each siren adding its voice to the cacophony the prospect got a little twitchier. To his credit, he hadn't cut and run. Yet.

This prospect was a lean, muscular dude of average height in his early thirties. His black hair was slicked back with gel and a carefully cultivated six o'clock shadow covered his strong chin. He wore a brand-new trench coat out of season—because I did—and he must've figured this was the Watch dress code. That, or he was going for the whole imitation-is-the-sincerest-form-of-flattery thing.

"Philippine energy beetles are nasty critters," I lectured him as we walked, straining to be heard over the noise. "They nest by the power lines and feed off the electricity. Those flickering lights the power company says are caused by faulty wiring are frequently a sign of an infestation."

Having finished with the cars, I fumbled with the lock on the front door of a vacant house.

"This place is lousy with beetles," I explained. "We're going to have to fumigate."

"That's just great," said the prospect. "I can't stand bugs. Now you tell me the Watch is in the exterminator business? This couldn't possibly get any worse."

But, of course, it could. He hadn't seen the beetles up close yet. The prospect's problem with insects was part of the reason I had brought him to this place. I needed to know he'd be able to handle himself when push came to shove. I needed him to overcome whatever phobias and preconceived notions he'd been living with before he learned about any of the really bad things out there. And with the Traveling Fair auction nine days away, I needed him to learn about them soon.

"Relax," I told him. "There's *some* good news. These critters hate loud noise."

The lock finally surrendered to my ministrations. As soon as I cracked the door open, hundreds of fully grown beetles surged out of the house. A mass of bugs scampered over each other and jostled us on their way out. Some stampeded over my feet. Their passing legs felt like being scraped with dried tree branches. Each beetle was two to three feet long and stood about a foot tall. The swarm rushed past us and toward the sewer as the poor things tried to get as far away from the roar of the sirens coming from the opposite side of the street as they could. The prospect turned white as a sheet, but he still didn't run. This one might be a keeper.

"They are …" The prospect gulped. "Enormous."

"This is New York," I told him. "We don't sweat the small stuff. You should see the size of the troll who lives under the Verrazano Bridge. Follow me." I took a careful step inside.

"Shouldn't we go after them?" the prospect called after me. "That brood will infest half of Brooklyn."

"The beetles we've scared off can't reproduce on their own and won't last a week outside the nest," I said while examining the foyer. "The root of the problem is in here." The house was a mess, foul smelling and covered with greenish goo. Dozens of semitranslucent eggs, each the size of a golf ball, hung from the walls and ceiling in batches like ornaments, cradled in the slime. If you squinted, you could see the larva gestating inside.

"Do we crack them open?" asked the prospect.

"No need," I replied. "I've come prepared." I pulled a small antique lantern out of my backpack and lit the candle inside with a Zippo lighter. The special candle, blessed by the Panchen Lama, activated the lantern's magic. Wherever its light shone, the eggs shriveled with a hiss and died, as though they'd been doused in DDT.

We made our way through the house, using the lantern to illuminate every corner and nook. The queen would not have abandoned the nest as easily as the other beetles, so I trod very carefully.

There was an ominous noise coming from upstairs, akin to the scraping of claws against a chalkboard. We followed the sound to the second floor. The scraping ceased; the queen must've sensed our approach.

The prospect opened the door to one of the bedrooms and there she was—three times larger than the drones we'd chased off—guarding a pile of eggs at the back of the room. The queen perched on one of the walls, near the ceiling. It turned toward us, trilled in warning, and opened its veiny, yellowish wings, each with the span longer than my arm. The stench of eggs and bug excrement blown toward us by the undulating wings stung my eyes.

"Blast her," I told the prospect.

Frazzled by the sight of the huge bug, the prospect mumbled the incantation, getting half of it wrong. Instead of a powerful blast of energy, he only managed to unleash a spray of flames that sizzled in the general direction of the queen like a faulty sparkler firework. The oversized insect charged and the prospect stumbled back, desperately trying to cast another spell. With the queen almost upon him, he managed to erect a force shield. The queen bounced off it as though the energy barrier were bulletproof glass. She was momentarily stunned by the force of the collision.

The prospect began another spell, fighting hard to keep his concentration as the queen recovered her bearings and scraped against his weakening shield. Casting several combat spells in a row isn't easy, even for an experienced gifted, let alone a rookie. The prospect's fear of insects inspired him to dig extra deep within his energy reserves. With a belligerent bug inches away and held off only by a thin, invisible barrier, the prospect spoke the words of power in a trembling voice. It was close, but he managed to finish the incantation before the shield collapsed. The queen was enveloped in an intense ball of fire for several seconds. The blaze cast bright orange shadows onto the slime-covered walls and a wave of intense heat washed over us. When the flames disappeared, all that remained was a charred chitinous shell.

The prospect was practically hyperventilating. "I could have used some help," he said.

"You have to rely on your own magic," I told him. "You wouldn't have been in trouble if you hadn't screwed up the energy bolt. Avoid the distractions and concentrate on your spells, just like you were taught. Do better next time."

I walked past him into the room and used the lantern to take care of the last batch of eggs. The prospect took another look at the singed bug remains on the floor and threw up.

Once outside, I took a moment to enjoy a few breaths of fresh air, then set about marking the house. Using chalk, I drew an arcane symbol on the brick wall. It was an abstract representation that vaguely resembled an iris set within a double eyelid. This symbol was called the Sigil of the Effulgent Eye and it was the official emblem of the Watch. A minor warding spell in its own right, the sigil served as a warning for other magic users to keep away from the marked structure. It was also an identifying mark for the Watch cleaning crew who would eventually be along to tidy up the place and make it appear as if nothing out of the ordinary had occurred here.

The sigil's symbolism was meant to imply that the Watch was keeping its ever-vigilant eye on threats with and without auras—hence the bonus eyelid—or something along those lines. When I was relatively new, an aging Watch desk jockey had once cornered me at the coffeemaker and expounded upon this for a greater period of time than I would've liked. I finally escaped once I held up my index finger and declared, "Ah! It means we are effulgent-eyed and bushy-tailed." The old-timer hadn't spoken to me for weeks after that, which had been a nice bonus.

I finished drawing the sigil, took a step back and admired my handiwork. Personally, I thought our predecessor had chosen this emblem because it looked cool.

I'd first met this prospect several weeks earlier, when I sprung him from a loony bin.

This wasn't unusual, as such things went. When people first begin to perceive auras and magic, their mind desperately wants to reject the truth, to pretend that the world is still safe and normal. They convince themselves, or those around them, that they're losing their marbles. Some try to drown out their newfound sight with liquor or pills. A few get themselves committed. They don't typically go so far as to burn their house down.

Back when the prospect went by a different name—real names carry power, so for the sake of anonymity let's call him George—his sight awakened, slowly. George began to notice things; things that mundanes were blissfully unaware of, such as some individuals having auras and other people not actually being people at all. Mostly he noticed a particularly nasty ghost that had been haunting his house since the early fifties.

The ghost had been more surprised by this development than the prospect. You would think the old spook might have appreciated finally having someone to talk to. Being stuck in that house for over half a century with no one but the cats even remotely aware of his existence couldn't have been fun. Instead, the ghost unleashed decades of pent-up frustration and anger on poor George. With each passing day George's sight became clearer, and the ghost's cursing and swearing louder. The ghost followed him around the house, wailing, nagging, and shouting abuse the entire time. It got so bad, George could no longer remain in his own home.

He went through the usual stages: denial, self-medication, and trying to share what he could perceive with the world. He even called for a priest to perform an exorcism, but the priest who came over wasn't gifted and couldn't banish what he couldn't perceive. Eventually, George had had enough. He'd bought a canister of gasoline, poured it all over his parquet floors, and set the house on fire.

Lucky for George, he'd been seeing a shrink, and his claims of ghosts and otherworldly creatures had been duly documented. Because of this, when the cops and firefighters sorted things out, he got sent to the nuthouse instead of prison.

The head physician at Bellevue's mental ward owed the Watch a few favors, and he knew to call us any time someone like George turned up. My Manhattan colleagues checked and confirmed that George had the sight. It's easy to tell a gifted apart from the other people because the gifted have a shimmering aura clearly visible around them. And no, their karma does not color the aura, or any of that new age crap. A person either has an aura or they do not.

My colleagues also realized that George's gifts were considerable; with proper training he could become quite powerful indeed. The Watch could always use someone like that.

After a couple of weeks, it was easy as pie for the head physician to declare George no longer a danger to himself or others, and release him into our custody. Everyone at the Watch took turns training newbies, and it was a duty I truly despised. Teaching requires patience, which has never been my forte. More importantly, it's extra difficult maintaining my secret when I'm trying to teach someone spells and incantations I cannot execute on my own. I did the best I could to pass each recruit off to another member of the Watch as early as feasible without making it seem suspicious.

I'd swaggered into George's hospital room like I owned the place. I've learned how to make a good entrance over the years. Perception is usually as important as reality, and it's crucial to immediately establish who's in charge.

"I've got good news and bad news," I told George in lieu of a greeting. "The good news is you aren't crazy. The doctor said so, so it must be true. You can pack your toothbrush and get out of here whenever you please."

George gaped at me, trying to puzzle out whether I was legit or just a fellow patient.

"The bad news? That ghost was real. So are all the other weird things you've been noticing out of the corner of your eye. You can see them now, but more importantly—they can see you."

I told him about the real world—beings and monsters that only a small fraction of people can perceive. A world the rest of humanity catches glimpses of through fairy tales and scary campfire stories. Not a nice place at all.

I explained about the Watch—a group of gifted who do their best to protect humanity. I gave him a choice. He could join us or go out into the night and deal with whatever's out there on his own. Few people ever turn us down when the facts are laid out for them like that. Then it becomes a matter of making sure they've got what it takes to join up.

The first order of business was to ditch his name. Real names have power, and one shouldn't casually volunteer them to every stranger one meets. Stripped of his name, George became a prospect. If found worthy, he would choose a new name for himself, a sobriquet that's safe to share with others.

I've been proudly wearing the name Conrad Brent for a long time.

After we finished taking care of the beetle eggs, our next stop was to visit the oracle of Eighty-Sixth Street.

She had sent word that she wanted to see me, and the oracle wasn't someone I liked to keep waiting. She might get annoyed and predict something unpleasant in my future, like an ingrown toenail. The oracle's predictions came true much more often than not, and no one was entirely sure whether she merely saw the future or influenced it. The whole cause and effect thing gave me a headache, so I tried not to dwell on it.

I left the prospect in the car. He wasn't advanced enough in his training to be meeting the major players. Besides, I suspected the oracle knew things about me that the prospect had no business learning.

The prospect grumbled something under his breath and cranked up the radio. I could tell he was growing to like me less and less by the day, but that was all right. Few people liked the tough teacher or the mean drill instructor. I had a way of growing on people. If the prospect made it into the Watch, I was certain our relationship would warm up again. Eventually.

The oracle operated out of a one-bedroom apartment above a Korean nail salon in a rundown building. She could do far better, for what she charged. One time I'd asked her about it. She'd smiled cryptically as she surveyed the peeling wall paint and leaky ceiling and had said she was exactly where she was meant to be.

She'd got up from the sofa to greet me. "Conrad Brent." Her voice strong and steady, in contrast with her small, wrinkled form. "Your future is fire. I see difficult decisions and you'll make the wrong ones. A flame wave will burn the buildings, char the churches, scorch the schools, and strafe the streets. Yours is a dark destiny of challenging choices and tragic tribulations—"

"Cut the crap, Agnes," I interjected. "I'm not a customer. Surely you didn't call me here just to reiterate the same doom and gloom prognostication you've been trying to scare me with for years?"

"Philistine." She sniffed. "People pay good money for the kind of insight I share with you free of charge. A day will come when you'll wish you'd listened more attentively. Fine, then. Let's tend to a more immediate problem. There is a charlatan in Williamsburg who calls himself the Crimson Prophet. He's been swindling the unwary and besmirching the good name of honest clairvoyants. A thorn in my side, he is. I would like you to remove him."

"Really, Agnes," I said, "this isn't like you. There are dozens of phonies out there taking advantage of the gullible, and they are hardly a threat to someone of your considerable and real talents. You can't expect the Watch to act as your muscle and lean on every two-bit fortune teller who happens to irritate you."

"Those were my sentiments exactly," the oracle replied, "until a few days ago, when this upstart somehow got his hands on an Atlantean shard."

I should have known the oracle had experienced serious difficulty when she contacted the Watch. Her own resources were substantial enough to handle lesser issues. A shard showing up in New York wasn't just a problem for her; it meant trouble for all of us.

Three thousand years ago, Atlantis had been the first global superpower. While most of humanity was muddling its way through the Bronze Age, Atlantis had skyscrapers, a public transportation system, and a power grid. Fueling it all was a giant crystal fused with science and magic more advanced than anything another human culture had accomplished since.

One day a crack appeared in the crystal. Some say it was an accident; others blame the Atlanteans themselves, who put too much strain on the crystal, greedily drawing ever more power. Their best engineers and alchemists tried feverishly to seal the crack even as ships filled with fleeing Atlanteans left its shores. Ultimately the alchemists failed, and the resulting explosion sunk the island and annihilated their culture. The crystal itself was broken into thousands of shards, of which even the smallest are still very potent and incredibly dangerous. A decent-sized shard is capable of increasing a magic-user's power tenfold, which often doesn't end well for anyone, most especially the hapless gifted who dare to use it. A minor personage, like this Crimson Prophet, getting his grubby little hands on a shard was even worse. It was like letting a child play with a suitcase nuke.

I jotted down the Crimson Prophet's address and said my goodbyes. The oracle of Eighty-Sixth Street would get the help she had asked for. This had just become the Watch's problem.

CHAPTER 3

I had to give the Crimson Prophet some credit—he knew how to live well. A stately brownstone in the nicest part of Williamsburg was in stark contrast to the oracle's decrepit abode. My feet sank deep into the luxurious sheepskin rug as I was ushered through a series of posh rooms by a pair of elegantly dressed men. A trained eye could detect holsters hidden under their tailored suits. These guys were muscle, but not the cheap, thuggish type. They were the upmarket variety, the sort who could handle themselves in a hoity-toity setting like this but hadn't forgotten how to break kneecaps out back when necessary.

The Crimson Prophet waited for me in the middle of a tastefully decorated study. Paintings reminiscent of the Old Dutch Masters in antique gilded frames decorated the walls. Armchairs, bookshelves, and tables appeared equally old, the wood molded and framed in the Louis XV style. The decor served to make the rich feel right at home, and to intimidate the rest. I did my best to appear unimpressed, bordering on slightly put off, on general principle. The Prophet himself was a tall, skinny man in his thirties. He wore a three-piece suit with a red velvet cloak draped around his shoulders. All he was missing was a top hat and a handlebar mustache and he'd be ready to perform as a Victorian villain in an off-Broadway play.

"Welcome." The Prophet flashed a blinding smile at me. "I must say, I was quite surprised when my men told me about a stranger showing up at my doorstep and demanding an appointment. My reputation must be spreading among the populace faster than I'd anticipated. You do, however, have me at a disadvantage. Whom do I have the pleasure of addressing?"

"My name is Brent. Conrad Brent." Who could resist the James Bond bit? "I'm with the Watch."

A blank stare was accompanied by several seconds of uncomfortable silence. Could it be possible that the Crimson Prophet did not know about the Watch?

"We're a group of gifted who protect the world from supernatural threats. We keep the fae and other magical creatures in line, and rein in any rogue humans who might choose to take advantage of the mundanes."

"Arcane cops." The Crimson Prophet's smile grew even wider. "How ... delightful," he added with the barest hint of disdain.

"We aren't cops," I said. "The Watch is a law unto itself. We recognize no greater authority, and those in whom we take an interest are most certainly not presumed innocent until proven otherwise."

"I see," said the Prophet. "And what can I do for your illustrious group? If you're looking for insightful and stunningly accurate divinations, you've come to the right place."

"No, thanks," I said, thinking of the oracle's fiery foretelling. "I'm trying to cut down."

The Crimson Prophet indicated his disappointment by shrugging in an it's-your-loss-not-mine way. "Something else, then?"

"It has come to my attention that you own an artifact that is of interest to the Watch," I said. "It's a small chunk of incandescent crystal. I was hoping to see it."

"I did recently acquire such a trinket," said the Prophet. He rummaged through a desk drawer to produce a leather carrying case. "It was a gift from a grateful patron, in acknowledgement of the fine work I've been doing."

He opened the case and there it was—a piece of Atlantean crystal the size of an iPhone, glowing warmly like a dimmed light bulb. He tapped it with his index finger and shimmers of energy spread across the surface like ripples in a pond. It was the largest Atlantean shard I had ever seen.

"This is it, precisely." I struggled to keep my voice level. "The Watch has been working to recover this, and several other items, stolen from a friend we owe a few favors to." I was making up the lie on the spot. "Would you be amenable to selling it to us?"

The Crimson Prophet extended his hand, inviting me to take another look around. "As you can tell, I am not in any financial straits at the moment."

"A trade, then?" I persisted. "We have access to a wide range of rare objects that could prove useful in your line of work. I can get you something flashy and magical, to impress your clients. A phoenix feather, perhaps, or a caged sprite? Plus, the Watch would owe you a favor. That is a valuable commodity in its own right."

"Those are some interesting possibilities." The Crimson Prophet sat behind his desk to indicate that our meeting was at an end. "I will consider your offer, but not until I've made further inquiries as to the crystal's value. You understand, I'm sure."

I thanked him and headed out. I hadn't seriously expected my offer to tempt him. While the Prophet was a dilettante when it came to magic, it was clear he understood money and power. Once he'd gleaned even a glimpse of its actual value, he would not relinquish the crystal voluntarily. Fortunately, this wasn't going to be an issue. I'd walked through his home, and there were no magical wards or other supernatural defenses in place. I'd be back that night to liberate the crystal.

A fool and his shard are easily parted.

Lacking arcane protections, the Crimson Prophet relied on mundane security. Nonmagical problems are best solved via nonmagical means, and there existed no better nonmagical solution than Petya.

At six foot seven, Peter "Petya" Kuznetsov stood an entire head taller than me and was at least twice as wide. He moved with the easy grace of a ballet dancer, which he wasn't, and the precision and purpose of a killing machine, which he most definitely was. Petya had been trained by the Spetsnaz and had worked for the Pennant, the Russian government's most elite special ops unit. Some said he had gone rogue after a series of unjustified kills; others claimed he'd been planted in New York City as a Pennant sleeper agent on a long-term mission. Either way, Petya was the best operative money could buy.

At approximately four in the morning, Petya disabled the security system at the Crimson Prophet's brownstone. The lock on the front door barely slowed him down. He slipped inside, motioning for the prospect and me to wait.

Two minutes later, Petya emerged and waved us in. The three of us quietly traversed the dark hallways. We walked past one of the goons I'd met the day before. His unconscious form slouched in a chair, his gun still in its holster. Another sentry lay sprawled on the floor of the next room, a small trickle of blood congealing at the corner of his mouth—a recipient of Petya's tender mercies.

Unlike the rest of the house, the lights were still on in the study. Petya paused by the door to disable yet another security widget, then we were inside. I reached into the drawer from which the Prophet had produced the case earlier, but it was empty. As I looked up from the desk, a searing pain shot through my body and brought me to my knees.

It was an arcane attack of immense power. My various charms and amulets had absorbed the brunt of it, yet I still felt like I'd just been tasered. Absent my protections, Petya and the prospect were not so lucky. Petya was out cold, his mundane body defenseless against hostile magic. The prospect had fared only a little better; he was moaning in pain by the door.

"Welcome back, Mr. Brent." The Crimson Prophet towered over me, the shard gripped in his right hand. "And yes, in case you are wondering, Atlantean crystal is everything it is said to be, and more."

I tried for something witty but was only able to produce a pained grunt. Enhanced by the shard's power, the Prophet's magic was too much for me to handle.

"How monumentally arrogant of you," said the Prophet, "yet so predictable. You presumed me powerless, and therefore felt justified in stealing my property. The Watch pays lip service to protecting ordinary people from the wielders of magic, yet here you are, breaking into my home like a petty burglar. Just as I expected you to."

The effects of the arcane blast were beginning to recede. The ringing in my ears decrescendoed from cathedral bells to one-horse-town church bells. Out of the corner of my eye I could see the prospect trying and failing to get up. I had to buy time—to keep the Crimson Prophet talking. So I tried again, and this time I was able to groan an actual word.

"Why?"

The Prophet smirked. "Because I don't like competition. Now that I've settled here, I intend to be the one and true power in this borough, able to do whatever I please. Others are mere nuisances, but the infamous Conrad Brent of the Watch, you were always going to be a problem. I could find and kill you, of course, but then the Watch would send others to avenge you, and the war would never stop until they overpowered me, or I killed them all."

He leaned in closer. "I posed as a mere fortune teller and set events in motion that would inevitably lead to this very moment. Lesser intellects are so easy to manipulate. Now I get to have everything I want, on my terms. Even the Watch recognizes self-defense. You invaded my home and were accidentally killed in the struggle. Your superiors will understand. Plus, once I've taken your magic and added it to mine, I will become so powerful that the Watch will be only too eager to let matters rest."

The Crimson Prophet grabbed me by the front of my shirt with his free hand and lifted me up to his eye level. He touched the shard to his forehead and began an incantation. The shard flared as guttural words spoken in a dead language hung in the air with an almost physical presence. The Crimson Prophet was casting a spell that would rip the magic right out of me, a spell so difficult and dangerous that even the most talented among the gifted would be foolish to attempt it. A spell that he could manage now, thanks to the power of the shard. In moments, he was going to drain all of my arcane powers and claim them as his own.

Little did he know.

New York City is a magnet for upstarts like him. It draws all manner of sorcerers and monsters drunk on their own Kool-Aid, who believe they've got what it takes to make it in the big city but grossly overestimate their power. I may have been dazed and in pain, but I'd dealt with worse threats than this pompous windbag every other week.

He struggled to finish the incantation, barely able to contain and direct the dark magic, even with the power of the shard. As the final words were spoken, a great jolt shot through my body, an unstoppable invasive force seeking to collect every shred of my magic and bestow it on the Prophet.

Nothing happened.

The Crimson Prophet still held me up at eye level. I could see his pupils widen with surprise, a realization that something had gone wrong.

I made a fist and socked him in the face.

There was a satisfying crunch, and the Prophet staggered back. Blood poured from his broken nose. I went after him, pummeling him to keep him off balance. He whimpered as he tried to pull away from me. I grabbed his hand and pried his fingers open, liberating the shard. Then I shoved him aside. I clenched the shard, feeling its cool, smooth surface, but it grew dim in my hand, like a useless chunk of glass.

The Crimson Prophet reasserted himself and lunged at me, trying to regain the crystal. Even with the broken nose, he was a fair match for me after I had been worked over by his spells. As he reached me, I turned around and threw the shard.

The shard landed on one of the sheepskin rugs, within an arm's reach of the prospect. He grabbed for it with both hands, then cupped the crystal to his chest. The Crimson Prophet went after him, but before he could cross the room, the prospect fired off a beam of energy.

The Crimson Prophet stopped and stared with disbelief at his own chest. In it there was a fist-sized hole burned cleanly through. Wordlessly, he crumpled to the floor. The air smelled of ozone and singed hair.

"Now that," I told the prospect, who appeared shocked by the intensity of his own spell, "*that* is how you cast an energy bolt."

The prospect stared at the corpse wide-eyed. Killing a jumbo bug was one thing. "Why did you make me do this? You had the shard. You could've ..." He trailed off. Killing a man, even a villain like the Crimson Prophet, that changed someone.

The Prophet's plan had been just shy of perfect. He couldn't have known that I was the only member of the Watch without magic. That I was an accident, a freak of nature, capable of perceiving the arcane while possessing no powers of my own.

When I'd first become a prospect, it had taken my mentor some time to figure out why I was failing to cast even the simplest spells. He was not obtuse; it's just that middlings like me are so incredibly rare. He kept my secret and trained me anyway.

I learned to get by. My weapons were bluster, information, and an array of enchanted tools and magical charms that could make Batman's utility belt turn green with envy. I performed my duties for the Watch and used its authority and resources to quietly look for clues—for hints of what was wrong with me and how to cure it.

And now there was someone else like me out there, another middling in trouble, waiting to be sold to the highest bidder. I was going to help them, rescue them, teach them how to blend in with the rest of the gifted the way I had. Or perhaps together we'd unlock this mystery and repair whatever broken link had crippled us. One day I would find a way to do magic. But I was glad I hadn't yet become a full-fledged gifted by the time I'd met the Crimson Prophet.

"Being a guardian is a demanding calling," I told the prospect. "You have to make tough choices and risk your life for others. Sometimes, you have to kill. Better you face the worst of it with me around than later, on your own."

I extended my hand, and the prospect handed over the shard without hesitation. I smiled at him. To experience such power and give it up voluntarily is no small thing. Yes, this one definitely had a future within the Watch.

First, we had to tend to Petya. Then I'd tell the prospect the good news, so he could spend a few happy hours picking out his new name.

CHAPTER 4

"**HE** went with Karl Mercado. Karl friggin' *Mercado*. How messed up is that?"

We were sitting in a booth at the back of a small diner in Woodhaven. An uneaten egg sandwich and fries sat on the plate in front of me. Across the table, Terrie Winter sipped a chocolate milkshake through a straw from an enormous glass.

"Dude, you're going to have to back up and explain. That name means nothing to me," she said.

Terrie Winter, the queen of Queens, was the Watch sorceress in charge of protecting that borough, just like I was in charge of Brooklyn. There was one Watch guardian per borough, plus a handful of support staff at headquarters, all of us reporting to Mose. The headquarters was called the Watchtower, a moniker likely invented by some snarky predecessor of mine, because the so-called tower was located in the basement of the Manhattan Municipal Building. And it also had nothing to do with that Jehovah's Witness magazine.

If you think a single figurehead trying to keep the peace in each borough of the city populated by millions is the definition of insanity, you won't get an argument from me. However, precious

25

few volunteers are willing to do the thankless job for no pay, and fewer yet are powerful enough to deter the sort of trouble we deal with. At five foot six, Terrie may not have looked imposing, but she was among the most powerful gifted I'd ever met, and she never allowed bad guys to underestimate her twice.

She was also plainspoken and down-to-earth, a rare gifted who didn't let her status and power and the soul-crushing job of dealing with literal monsters change her personality. I liked her best among all of my colleagues.

"Okay, so you know how I picked the name Conrad Brent because that's what the lead character is called in the Detonator novels?"

I'd devoured dozens of the Detonator paperbacks as a kid. They were trashy, over-the-top pulp novels about a rogue operative who was a cross between James Bond and Rambo, and who fought everything from Russian spies to genetically modified sumo wrestlers. When the time had come for me to pick an alias, I didn't have to think twice.

Terrie sipped her milkshake. "You're a huge nerd. That's not news. So what?"

"Karl Mercado is Brent's rival in the Detonator novels."

She looked up from her drink. "He chose the name of a villain? That's interesting."

"Mercado isn't a villain," I said. "He's a fellow agent, but he's kind of a dick. Always a thorn in Brent's side. They butt heads all the time, and they're often forced to work together, and he's the one guy that occasionally gets the better of our hero."

"This means your prospect is a nerd too, and his dumb male fantasy is to be just like you, but even more badass." Terrie plucked a French fry off my plate. "That's not messed up. That's kind of sweet, actually."

"It would be. Except he'd never heard of the Detonator books before I explained the whole alias business to him. He looked up Karl Mercado on Wikipedia for the express purpose of annoying and upstaging me. He told me so right before he asked to be reassigned to somebody else—anybody else—within the Watch for the rest of his training."

"Ah." She chewed the fry thoughtfully. "Your sink-or-swim teaching method has never been especially popular with the prospects."

26

I couldn't tell her the truth, so I took a bite of my sandwich and said nothing at all.

"Okay," she said. "You take me out to lunch, ply me with milkshakes, make me think it's because you enjoy my winning personality, but you really just need a favor, dontcha?"

"You've got to take him off my hands, Terrie. He's a prickly bastard, but he's got a lot of raw power, a lot of potential. He needs a patient teacher, someone with a steady hand who is clearly more powerful than he is. Someone he can respect."

"Flattery will get you nowhere, Conrad," Terrie said without bothering overmuch to hide the fact that she was, indeed, flattered. "What's in it for me?"

I smiled and reached into one of my pockets. "Tickets to the Knicks game." I drew out a pair of blue-and-orange slips and slid them across the table to Terrie.

Her eyes lit up. "They say the way to a girl's heart is through Madison Square Garden, and they're right." She snatched and examined the tickets. "Not quite courtside, but close enough to see Spike Lee go berserk when they score a three-pointer. Respect."

"I knew you'd like them, Terrie."

"Just like you knew I wouldn't turn away your stray prospect, bribe or no bribe." She put away the tickets. "For future reference, I prefer bribe."

"Sure. But you've got to promise to make fun of Karl Mercado's name for me."

"It's a deal," Terrie said solemnly. "Care to join me at the game? I seem to have an extra ticket."

"I really wish I could, but I have a prior engagement that evening."

"Aww," she said. "Hot date?"

"Something like that."

I thought of the Traveling Fair auction scheduled in her borough on the evening of the game just under a week away, and felt a pang of guilt over manipulating my friend. I couldn't predict what lengths I might have to go to in order to rescue the middling, and what rules of the Watch I might have to break. The less Terrie knew about any of it, the better.

27

"Story of my life," said Terrie. "All the good ones are either taken or gay."

I stuffed my face with the sandwich so Terrie wouldn't see me blush.

While I didn't know exactly how I might rescue the middling from the Traveling Fair, I knew the Atlantean shard could prove to be just the advantage I needed. Not because of its abilities—I still couldn't tap into the sort of power it amplified—but because of its rarity and value.

After lunch with Terrie I drove from Queens straight to Mordecai's Jewelers in Borough Park. It was one of several locations in Brooklyn where the gifted traded in magical artifacts behind the façades of everyday businesses. I was a regular customer at all of them: the second-floor walk-up above a Russian bookstore in Brighton Beach, the converted bank vault at a community credit union in Boerum Hill, the game shop in Midwood. I made my rounds, buying and selling, always on the lookout for trinkets I could use.

Two things set Mordecai's apart from the other shops. First, he always had the widest selection. A shop stocked with diamonds and gold watches is easier to secure than a bookstore or a cafe without the security measures drawing undue attention. This allowed Mordecai's to keep more inventory on hand with somewhat reduced risk. Second, Mordecai, the proprietor, was by far the most honest and straightforward dealer in the business. His prices weren't the lowest, but he stood by his merchandise and unfailingly offered a fair value for the items he picked up in trade.

I was ushered past the glass displays filled with engagement rings and fancy watches into the private showroom. Back there, similar displays were filled with rings enchanted and cursed, spellbooks, and other arcane miscellanea. Mordecai sat on a barstool, engaged in a backgammon game against his ten-year-old grandson who stood on the other side of the counter.

"Think about that move, Chaim," Mordecai told the gangly boy who scratched his head under a yarmulke that was perched dangerously askew and hung onto his hair by a small metal clip. "Never rush your play. Consider all the options first."

He turned his attention to me. "Conrad! Good to see you, old friend."

I approached, and we shook hands. He sent Chaim away and waited until the child was out of the room before he asked, "What will it be today? Buying or selling?"

"Selling," I said. "Maybe."

Mordecai waited for me to elaborate, but I handed the Atlantean shard over instead. Mordecai's eyes grew wide. He didn't need to test its authenticity. I knew he could feel its power in a way I only aspired to.

"This is the nicest thing you ever brought me," he said.

"What do you think it's worth?"

"Six hundred thousand," he said without hesitation. "Maybe six-fifty if I find the right buyer."

Arcane artifacts are an expensive habit. Even so, I was used to dealing in figures ranging between four and low five digits. Under different circumstances I'd be over the moon, but just then my main thought was, *will this be enough?*

Mordecai sensed my unease even if he didn't know the reason behind it. "I could try to get more if there's no rush. If you want to leave it on consignment, I'll get you as much as I can, minus a fifteen percent fee. If you need cash up front, I can pay you five hundred thousand now."

Half a million dollars in cash. Damn.

I wondered about the sort of customer who'd pay even more than that to amplify their magic. It was possible—likely, even—that this person would be far worse than the Crimson Prophet. It wasn't a risk I was taking lightly.

"It's a fair offer, but I'm not certain I want to sell. What I'd like is a line of credit—a note from you saying I'm good for five hundred large." I pressed on as I watched him frown. "This is not a means to leverage another buyer. You know me well enough to believe that. It's just that I may or may not need the money for another transaction. If I do, the shard is yours."

"I don't run a pawn shop, Conrad, but I suppose if you leave the crystal as collateral I can lend you the money."

"I'll need the shard and the note both, for what I'm doing. Please. You'll be helping out both me and the Watch. I'll owe you a favor."

He thought about it. Mordecai and I had enjoyed a good business relationship over the years, but a note of credit from him meant he might possibly be on the hook for whatever shenanigans I became involved in. I really couldn't blame him if he chose to turn me down.

Mordecai fidgeted with the backgammon checkers. "Two years ago, a child went missing from a family in Brooklyn Heights. Esther was ten, about the same age as my grandson is now. I don't know her family personally, but some of their relatives belong to my congregation." He looked up from the board. "You brought her back."

"I did."

I remembered the incident well. The girl had been abducted by cultists who'd thought they could summon their evil god through human sacrifice. In the end, there had been plenty of blood on their altar that night, but none of it had belonged to the child. That wasn't the sort of detail I'd shared with Esther's parents when I brought her back home in one piece, nor what I would choose to share now.

"You performed what we call a *mitzvah*, a good deed," said Mordecai. "I don't always agree with the actions of the Watch, but I believe you to be a good man. Tell me what you're doing is for a worthwhile cause, and I'll do as you ask."

I thought of the anonymous middling. Was it a child? Was he or she scared, shivering like Esther had on that cold marble slab of an altar?

"It is," I said with conviction.

Mordecai nodded, placed a sheet of stationery with his letterhead onto the counter, and began to write.

I was being followed by amateurs. The black Lincoln Town Car lingering in my rearview mirror had stalked me all the way from Borough Park and along the congested Brooklyn streets without any grace or subtlety. Its driver must have thought he was very clever, always keeping one or two vehicles between us. I made a few turns, just to be sure. The Lincoln stayed with me, conspicuous as a polar bear in the desert.

Sensing my concern, my car's various magical protections began to activate. To say that my car didn't look like much would be an understatement. It was an '84 Oldsmobile with crooked bumpers, a few months overdue for a car wash. On the inside, though, it sported more nasty tricks than the Batmobile. It had the best defensive enchantments money could buy, and a few that were literally priceless. All of them woke up as the car prepared itself for a possible confrontation. Some of the arcane shields interfered with the radio, mixing "Tom Sawyer" by Rush with static, which only served to annoy me further. I pulled over and watched the Lincoln slide into a parking spot a few yards behind me.

I got out of the car, strolled over, and tapped on the tinted driver's-side window.

"Hey there, chum. I got news for you: you aren't very good at this trailing thing. Either leave me alone and go back to picking up fares at the airport or roll down this window and explain what it is you want."

The driver didn't respond. Instead, the passenger door opened and a petite redhead in a business suit climbed out.

"Don't frighten the help, Mr. Brent. He was simply doing his job." There was a healthy amount of amusement in her voice, as though she was delighted by this turn of events. She spoke with a hint of a British accent. Her looks and voice were almost enough for me to forgive the imposition. Almost.

"Maybe so," I grumbled, "but he wasn't doing it very well."

"On the contrary," she said, "I intended for you to see us. I had no doubt that a man of your reputation would notice being followed. What I really wanted was to see how you'd handle it."

She offered me a business card. According to the fancy font her name was Moira O'Leary and she was a freelance security consultant.

"Watching someone react to a perceived threat is very instructive. I like to learn as much as I can about the people I'm going to work with. I'll admit that your rather … *direct* approach was pleasantly unexpected."

"I'm glad I managed to entertain you," I said, "but what makes you think we're going to be working together?"

"Oh, we will." She smiled. "Your boss owes my client a favor or two. I'm sure Mose will be in touch with you shortly. He might even say 'pretty please.'"

Not bloody likely. Mose didn't have to say please because no one was foolish enough to question his orders. When he said jump, you jumped, and you didn't dare to ask how high.

"My organization doesn't owe favors to many people. Your client must be pretty special," I said, fishing for a little more information. Turned out, Ms. Security Consultant wasn't going to make me guess.

"Of course he's special," she said sweetly. "He's Bradley Holcomb."

Bloody hell. I struggled to keep most of the surprise off my face to avoid giving her the satisfaction, but I was pretty sure I'd failed spectacularly.

She enjoyed my reaction. "I look forward to working with you."

"We'll see about that." I turned on my heels and stomped back toward my car.

I drove off and the Lincoln didn't follow. I checked my cell phone and, sure enough, there were several missed calls and a text message from the Watchtower demanding that I check in ASAP.

CHAPTER 5

I don't like venturing into Manhattan. It is the capital of Weird in the New World. Beings of immense power walk the streets beneath its gleaming skyscrapers. Terrible schemes are hatched behind closed doors in offices with prestigious addresses—and I'm not just talking about the Wall Street financiers. Dangerous humans and creatures of all kinds congregate there, and they make Brooklyn feel like a sleepy suburb. I tried to keep my visits into the Big Apple's rotten core brief and infrequent. But sometimes, things couldn't be helped.

O'Leary hadn't been kidding; people at the Watchtower were falling all over themselves to accommodate her real estate magnate boss. I was told to assist him in any way I could, with special emphasis on the fact that these orders came from Mose himself. I had called the number on Moira's business card and had been summoned to an audience in Holcomb Tower the next morning.

I was ushered into a large office furnished with a mismatched collection of objects of art and antiquity. Ancient Greek marble statue heads in freestanding display cabinets stared across the room at bookshelves filled with Ming vases and Faberge eggs, but no actual books. These items may not have fit together particularly well, but they all shared one common trait: hefty price tags. A supersized mahogany desk had been installed in the center of the room. Leaning back in a lambskin office chair was the man himself.

Bradley Holcomb, real estate king of New York, reality TV host, and—at least in his own mind—a curator of the upwardly mobile lifestyle. His name, slapped indiscriminately on everything from condo developments to cologne, was the gold standard for the bourgeoisie. Even surrounded by the opulence of his office, Holcomb looked less impressive in person than he did on TV. They always do.

"Mr. Brent," he said, studying me intently, "thank you for coming to see me on such short notice. Also, forgive me for staring. Very important people visit my office all the time, but I've never had the pleasure of meeting a wizard before. I imagined you to be"—he paused, looking for the right words to express his disappointment with my being so ordinary—"older."

"In my experience people rarely live up to their hype," I said. Holcomb either chose to ignore the barb, or it went over his head. He continued to ogle me as though I were a circus freak.

"What is it I can do for you, Mr. Holcomb?" I prodded.

"I've been working on a fascinating project," he said, snapping out of it. "I acquired a huge plot of land adjacent to Marine Park. Beautiful space. Naturally secluded, yet right off of Belt Parkway, so it's easy to reach. I'm building a high-end theme resort there. Gonna make the place look like ancient Rome. This will be huge, believe me!"

Holcomb's face lit up and his entire demeanor shifted when he started talking about his hotel. He became almost tolerable.

"It'll be the best combination of classic style and ultramodern amenities. Really something very special. I'm even building a miniature copy of the Coliseum, with a boxing ring in the center. Holcomb's Rome is going to make theme hotels in Vegas and Atlantic City look like gaudy McMansions in comparison."

I nodded patiently. Holcomb would know a thing or two about gaudy.

"It took forever to get the permits," he said. "But once construction began, strange things started to happen. Floor plans went missing from a locked safe. Every worker on the demolition crew

34

simultaneously came down with diarrhea. Sabotage of all kinds has been derailing the project."

Holcomb reached for a stress ball on his desk and squeezed it, hard.

"I'm a practical man, not taken to flights of fancy. When it was first suggested to me that my problems were supernatural in origin, I laughed it off. But I'm not laughing any longer. I tripled security, accomplishing exactly nothing. Those security guards aren't going to see a dime for their terrible job, believe me! Then a business associate recommended that I hire O'Leary as an arcane consultant. I always hire the best people, you know, and she's been great. She was the one who filled me in on the crazy stuff going on in the world that we muggles aren't supposed to know about."

"We prefer to call you mundanes," I said.

"Whatever you need to tell yourself," said Holcomb. "I may not be able to do voodoo, but I'm hardly mundane. I'm the best businessman and negotiator in New York!" He seemed to expect me to argue, or better yet, to agree with his claim. I did neither. After a few seconds of uncomfortable silence, he went on, deflated. "O'Leary told me about the Watch and helped me get in touch with Mr. Mose. It wasn't all that difficult to persuade him. Money, it seems, can buy magic as reliably as any other service."

Mose must've charged this arrogant fat cat a fortune to make me do house calls like a plumber. Still, someone was using magic to mess with the mundanes—exactly the kind of thing the Watch was created to guard against. The fact that the victim was Holcomb didn't obviate my obligation to look into the matter.

"All right," I said. "Fetch whatever maps and floor plans for this thing that weren't stolen from your safe and let's take a look."

Perched between Marine Park and the coastline of Deep Creek was one of the last undeveloped areas remaining in the borough of Brooklyn. Thousands of people drove past it every day, commuting via the always-congested Belt Parkway. There was no off-ramp by Marine Park. Drivers could only marvel from afar at the glimpses of primordial wilderness and the scenic view of the Atlantic.

Holcomb planned to change that. His blueprints called for building an Exit 10 off Belt Parkway, which would deliver travelers right to his new hotel's front door. For now, I had to drive all the way to the Flatbush Avenue exit, park at the Gateway Marina, and walk.

On Monday afternoon I spent several unpleasant hours slogging around Holcomb's construction site. Whoever was messing with the project was thorough, devious, and definitely supernatural. Signs of arcane interference were everywhere. Tree trunks had runes carved into their bark, enchantments spun like shimmering spider webs hung from the branches, and glyph-covered stones were sprinkled along the sandy beach. An ancient magic was at work, intent on disrupting the construction. It was effective and considerably unpleasant, but never lethal.

This magic was different from the types I'd encountered in the past. I was clueless as to what manner of creature was protecting its territory but had a pretty good idea of how to flush it out. I set to disarming the traps and clearing the area of supernatural hindrances.

It was slow going. With no magic of my own, I had to rely on various arcane tools. Each action that any other gifted could perform by merely flexing their abilities took me minutes of careful tinkering with artifacts that operated on other people's stored power. My feet got wet and the bottom of my trench coat was caked with mud. The briny scent of the ocean clogged my nostrils. I cursed as the wild shrubs scraped my skin. There was a reason I'd chosen to live in an urban environment. I'll take nice a paved road over a grassy path any day of the week.

"You shouldn't do that."

I was knee-deep in disrupting a particularly elaborate enchantment when the voice caught me by surprise. I spun around to see who'd managed to sneak up on me. It was a man in his late forties, dressed in an earth-toned windbreaker, tough khaki pants, and hiking boots. He was far better prepared for an excursion to this area than I.

"Don't break it," he said. "Do you have any idea how much effort goes into weaving an enchantment like this one? It'll take us weeks to repair all the damage you've caused today."

"Repair?" I said. "Oh no, no. We can't have that. The Watch takes a dim view of magic being used against the mundanes."

"I know who you are and what you represent, Mr. Brent," said the stranger. "My people have deep respect for the Watch. It is a grave disappointment that you choose to side against us."

"Back up for a moment," I said. "I'm not picking any sides. I don't even know who or what I'm dealing with, and I don't like that one bit. Care to bring me up to speed?"

"My name is Graeme Murray. I sit on the ruling council of the Circle of the Sacred Oak." He saw a blank expression on my face and elaborated, "We're druids, Mr. Brent."

I displayed my encyclopedic and brilliant command of history: "I thought druids were, you know, extinct?"

"There are still a few of us around, carrying on the traditions of our forefathers. Walk with me, Mr. Brent, and I will endeavor to, as you put it, bring you up to speed." The druid headed deeper into the brush. I followed him, the still-active enchantment threads glowing faintly behind us.

"My people were rulers of the British Isles since the beginning of history," said Murray. "Openly at first, then behind the scenes, after the Romans came. But things were changing. Over time, our numbers and influence waned. To make matters worse, in the 1700s the ruling council got us mired in the war against the Cabal."

I'd heard about the Salzburg Cabal before. It was a shady organization of European mystics and sorcerers that had first come to prominence in the early days of the Austro-Hungarian Empire. They'd spread across Europe and had been vastly powerful in the Victorian era. They were still influential in the present day. The Watch and the Cabal had butted heads in the past, but that was before my time.

"The Cabal devastated us. Druids were hunted in Britain and Ireland like common criminals. Siobhan Keane, one of the few among the ruling council to have opposed the war, gathered her remaining loyalists and set sail for the New World."

We walked toward the far end of the property, near the edge of Marine Park.

"Druids share a bond with the land; most would rather die than abandon their sacred groves. To convince so many to leave the British Isles and begin life anew elsewhere was a gargantuan feat. Siobhan Keane wasn't merely a leader—she was our group's founder, our savior, as important to us as Jesus and Mohammed are to their followers."

We arrived at a small clearing, surrounded by ancient oak trees overgrown with mistletoe.

"This," said Murray, "is Siobhan Keane's final resting place. It's the most sacred site for my people in exile, and we'll do whatever we have to in order to prevent anyone—gifted or mundane—from bulldozing it down."

The two of us stood quietly for a moment and listened as the Atlantic breeze rustled the yellowing leaves in nature's requiem for the queen of the druids.

It took some doing, but I managed to set up peace talks.

We sat in the conference room of a nondescript hotel by the JFK airport. Holcomb probably didn't feel comfortable inviting a bunch of hostile gifted into his home office. He wouldn't even take my calls, leaving it up to O'Leary to handle the preliminary negotiations. The man was a big fan of delegating, at least according to his reality TV show. To her credit, O'Leary got him to consider the druids' situation and consent to a face-to-face meeting with the ruling council of the Circle of the Sacred Oak.

Six rather ordinary-looking people, my new pal Graeme among them, sat around the large, oval table. They were broadcasting various degrees of annoyance, frustration, and overall bad karma. Holcomb was running late. Really late. The druid leaders didn't appreciate being made to wait. Several of them took to shooting accusing glances my way, as though the real estate mogul's tardiness was somehow my fault. I kept a neutral expression, hating every moment of it.

After what felt like hours, the conference room door finally swung open to admit Moira O'Leary and a dozen grim-looking men. They fanned out in a semicircle, taking positions against the walls and blocking the entrance. Every one of them was gifted and every one of them was heavily armed. They aimed their weapons at the druids.

"What is the meaning of this?" demanded a councilman. "Where is Holcomb?"

"He won't be coming," O'Leary said. "Mr. Holcomb has left it up to me to deal with this nuisance." She turned her attention to me. "I want to thank you, Conrad, for flushing out the pagan scum. We'll take it from here. You should leave. Now."

Moira's voice, posture, speech pattern, her entire demeanor changed drastically. It was as though a dedicated character actor finally dropped their cultivated persona or, more accurately, a venomous snake shed its innocuous-seeming skin.

The double-dealing, two-faced mercenary had played me. And I'd been just beginning to like her.

"These people are here to negotiate." I remained seated, so O'Leary and her goons couldn't see me rummaging through the pockets of my coat. "You wouldn't want to jeopardize that with rash vigilante action."

O'Leary laughed.

"Rash? We've been hunting their kind for centuries. Don't let the nature-loving act fool you. They are terrorists, ruthless killers of women and children. They've waged a guerilla war against the Cabal for several hundred years, and their hands are elbow-deep in blood."

She was a Cabal agent, and the hate in her voice sounded genuine. I wished I hadn't gotten out of bed that morning.

"Our faction wants no part of your war," said Graeme. "Our ancestors traveled across the ocean so that we could live at peace."

"These people are civilians, Moira. Look at them. They didn't try to hurt Holcomb's workers and they're certainly no threat to the Cabal." I waved my right hand, palm out. "Come on. You know these aren't the druids you're looking for."

No one even chuckled. So much for diffusing the situation with humor.

"Do keep in mind that these negotiations are guaranteed by the Watch. I'm sure both of us would rather avoid the possibility of friction between our organizations?"

O'Leary was having none of that. "We have no quarrel with your band of do-gooders, so long as you stay out of our way. You're free to go and play at policeman somewhere else. But if you stay, you die with them."

The smart move would've been to take her up on her offer. I had no business interfering in a centuries-old war. Besides, what chance did I have against a half-dozen gifted? Yet, I couldn't bring myself to walk out and leave six innocent people to their doom. After years of making careful, calculated decisions I surprised myself by abandoning caution and following my gut.

"You really shouldn't have called me a cop," I said, rising from my chair. "It upsets me."

Before anyone could react, I drew a pencil-thin, turquoise glass vial from one of my pockets and threw it as hard as I could against the wall.

The vial shattered, unleashing a Chinook wind bottled inside. Powerful gusts wreaked havoc in the confines of the room. Hurricane-like currents lifted people and chairs from the ground. Intense fog made it impossible to see beyond arm's length. The air became hot and moist, as though someone had run a long, steamy shower.

The pandemonium kept the bad guys busy and gave me a chance to set up a portal. Transportation magic is unreliable overall, and this artifact took at least a dozen heartbeats to activate. What's worse, the portal charm was only good for a single one-way trip and was very difficult to replace. I winced as I activated it—but using up a prized possession was better than facing a Cabal army.

Someone managed to open the conference-room door and the Chinook swooshed out into the hallway. As the fog began to dissipate, everyone could see a shimmering portal the size of a manhole cover floating a few feet above the floor.

"Go!" I shouted at the druids while ripping a golden bracelet off my wrist. The action triggered a force barrier, cutting off the other half of the room. That particular toy was reusable, but it would take four lunar months to recharge. This mess was costing me dearly.

Druids stumbled toward the portal while the Cabal mages got their act together. They unleashed a coordinated attack on the barrier and within seconds it began to collapse. I desperately tried to think of a way to buy us more time, but this was supposed to have been a boring real estate meeting. I'd brought no trinkets capable of stopping a dozen hostile gifted working in unison.

A druid woman in her early fifties turned around. In a few steps she was at the barrier, touching it lightly with her fingertips. Her entire body glowed as she worked her magic. Infused with whatever power she lent it, the barrier strengthened despite the continued attack from the other side. She appeared calm, almost serene, but I could see the new wrinkles forming on her face and her hair turning gray as she surrendered her life force to maintain the barrier.

The rest of the druids were through the portal now. It was beginning to wobble and would disappear soon. I took one last look at the woman, who had not hesitated even for a moment before choosing to sacrifice herself in order to save her people. A small part of me wanted to stay, to fight, and probably die alongside her once the barrier failed, but I knew better. I was no martyr. I was just a guy with a few arcane gadgets and lots of bravado.

I hurled myself into the portal, hoping its erratic magic wouldn't teleport me into a concrete wall.

The portal spat me out in a parking lot. The five druids were just getting their bearings when I arrived. Graeme helped me up.

"Thank you," he said as I brushed dust off my coat. "It seems you've chosen a side after all."

"Couldn't just walk out on you lot. Would've been bad for my reputation."

We watched the portal flicker and collapse. No one else would be coming through.

"They got Alice," said one of the druids, tears rolling down his cheeks. "This can't be left unanswered."

"We must gather everyone," said another. "Sound the call. We will march to the Holcomb Tower and bring it down on the treacherous bastard's head."

"Hold on," I said. "Holcomb isn't gifted. He told me that, until a week ago, he didn't even know magic was real. I don't buy the idea of him as a member of the Cabal."

"You only have his word for that," said Graeme.

"I've watched this guy on TV," I said. "He isn't that good a liar. I bet O'Leary set up the trap by herself and never even told him about you."

"We will rip the truth out of him," growled another druid. Everyone began to speak at once. The druids were primed to take action, anything to avenge Alice and lash out at their persecutors. Then my phone rang; O'Leary's name and number showed up on the caller ID. I answered.

"Yeah," I grunted, taking a few steps away from the druids. Bent on their revenge plans, they barely noticed.

"That was very impressive," O'Leary said with that hint of cheerful amusement in her voice I would find endearing had she not just betrayed and tried to kill me. "I suppose I should have expected no less."

"What do you want?" For once, I wasn't in a mood for banter.

"I assume you're still with the druids," said O'Leary. "I want you to pass along a message. We'll be waiting for them at the tomb of their precious founder. If they don't show by sunset, we'll burn down the trees, demolish the stones, then dig up her grave and spend a fun evening coming up with ways to desecrate the remains."

"That's a mistake," I told her. "You and your people should leave town, before the Watch stomps on you, hard."

"Nonsense," she said. "Mose will never get the Watch involved. After all, the druids were the ones picking on the mundanes. I'm merely trying to set things right on behalf of poor, defenseless Mr. Holcomb. Beyond that, whatever disagreements my organization may have with the druids fall well outside of the Watch's purview."

I said nothing, hating the fact that she was right. As far as the Watch was concerned, Cabal agents could slaughter the druids and none of it was our business, so long as they never went after the mundanes.

"I suspect," she went on, "that Mose won't be too pleased with you for siding with them just now. So why don't you be a good little rent-a-cop and give the tree huggers my message. They won't be able to resist trying to protect their sacred swamp and we'll mop 'em up. Everybody wins. Mose doesn't even have to know about your error in judgment. What do you say?"

"I'll pass the message along," I conceded. "This isn't over."

She started to say something snide, but I ended the call.

I relayed the message to the druids and contemplated my next move. There were less than four hours of daylight remaining.

O'Leary's plan was working perfectly. Compelled to defend their grove, the druids showed up in force, like so many lambs to slaughter. Nearly thirty of them had joined their leaders in an effort to protect their sacred ground. They were all gifted—but they were no warriors, and no match for the hardened Cabal mercenaries.

I walked with them, prodding along a prisoner. By my side, disheveled and dragging his Italian loafers through the brown mud, was Bradley Holcomb.

Moira O'Leary and her people waited for us at Siobhan Keane's gravesite. There were nearly three dozen Cabal fighters this time, weapons and magic at the ready. They parted to let our procession approach.

"I've got your boss," I told O'Leary once we reached the clearing. I shoved Holcomb back into the arms of several druids. "If any fighting takes place here, I'll make sure he's among the first to die. Why don't we talk things out instead?"

"You're a fool," said O'Leary. "And a desperate fool, at that. I heard that you abducted Holcomb from his office in broad daylight. Talk about abusing the mundanes! And for what? Did you really think that a chance at saving his skin would get me to back off? Now that we've lured the druids here, Holcomb is useless to me."

Bradley Holcomb straightened up, stepped forward, and looked down his nose at O'Leary.

"You were right, Mr. Brent. It appears my arcane security consultant never had my best interests at heart after all. Moira," Holcomb said with as much aplomb and dignity as he could muster under the circumstances. "You're fired!"

That was all we needed to hear. Holcomb stepped back into the relative safety of the cluster of druids and my fellow members of the Watch dropped their concealment spell. I would take any two of them against all the Cabal goons present. Together they were an overwhelming force that should make any sensible gifted think twice.

Cabal agent Moira O'Leary wasn't the sensible type. She sized up my friends the way a matador examines a bull.

"Half a dozen do-gooders against an army. Is that all you've got?"

O'Leary signaled her men to attack. The tranquil burial site turned into a war zone. Energy blasts, curses, and bullets flew as both sides unleashed everything they had at each other.

Terrie Winter of Queens wielded an enchanted staff so powerful you could physically feel the presence of its magic. She moved gracefully, jabbing at enemies and dodging their attacks in fluid, ballet-like motion. Our mutual trainee, Karl Mercado, was at her side. Although he had no powerful artifacts of his own, he used his considerable abilities combined with our training to unleash a barrage of small, fast fireballs.

Father Mancini from Staten Island held a large silver cross with sharpened edges in one hand and a .44 Magnum revolver in another. He had no trouble reconciling his arcane ability with his faith, and Lord help any gifted sinner who got in his way. The good priest stood his ground, striking down any Cabal fighters within reach while quoting scripture.

Gord from the Bronx stood seven feet tall, courtesy of the giant blood somewhere deep in his family's past. He carried a sawn-off shotgun that could blast through any obstacle, physical or magical. Gord fired off a few shots, and then took several large strides that placed him in the midst of the enemy. He used his shotgun as a club, tossing men around like rag dolls.

Manhattan's John Smith stood empty-handed and smiled nastily at his enemies, his own magic far more powerful than any weapon. He was elegant in a three-piece Armani suit and a white silk scarf tied around his neck. The scarf contrasted smartly against his ebony skin. John cast spell after spell, conjuring ephemeral horrors. They materialized in the air, swooping from above to maul the Cabal mages with their ghostly fangs and claws.

I used whatever protective charms and devices I had to keep Holcomb and myself out of harm's way, but my supplies were dwindling fast. I found myself fighting back-to-back with Karl when several Cabal mages cornered us. They worked in concert, unleashing a wave of energy that nearly penetrated our defenses and knocked both of us to the ground.

One of the bad guys read from an ancient scroll, its magic undoubtedly lending power to their attack. I didn't have a charm handy to counter it, so I threw a rock at him, hoping to buy a few seconds. The rock went wide, landing a good three feet away from my target. Karl gave me a disgusted look and recited an incantation he must've learned from Terrie. Wind gusted, not quite ripping the scroll from the Cabal mercenary's hands but disrupting his reading. We were still outmatched but it gave me the time I needed.

Suddenly, a ten-foot monster appeared between us and our enemies, gnashing its teeth and growling loud enough to be heard over the sounds of the fighting. Cabal goons took a good look at it and decided that they were needed elsewhere on the battlefield.

I would have to recapture the Sumatran changeling after this was over. The clever charm that had emporarily miniaturized and kept it suspended so it could be unleashed like a Pokémon had been used up forever.

Unable to defend against the far superior talents of the Watch for long, those Cabal fighters who could still move broke ranks and fled. I watched O'Leary and a handful of her people escape through a portal similar to the one I'd used earlier. After being routed so thoroughly, I didn't expect to be seeing her again anytime soon.

"Guess this means you owe each of us one, for a change," said Father Mancini afterward.

"That," added Terrie Winter, "and you're the one who has to explain this mess to Mose. He won't be pleased about being kept out of the loop. I think I'll go ahead and skip that meeting."

Reporting to Mose wasn't something I looked forward to. This was definitely one of those scenarios where begging forgiveness was easier than asking permission. The big man wouldn't have approved—and my theory about Moira becoming fair game for the Watch once Holcomb severed his connection with her was tenuous at best. Still, everything had worked out, and Mose wasn't the type to punish success.

My colleagues had really come through for me this day. After all, this wasn't the Watch's fight. They were there because the Cabal had attacked *me*. Whatever our occasional disagreements and however each of us felt about the Watch's rules, we closed ranks to defend our own.

I walked over to Graeme and the rest of the council. Holcomb was pitching at them in the rapid-fire fashion of a used car salesman.

"It's gonna be great," he said. "Just picture it: Holcomb's Stonehenge! We'll build a replica of those standing stones instead of the Coliseum. Make the hotel druid themed. We'll leave the shrine alone and fence it off from the tourists. Your people can come and go whenever they please, and no one will be the wiser."

Holcomb's plan was actually making sense. The druids must've thought so too; they were listening intently to what the real estate mogul had to say. After all, who would suspect one of Holcomb's resorts to be anything more than it appeared? Besides, Holcomb's legal ownership of the site would help secure the Watch's protection in case the Cabal ever decided to take another run at the druids.

I left them to talk business. The man was about to convince an ancient order to let him build a theme resort around their sacred site. And if that sort of salesmanship doesn't take a bit of magic, I don't know what does.

CHAPTER 6

THE waiting felt like forever, and when the day of the auction finally came, I showed up at the Traveling Fair early.

The Fair had taken over a McMansion on Midland Parkway, one of the more posh neighborhoods in Queens. A dozen heavies, who looked like carbon copies of the Crimson Prophet's security people but who were also gifted as per their auras, surrounded the property. One of them studied my golden ticket and looked me up and down with obvious distaste.

"Name?" he asked in the blandest, most disinterested voice possible. I've only heard the like at the DMV.

"Conrad Brent."

"You're not on the list."

If he had a list, he must've memorized it, because there was no physical evidence of one.

"Try Demetrios Sanna. I'm here on his behalf."

The heavy half turned away from me and muttered something into his earpiece. He listened to the response and his frown deepened. He scanned me for weapons, magical and otherwise. Expecting this, I had left anything that could be considered dangerous in my car.

47

"You may enter." He handed me a white paddle with number 19 printed on it in bold font.

I entered a large vestibule that took up a significant portion of the building's innards. Rows of cushioned chairs were set up, enough to seat over fifty people. A few individuals were in their seats already. As I looked around, a waiter approached with a tray of champagne glasses. Now that I was inside, I was a valued client rather than riff-raff trying to get in, so everyone was super nice. I accepted the glass and took a sip of bubbly, which, I suspected, had cost as much as my average dinner.

It tasted good, but not so much better than what I was used to drinking. Perhaps I just wasn't cut out for the life of a wealthy socialite.

My phone vibrated. It was the Watchtower. I sent the call to voicemail. I hadn't fallen on my sword in front of Mose about the Holcomb affair yet. I needed to do that soon or risk making him even more annoyed with me, but this took precedence.

As I sat in the back row, I went over my sorry excuse for a plan.

I had Mordecai's credit note, so I could participate in the auction directly. That seemed to be the path of least resistance, except I had no idea what might be the going price for a human being whose only value to the people in this room was as a murder victim.

If the bidding exceeded my price range, I would have to find out who won, follow them out, and persuade them by whatever means necessary to part with their prize. I suspected that many among the sort of characters who'd bid on a person would also be very much interested in an Atlantean shard. A straight-up trade was not out of the question.

I expected the who's who of New York's gifted, but as the seats filled, I recognized no one among the people around me. The truly wealthy and powerful would send trusted proxies rather than attend this sort of a shindig, its outward opulence straining to conceal the lingering stench of impropriety.

Most of the bidders were dressed for a night out at the theater, in tuxedos and designer ball gowns. They flashed their platinum watches and diamond rings, preening like a murder of haughty crows. I counted thirty bidders in all. Each tended to keep to themselves. It seemed no invitation had come with a plus-one.

The auctioneers didn't offer us a chance to examine the merchandise. I suppose their reputation was guarantee enough for the gathered crowd.

The soft classical music they were piping in through the speakers cut out and the auctioneer stepped to the podium in front of the room. He was a tall, thin man with an even thinner mustache, dressed in a bespoke suit.

"Ladies and gentlemen, welcome to the Traveling Fair." I couldn't decide whether his British accent was real or if he was faking it to make the affair seem fancier. It reminded me of Moira, as if I needed an extra reason to dislike the auctioneer. "We encourage everyone who has accepted our invitation to participate in the bidding. Although no more than three of you will have the distinct privilege of placing the winning bid, rest assured that our staff will keep track of all bids." He lowered his voice and continued almost conspiratorially. "The bid records will be a factor in determining who is invited to the next Fair." He added, louder, with a touch of steel in his voice, "All bids are, of course, binding."

Got it. With so few scumbags invited to this shindig, the Traveling Fair organizers wanted to ensure most of them weren't merely spectators, there for some free food and entertainment. Fail to bid, and they'll invite somebody else next time. Meanwhile, if you bid just for show but end up the winner, you better pay up or those goons outside will get the opportunity to earn their paychecks. This was just like Sotheby's, all right, if Sotheby's conducted their business in North Korea.

A scantily clad woman brought out a large ring on one of those little red felt pillows.

"Our first item today is an Etruscan gold ring, circa 600 B.C.E." The anonymous auctioneer launched into a long-winded tirade about how rare and valuable the ring of invisibility was. I suppose it had historical value because its practical application was nothing special. I could buy a similar modern ring from Mordecai for under ten grand. The opening bid for the gaudy bauble on display was a hundred large.

I placed a couple of early bids while the price was still relatively low. I figured it might be useful to get Demetrios invited again. Also,

I'd never participated in a live auction before, unless you counted eBay, so I scratched that itch. There was plenty of activity for a few minutes as other guests got in on the action and worked to secure their own golden tickets to future Traveling Fair events. By the time the price reached $150 thousand, it was down to three bidders who were genuinely interested in the trinket. After a spirited bidding war, the ring went to a skeletal old woman who looked like she was cosplaying Cruella Deville. Ms. Moneybags shelled out $210K, which made me wonder how it was that some people had more money than sense, and how those same people managed to hold on to all that money.

The auctioneer and his lovely assistant trotted out the da Vinci manuscript next. The single sheet of paper or vellum or whatever it was people used to write on looked appropriately frail and yellowed and was encased in a protective glass display case. There was some handwriting and a couple of doodles on there, and the auctioneer once again went on and on about the historical value of this thing.

Da Vinci had been a powerful sorcerer and a talented artist, but he was also bat-shit crazy. Were he alive today he'd be wearing tinfoil hats and raving about alien butt probes and the government spying on people through their microwaves. Back in his day, he wrote equally stupid screeds on a variety of subjects. His thoughts on weather control had *historical value* because they sure as hell possessed no other redeeming qualities.

Which didn't stop the rich idiots around me from slobbering over this thing like it contained blueprints for a functioning fountain of youth. The opening bid was a quarter of a million dollars, and it didn't take long for the bidding to reach into seven figures. Cruella was in the running again but dropped out eventually, and the remaining two bidders fought over the prize for a while. In the end, the winner—and I use the term loosely—parted with $1.8 million in exchange for the sort of thoughts about weather control one could get for free by talking to bums at the Port Authority Bus Terminal. Then there was a short break and they brought out hors d'oeuvres.

My mood was dark as I munched on bite-sized duck Wellington puff pastries. Going in, I had no idea what value the Fair and its patrons put on the life of a middling, but the fact that they'd left this particular collector's item for last meant it was the main event. Which also meant the line of credit Mordecai had extended definitely wasn't going to cut it. I still had the shard to bargain with. I studied the other attendees as I ate—most either didn't recognize me or made a point of ignoring me—and waited for the auction to resume.

When the auctioneer took the stage again, he spoke with gleeful anticipation. "Ladies and gentlemen, our final item of the evening is a true rarity, a creature many of you have never previously encountered except in the holy books, which—across many cultures—are unanimous in their attitudes." The thin Brit reached into his jacket pocket for a leather-bound tome. "Exodus 22:18," he said, holding up the book. " 'Thou shalt not suffer a witch to live.' The word they translated as 'witch' from the original Hebrew meant a void, or a middling. Someone like *her*."

A pair of security goons led a young woman onto the stage. She staggered rather than walked. Her gaze was unfocused and her jaw slack, a bit of drool pooling at the corner of her mouth.

She looked to be in her mid-twenties, of medium build and height, her skin pale enough to suggest she spent most of her time indoors. She wore blue jeans and a knitted sweater. Strands of unbrushed black hair framed her face and dangled in front of her eyes. Her aura was indistinguishable from everyone else's in the room, same as mine. Middlings aren't easy to tell apart from the gifted.

The auctioneer must've thought the same thing. "This specimen has been thoroughly tested by independent experts to confirm that she is, indeed, a void. Authenticating documents shall be furnished to the winning bidder prior to payment."

As best I could tell, not a single person in the place blinked at him referring to this young woman as a "specimen." She stood there, propped up by the two guards, her head swaying like a flower in a shifting breeze. Those around me gaped at her like they would at a rare caged animal in a circus or, perhaps, a lobster in the fish tank of a seafood restaurant.

I caught myself rising from my seat and made a conscious effort to stay in place. My instinct was to fight, to unleash my wrath upon this gathering of villains, but I knew it was a battle I couldn't hope to win. For my own sake and for the sake of my fellow middling I had to keep my cool.

The bidding started at half a million dollars and the number climbed rapidly. As many as half of the people in the room were in on the action. I watched in amazement as the rich and powerful among the New York City gifted competed for the chance to murder a defenseless girl.

In retrospect, I shouldn't have been surprised. Many of the world's religions demanded that their followers kill middlings on sight; from the line the auctioneer quoted from the Bible to the dark edicts of the terrible gods worshipped by the elder races long before humans invented the wheel. Crusades and holy wars had been fought over such commandments, atrocities that made the murder of a single person pale by comparison.

I gripped the sides of my chair and watched as they raised their numbered paddles. I should have been terrified. They would've just as gladly killed me as they would her. But I've long since exhausted my fear. Its edge has become dulled with each day of living as a chameleon among the gifted until I can barely notice it anymore. It has been replaced with yearning and determination to find a cure. And as I sat there and watched the proceedings, it was cold fury rather than fear that filled my heart. I memorized each bidder's face. New York is a large city, but I was certain I would someday cross paths with many of these characters.

The bidding reached two million dollars, with four scumbags still waving their paddles like they were directing a passenger jet landing at LaGuardia. At this point the value of their prize far exceeded the value of my shard, so the only path still open to me was to find a way to rescue the other middling somehow. It was down to just two bidders at the three million dollar mark. They contemplated the standing bid and each other like they were playing a game of poker. They took their time and there was none of that "going once, going twice" business—the auctioneer was happy to wait since every bid placed at this stage increased the price by a hundred thousand dollars.

One didn't have to be an especially good poker player to see that the younger of the two bidders was wavering. He was twitchy, wiping sweat off his brow, and—if there was any justice in the world—perhaps rethinking his life's choices. But he was still in it against an immaculately dressed silver-fox type who maintained an emotionless façade, even if he didn't rush to place the next bid either. Perhaps he had calculated that making his younger competitor sweat for a while was the superior strategy.

At three point three I thought it was over. The younger bidder lowered his paddle and stared at the floor, his shoulders slumped in defeat.

"Four million." The bid came from the bespectacled man who sat at the end of my row and, until then, had placed no bids at all.

The new bidder appeared to be in his fifties, his gray hair cut very short, and wearing an off-the-rack gray suit. The only thing that could've made him look even more like a giant rodent was a hamster wheel.

Silver Fox appraised his new rival. "Four point two million," he said, enunciating his words with the crisp, neat vowels of a Connecticut private yacht club member.

All eyes were on the new guy. His shock-and-awe bid hadn't ended the auction. Would he try this strategy again or give his wallet a break and bid in smaller increments? I tried to sort out who would present an easier target for me, but it was difficult to decide. Both men were complete unknowns, and both were willing to spend unfathomable amounts of cash to snuff out a life.

The rodent-looking guy adjusted his glasses and said, "Four point five."

The poor woman up front stared into the distance, oblivious to her fate being decided and helpless to intervene. I felt the same way—itching to act but unable to come up with a viable plan.

"Four point seven million," said Silver Fox.

"Five," countered Glasses.

Silver Fox sighed audibly and ran his manicured fingers through his hair. I thought he was ready to give up, but there was fight left in him yet. He straightened his tie and pushed back his shoulders in a dominance display worthy of a nature documentary.

"Six million dollars," he declared.

"Seven," said Glasses without missing a beat.

Silver Fox maintained his composure, but only just. He stared at Glasses for several long seconds, then tossed his paddle onto the empty seat next to him.

And just like that, the only other middling I'd ever encountered was sold to an anonymous stranger for seven million dollars. With the auction at its end everyone was on their feet. Although the bidders had barely acknowledged each other prior to and during the auction, now they all seemed to be talking at once, discussing the events of the evening.

"Thank you for participating in another exciting event brought to you by the Traveling Fair," said the auctioneer, as waiters rushed in with more trays of tall glasses. "Please enjoy another glass of bubbly and toast our winners. After that we request that everyone except for the winning bidders exit the building. The Fair will be arranging direct and *secure* delivery of the items once payment details have been taken care of."

I knocked down a glass of expensive champagne like it was a shot of tequila and maneuvered past several attendees toward Glasses. Others had the same idea—as I approached, I saw him disengage with only the barest modicum of politeness from several people who were trying to talk to him.

I stepped up to Glasses, invading his personal space, my face inches from his, and exhaled, making him smell the alcohol on my breath. I slapped his back with my palm and spoke, intentionally slurring the words. "Congratulations, bud. That was quite a show."

"Thank you," he said tersely and took a step back then worked his way around me as quickly as he could while maintaining some dignity.

I watched him escape toward the Traveling Fair officials, to arrange his payment. With any luck, he would think little of our encounter, believing me to be nothing more than an overbearing drunk. If he was smart, he'd examine the cloth of his jacket where I'd touched it for signs of magical tampering or an electronic bug. And if he was especially careful, he'd ditch the jacket altogether, just in case.

I was counting on him to attempt some of those measures because while his attention had been on my face and my hand, my shoe had brushed gently against his.

The tip of my shoe was coated with a special type of fairy dust. Its magic was tied to a compass that could zero in on the dust's location from up to a thousand leagues away. It was colorless, odorless, and virtually undetectable by magic. The dust was held in place by a tricky little enchantment and was only released by me vocalizing the word "bud."

I could now find Glasses so long as he didn't travel farther than London or Los Angeles. With any luck, he and I would be seeing each other again real soon.

I parked the Oldsmobile a few blocks away from my apartment and walked, cutting through a small park to make sure no one was following me. Most nights I stayed at a studio I rented in Midwood. That's where I received my mail and where my few friends knew to find me. But there was also this safe house no one knew about: a two-bedroom apartment on the ground floor of a two-story private house in Sheepshead Bay.

The Russian immigrant family that owned the house lived on the top floor. When I'd first come to see the apartment for rent a few years back, the patriarch had sized me up and informed me that no cigarettes, no loud noise, and no animals would be tolerated in his house. I assured him that I didn't smoke, owned no pets, and spent much of my time traveling on business. I also didn't haggle on the rent and offered to pay in cash, which had sealed the deal.

I'd been a model tenant since, paying on time and leading a noise-free, pet-free, and smoke-free existence. As to the arsenal of magical weapons and other artifacts I kept there, protected as much by my wards as by the anonymity of the place? The less my landlord knew about that the better he'd sleep at night.

Once inside the apartment, I set the grapefruit-sized magical compass on my desk. It had been designed by Dutch warlocks in the early twentieth century and looked like a jumbo pocket watch: a golden onion with ingeniously crafted dials visible through a series of apertures. The numbers they displayed kept shifting via gears powered by the compass' magic. They represented the latitude and longitude where the fairy dust could be found, while the compass arrow pointed southwest.

Back when it was created the compass must've been a real pain to use—the practitioner had had to rely on a stack of maps and atlases. They'd had to arm themselves with a pencil and a protractor to figure out where their quarry was headed. Thankfully, we lived in a more enlightened age. I powered up my laptop and typed the coordinates into Google Maps.

It appeared Glasses had traveled from Queens into New Jersey. Given the princely price he'd spent on the middling, I was sure he'd be keeping her in his sights the entire way. I kept an eye on the coordinates for another half an hour or so, until the arrow and the numbers both stopped moving. The destination Glasses arrived at was an industrial area in Woodbridge Township. I zoomed in on the satellite images of the neighborhood to find a pallet manufacturer, several warehouses in various stages of disrepair, a recycling plant, a bunch of empty lots overgrown with vegetation, and a newly constructed four-story office building owned by a multinational pharmaceutical conglomerate. One of these things was not like the others.

According to the internet, the building housed a branch of Nascent Anodynes International, a company with a name so bland and generic that one had to assume their primary enterprises were kicking puppies and the ritual sacrifice of middlings.

I'd get a more precise match from the compass when I went there, but having met Glasses, my money was on the multinational pharmaceutical conglomerate over the pallet manufacturer.

CHAPTER 7

AT 11:05 A.M. a beat-up Honda pulled into the mostly empty parking lot of a freestanding office building in Woodbridge, New Jersey. Both sides of the vehicle were emblazoned with the Pizza Kid logo featuring a cartoon toddler holding a pizza pie. The child was portly, perhaps to indicate his predisposition toward a steady diet of cheese, dough, and tomato sauce.

Mikey, a lanky teenager in a Pizza Kid T-shirt and a New York Giants baseball cap, climbed out the driver's side door and pulled a thermal bag from the shotgun seat. He stepped through the building's rotating door and into the air-conditioned comfort of a capacious lobby.

An abstract art mural covered the walls of the football-shaped lobby, with splashes of color—that looked splattered rather than painted—over the sheetrock. The walls extended in both directions from the front entrance and terminated at the rectangular waiting area on the opposite end of the oval, which contained a pair of elevator banks and a staircase. Above the waiting area hung the company logo, capital letters *N* and *A* in dark blue followed by the lowercase cursive letter *i* in red. Soft elevator muzak piped into the lobby from hidden speakers.

Halfway between the entrance and the elevators stood an enormous reception desk. There, barricaded behind a gaggle of computer monitors, sat a pair of grim-faced gentlemen who looked like they might feel more at home at a *Sopranos* extras casting call than in any position where greeting people was part of the job description.

Mikey took it all in, pausing to appreciate the mural as he approached the desk. Underneath the Jackson Pollock-style drips of color it was teeming with lines and dots and vague shapes that almost made sense until you looked at them more closely. The two men watched him placidly.

"Delivery," said Mikey. He glanced at the sticker slapped onto the side of his thermal bag. "For Mr. Dover."

The two guards exchanged a look. "There ain't a Mr. Dover here," said one of them, perpetuating the Jersey accent stereotype.

Mikey looked closer at the sticker. He rattled off the address of the office building, and the guard nodded.

"Dover," he repeated. "Mr. Benjamin Dover?"

Four seconds later the other guard, who had remained quiet until then, guffawed.

"You've been pranked, kid," he said. "*Ben Dover*. Get it? Some wise guy thinks he's in a *Simpsons* episode."

The first guard demonstrated that he was not, in fact, the brains of the operation, by finally grasping the joke and laughing uproariously. Mikey frowned and scratched at the stubble on his chin.

"That's just great," Mikey said. "Took me fifteen minutes to drive out here." He hefted the thermal bag. "Any chance you guys wanna buy a large ham and pineapple pie?"

"Nah. I'm trying that Atkins diet," said the smarter guard. He eyed the bag with regret. "Going on the second week."

"That's how you shoulda known it was a bogus order," said the dumber guard. "No one in Joisey ruins their pizza by adding pineapple."

A brief but passionate debate about the merits of pineapple on pizza ensued between the two guards. Mikey listened to some of it, hefted the thermal bag, and headed toward the exit.

"Hope the rest of your shift gets better," called out the smarter guard.

Mikey flashed him a smile and waved thanks, then used the bag to push at the revolving door.

He left the parking lot and drove to the Holiday Inn Express a few miles down the road.

Mikey knocked on the door of the room I'd rented for the day and handed me his Giants cap. I gave him a pair of crisp hundred-dollar bills.

"Wait," I called out as he turned to leave. "Hand over that pizza. I did order and pay for it, after all."

Mikey grinned at me, opened the Velcro cover of his thermal bag, and liberated the cardboard pizza box.

When he left, I tossed the pizza on the little hotel room writing desk. "Dig in."

Herc, who was lounging in the armchair, reached over and opened the lid. The smell of baked dough filled the hotel room. "Pineapple? That's whack, man."

"We all have our crosses to bear in this situation," I told him. "If I'm hungry enough to eat Jersey pizza, you're hungry enough to eat pineapple pizza."

"Spare me your 'New York food is the bomb' act," Herc said. "You used to order from Pizza Kid all the time when we chilled at your crib."

Herc had been a prospect when I'd first met him. He had manifested young, a nineteen year old from Newark who dressed and talked like he was on *The Wire*. Once you got to know him even a little and peeked past his camouflage, he was this really smart, really sweet kid. He was a quick study and possibly the most powerful natural practitioner I've ever met, save Mose himself.

Needless to say, he hadn't stayed with me in Brooklyn for long. I'd taught him the lore and what to watch out for out there; spell-casting was something he took to naturally. I think he was better at it than any of his Watch tutors by the second week of training.

When he had been told to choose his new name, he hadn't hesitated for a moment.

"Hercules Mulligan," he had said.

"Like the Irish guy from the American Revolution?" I'd asked.

"Like the Black guy from *Hamilton*." He had chuckled. "Man, do I look Irish to you?"

"It's a good name, but … Hercules? You're way too scrawny for that," I'd said.

"How about Herc?" he'd suggested.

It had stuck.

Herc had worked for the Watch for about a year in Philadelphia, before quitting. I couldn't blame him. Volunteering for a dangerous and thankless job isn't for everyone. Herc had come home to Newark and continued to protect it from monsters and overly ambitious sorcerers in an unofficial capacity—a vigilante of sorts. He was tolerated and even liked by the Watch as he kept his nose clean and followed the rules. He was basically doing the same job, but without the headache of reporting to the Watch higher-ups. When I needed help with an unauthorized mission to New Jersey against a mysterious foe, there was no one I would have rather turned to for help.

I removed the miniature spy camera from the brim of Mikey's cap and fumbled with a tiny cable to connect it to my laptop.

"Moment of truth, Herc," I said, loading the video.

"I gotta tell you, if big, scary wizards were headquartered in a corporate park in Central Jersey, I would have heard about them by now," Herc said. He grimaced as he looked at the slice of pineapple-and-ham pizza, picked off a piece of tropical fruit, then took a big bite. "Things I put up with for my friends," he added, chewing.

"None of my plethora of charms and spells can see inside that building," I told him. "Not a one. The tracing charm is the only thing that worked. I'm confident the guy I tagged with it went inside, but I can't pinpoint him, not even from their parking lot. I can only think of a dozen places around the country with that level of arcane security."

"So you've said. Sending in a mundane to scope the place was a dope move. No aura for them to detect."

"Good thing you recommended this Mikey kid," I said, loading the video.

"One of my Irregulars," said Herc. He'd gotten that from Sherlock Holmes and really liked both the idea of developing a network of useful informers and the moniker for the foot soldiers of the said network. "I like him. He doesn't ask questions." He got up from the armchair, stretched, and positioned himself where he could see the screen.

We watched the recording of Mikey's encounter with the guards.

"Check out the walls," said Herc.

"Yeah. Industrial-strength protection runes in several dead languages, hidden throughout the mural in plain sight and masquerading as modern art," I said.

"I'm starting to buy into your theory about these guys," said Herc. "Listen."

After a few seconds I nodded. "The music is a warding chant mixed with some atrocious pop tune. Good catch."

We watched the rest of the encounter, until Mikey had left the building.

"Okay, so you were right," said Herc. "There *are* scary wizards there. Now what? We still don't know what's beyond that lobby."

I thought about the drugged middling they had in there.

"The two of us can take them," I said. "Recon by combat. We go in fast, hit them hard."

Herc sighed. "You know I got your back, but are you sure that's wise?"

"I don't think their bite is as bad as their bark." I plucked a slice of pineapple off the pizza and popped the sweet morsel into my mouth.

"How do you figure?"

"Let's logic this out," I said. "We know whoever owns this place has access to serious magic, and we know they don't want their presence known. So why put up artwork that screams Here Be Dragons? Or rather, Here Be Scary Wizards, whatever. Why not hide the wards beyond the lobby? That way, a gifted walks in, sees nothing interesting—assuming the rent-a-cops are mundanes—no magic, no auras. Everything is hidden elsewhere in the building, right?"

Herc thought about it. "That's what I'd do."

"But instead they figure, okay, no gifted has a reason to be here, but should one show up, we make the place look more impregnable than Fort Knox, make any reasonable person think twice about what sort of horrors await inside, convince the visitor to turn around on their heels and leave. Now, why would they do that?"

"Because the guard dog in the huge, scary-looking doghouse behind the fence is a Chihuahua?" asked Herc.

"Bingo. I don't think whatever or whoever is in there is beyond our ability to deal with. Their bosses may be another story, so I figure we grab the hostage and get out before their cavalry arrives."

"We ride into an enemy castle to rescue a girl," said Herc as he wiped his fingers on a napkin. "What's not to like?"

As we drove toward the bad guys' lair I didn't feel as confident as I'd made myslef sound to my friend.

I walked into situations like this all the time. It was part of the job description. But when I did, it was knowing that the combined resources and power of the Watch was behind me. Their name alone was enough to make thieves and necromancers surrender, to make monsters and cannibals hesitate, hold back, or try to run. And even those who stood and fought knew that if they somehow took me down the Watch would hunt them to the ends of the earth.

This time around, I was up against an enemy that seemed powerful enough not to be intimidated, and I was here on a personal mission; if things went wrong, Mose and the others wouldn't even know where to look for my body. What's worse, I was also risking the life of my friend. A good enough friend to help me on a dangerous mission without prodding for details. When I'd said I couldn't explain why I wanted to rescue the middling, he'd simply accepted that I had my reasons for keeping the details private and had focused on the *how* instead of the *why*. That was the sort of man Hercules Mulligan had always been.

I tried to put these thoughts out of my mind as Herc parked his Jetta by the Nascent Anodynes entrance. I couldn't let worry distract me. I grasped a short silver wand in my right hand and a string of wooden prayer beads in my left, wrapping them twice around my fingers.

Herc needed no knickknacks. He arrived dressed in jeans and a Public Enemy T-shirt. His natural talent was superior to whatever I could accomplish with my arsenal. He stepped out of the car and sized up the building.

"Giddy up, Conrad," he said. "Let's go storm the castle."

Even as Herc and I approached the front door we felt the power of the wards. A subtle suggestion spell whispered in my ear, attempting to convince me that I had urgent business elsewhere. A not-so-subtle spell on the door itself detected our auras and attempted to physically repel us. We walked forward as if wading through a shallow pool. An alarm began to wail inside the building.

The lobby was overflowing with magic. I felt its malevolent presence deep in my bones. The guards huddled in the far corner. They observed us from a distance but didn't interfere. They were mundanes and must've been told to keep out of the way if the special alarm ever went off. We paid them no mind as we marched toward the elevators. As soon as we reached the halfway point, the entire lobby turned into a kill box.

It was like the Magic Kingdom in there, except not adorable, and everything was trying to kill us. Sigils on the walls lit up with the color of hellfire. The sound system piped in ancient curses. The abstract images of the mural swirled and rearranged themselves into hexes.

I was pretty certain our unseen enemies didn't even know who we were. They didn't know why we were there, and they didn't expect we were coming. The trap was set up to go off the moment any gifted entered the lobby. The owners of this place must've really hated visitors.

I clutched the prayer beads. They made the air around me shimmer like a full-body halo and blocked the brunt of the hostile magic. The fact that I felt even a little of it spoke to how lethal the attacks were.

Herc surrounded himself with a personal ward. It enveloped him like a cocoon, protecting him from the assault. He had power to spare, yet even he was struggling to shrug off this attack. His fists were clenched, as was his jaw. Sweat trickled down his brow.

"These are static defenses," I said. "We need to keep moving."

Get past the lobby and the big, bad defense system will stay behind.

I pushed forward and it was like walking toward a hurricane with not so much as a cheap, disposable umbrella.

CHAPTER 8

WE pushed toward the elevators, past the curses and spells flung at us like bullets fired from enemy trenches. I pointed toward the EXIT sign that hung above the staircase. There was no chance in hell we were getting into one of the elevators—they were too easy a trap, with or without magic. We were almost to the stairs when the floor indicator dinged and the door to one of the lifts opened.

Out spilled a menagerie of monsters that would have given Dr. Frankenstein and Dr. Moreau instant erections. Half a dozen of them strode toward us, ignoring the barrage of pernicious magic around them. They were each roughly five feet tall, with alligator heads and lithe muscular panther torsos. They stood upright on short but powerful hind legs that might or might not have come from gorillas. Catlike tails with scorpion stingers bobbed back and forth behind them.

"This may be a terrible time to pun," I told Herc, "but I do believe they bear arms."

The creatures had thick grizzly arms covered in brown fur. Black razor-sharp four-inch claws extended from their paws.

"Puntastic," Herc muttered through clenched teeth.

Then the weaponized nature collages were upon us.

Herc spoke an incantation and intense flames engulfed the nearest monster. I pointed the silver wand and it crackled with magic, unleashing a bolt of electricity powerful enough to fry an elephant. It caught one of them in the chest, but instead of collapsing in a heap of charred multi-species barbecue, the monster staggered back a few steps before resuming its attack, despite the smoldering wound that now decorated its fur.

The nearest monster swiped at my arm and caught me just below the shoulder. Its claws sliced through my coat and shirt like my clothes were made of heated butter, grazing my skin, leaving several shallow gashes. It hurt pretty bad, and I wondered how many of the animals that comprised that living jigsaw puzzle might carry rabies.

Herc conjured a force barrier between us and the collection of snapping jaws, claws, and stingers while I kept firing bolts to little effect. I made myself lean closer to the invisible barrier for a better look and noted the strings of amulets stitched into the creatures' flesh along the lines where different animal parts were fused together via magically grown bone, muscle, and skin.

"They each have half a million dollars' worth of protective charms embedded," I said. "We have to hit them with a physical attack instead of an arcane one."

Herc was sweating profusely. Even someone of his ability couldn't maintain both the force barrier and the ward against arcane attacks for long. Which, I felt certain, was the point of this two-pronged assault.

"Sorry, Conrad," he said. "I left my big game rifle in my other pants."

I scanned the lobby for something to use as a club but quickly discarded the idea. There was no way we'd win a physical fight against these things. The gashes on my arm really stung.

Herc was backing away in the direction of the front door, and since the force barrier moved with him I had no choice but to follow.

We had underestimated the power and resources of our faceless foes. Retreating was the right move. Except I couldn't give up. I couldn't leave the middling in the hands of whomever had mutilated animals to create the things that were menacing us from beyond the force shield.

I had a trump card to play. Wincing from the pain, I reached deep into the inner pocket of my coat for one of the rarest artifacts I owned. I placed an orb the size of a human heart onto the tiled floor. It sat there, pulsating deep red, priceless and irreplaceable. I crushed it under my heel.

The magic attack ceased instantly. The lobby reverted to its normal state, as though someone had flipped a switch turning off the defenses. Even the sound system went back to playing some milquetoast tune. The monsters in front of us collapsed into piles of gruesome body parts splattering the floor, walls, and force barrier with blood.

"Ugh." Herc released the force barrier and we watched the crimson droplets fall to the floor. "What the devil was that?"

"The Heart of Ur," I said. "Think of it as an EMP for magic. It fries amulets, charms, anything that stores magic, within a city block when you set it off."

"That explains my force barrier remaining in place while everything else got KO'ed. I was using my own magic instead of an imbued artifact to maintain it," said Herc. He was always quick on the uptake. "Nice toy."

I ran a hand through my hair. This *toy* might have been the last of its kind. Moreover, it had destroyed all of my other tools and protections. It had left me completely unarmed in the face of whatever else awaited us in the building.

Herc walked over to where the monsters had collapsed, leaving boot prints in the blood on the floor. It smelled pretty much how you'd expect a pile of severed animal parts to smell. He picked up a grizzly arm and studied it.

"What is it with me and bears?" he asked. "Since coming back home I've had to fight a werebear once, and a zombear on two separate occasions. I guess frankenbear makes it a trifecta."

I shrugged, sending another jolt of pain up my arm. "That's Jersey for ya: bears and chemical plants."

Herc dropped the bear arm, wiped his hand on the side of his T-shirt, and gave me the middle finger.

"Your arm okay?" he asked.

I nodded. "It's just a flesh wound."

"Good thing you're the weirdo who wears a coat regardless of the weather," he said. "Gave you some protection."

I nodded again.

"Come on, then. Let's see what's behind door number one." Herc stepped over a jumbo-sized scorpion stinger and headed toward the staircase.

Wounded, unarmed, and as defenseless against all magic as a newborn babe, I followed him.

The staircase was immaculate and boring: gray concrete flights of stairs leading up and down. There were three floors above us and who knows how many underneath. I hesitated momentarily. Which direction should we head in? Splitting up seemed like a terrible idea—and making a wrong decision could easily lead to the bad guys sneaking their prize out the door.

Herc didn't break his stride. He headed downward.

"Are you sure?" I asked as I followed him.

"New construction in this area isn't supposed to have basements. Floodplain management, and all that," Herc said. "Also, when the elevator delivered our frankenfriends back there, it was going up."

Even while fending off an attack Herc had noticed a detail like that. The Watch was truly poorer for him leaving.

We reached the bottom of the stairs and Herc pushed the door open. I hung behind him praying that he wouldn't over-rely on the backup I couldn't provide, and that my uselessness wouldn't get us both killed.

We encountered no resistance.

The basement was a series of rooms, each the size of a spacious New York apartment. They were connected to one another with wide double doors that swung open with a push.

The first room housed a cubicle farm with laptops and sheaves of printouts on desks, a water cooler and a coffee pot in the corner. There were several employees still at their desks, ordinary-looking men and women. They wouldn't meet my gaze. They stared at the floor meekly instead, looking about as comfortable as bank tellers during an armed robbery. They had no auras. I wondered briefly what it was like for the mundanes to work in this environment. Were they in on the truth, or did they think the animal monsters were created through science, Mary Shelley style?

The second room was a chemistry lab. Various beakers filled with liquids of unhealthy hues sat on chrome tables along the walls. Industrial-sized refrigerator units hummed and probably contained things I didn't want to see while there was still pizza in my stomach. One wall was lined with rectangular storage units. Based on what I'd seen on TV, they looked like the cold chambers in the morgue. Another pair of mundane employees stared at us in abject fear.

The third room was a vivisection chamber. It smelled strongly of rubbing alcohol. Billiards-sized metal tables had elevated edges and small drain pipes. What looked like medical equipment units on wheeled tripods were positioned next to those tables. Knives and bone saws hung on the walls and a collection of scalpels and other shiny, metal surgical instruments were stored in sealed see-through containers. The room was clean and tidy, like an operating theater, but I could see nicks and scratches on the tables from where sharp implements must've bit through flesh and bone to connect with the metal surface.

An entire shelving unit contained a collection of magical artifacts these people must've used in their grim work. I stared at them through glass: there were hundreds of thousands of dollars' worth of gem-laden amulets, charms made of teeth and tusks and bones, saws and scalpels and other sharp tools inscribed with runes and sigils. Up until a few minutes ago, all of these artifacts must've been enchanted with powerful spells, imbued with vast amounts of magical energy. The Heart of Ur had turned them into a heap of impotent curios. And although a part of me mourned the lost opportunity to loot the trove, I was glad they'd never again be used for their grisly purpose.

The next room was filled with cages, most of them empty. This is where the monsters they'd set upon us had been kept. Animal odor combined with the stink of wet fur and the stench of feces to create a gag-inducing stench that the powerful air conditioning unit was trying desperately and failing to keep up with. Several of the locked cages contained living animals. There was an alligator or crocodile in one—I couldn't tell the difference—lying still under a lamp that emitted warm light. A brown bear shifted in a cage that was barely large enough for its massive size. The bear was all matted fur and sad eyes. It raised its head to stare at us as we passed by.

The next room looked much like the lab we had encountered earlier, except there was a hospital cot in the center. In it the middling slept amidst a tangle of tubes and wires. Sensors of all kinds were attached to her skin. An IV drip connected her left arm to bags of greenish-looking goo that hung on the pole.

Next to the cot stood two men in lab coats and surgical masks. Of everyone we had encountered in the building, they were the first to possess auras. They turned toward us.

I recognized Glasses immediately despite the mask. The man next to him was squat and stood about five feet tall. He appeared to be in his late thirties. His black hair was slicked back with a ton of gel. The shorter man took off his mask. He wore a petulant expression on his pale face. Unlike everyone else we'd encountered thus far, neither man appeared afraid of us.

"Gentlemen," said the younger man. "Before you do anything rash, direct your attention at the cameras." He pointed at several opaque globes along the ceiling. "The recording is being stored offsite for use by our legal department."

"What are you doing to her?" I asked, rage barely contained in my voice.

"My name is Marko Hanson and I'm in charge of this facility," said the younger man, ignoring my question. "And you're Mr. Brent and Mr. Mulligan, yes?"

Herc and I exchanged a quick look. We'd figured our adversaries would eventually discover our identities, but we hadn't thought it would happen so quickly.

"Our facial recognition software is top-notch," said Hanson. "We have the resources to do that at Nascent Anodynes." He looked me in the eye. "A member of the Watch moonlighting as a brigand? *Tsk, tsk*. What will your superiors think?"

I ignored his words as he had ignored my question. "What are you doing to her? Last chance."

"What are you being paid for this smash-and-grab?" asked Hanson. "I'm sure we can offer you more. All you'd have to do to earn that money is tell us who hired you and walk away."

"Not happening," said Herc. "Disconnect her from those machines and get that needle out her arm, now. And she better be breathing after that if *you* also want to keep breathing."

"Two million dollars," said Hanson. "A million each for you to walk away, or …" He smirked. "Should one of you decide to take the other out, we'll pay the two mil to whoever's left standing."

I took a pair of steps forward and punched Hanson hard in the solar plexus. He doubled over, wheezing.

Herc turned to Glasses. "Best do what I said, or my associate here is gonna punch the smirk off your face, too."

My buddy had to be making an assumption about that smirk, because Glasses still had his mask on and his eyes definitely weren't smiling. He raised his hands, palms up, then turned to the hospital cot and set about removing sensors and needles and what-have-you from the unconscious middling.

"You're going to regret this," Hanson hissed. "I'll make sure you die slow. You can't hide from—"

I raised a fist but before I could punch him again, Glasses spoke.

"Stop! We got what we needed from her, Mr. Hanson. Let their employer dispose of her for us." He kept working, his hands and voice steady. He glanced at me. "I'd like your assurances that you will not harm us and will leave this place immediately once we hand her over."

I wasn't happy one bit about the ominous declaration Glasses had made regarding them getting what they needed, but time wasn't on our side. My primary concern was to get her out. Everything else would have to play second fiddle.

"What's your name?" I asked.

"Vaughn."

"Here's the deal, Vaughn. We're going to take her with us and we're going to leave now. *If* she hasn't been harmed, and *if* your pharma bro boss does nothing stupid, such as try to retaliate against any of us, our interaction will have come to a satisfactory, violence-free end. Otherwise, remember how easily we found you this time and that my friends and I can *always* find you again."

Hanson muttered something under his breath but didn't challenge us. Vaughn finished what he was doing and stepped away from the woman, his face impassive. He radiated this cold confidence that was more disturbing than Hanson's hateful glares.

Herc tapped the woman's shoulder. She didn't move. Her breathing was even and deep.

"Wake her up," Herc said.

"She'll wake up in a few hours," said Vaughn. "She's under sedation, and if you want her unharmed, I advise against rousing her sooner. Here." He bent down and unlocked the brake. "The bed has wheels."

I grumbled and grabbed the handles pushing the cot forward. It wobbled. Herc steadied the side of the cot with one hand, keeping a watchful eye on our adversaries.

Vaughn hesitated a moment, then approached the other side of the cot and elevated a metal railing at the woman's feet. He grabbed hold of it with both hands and pulled. "A two-man job. Like so."

I didn't think this cold bastard had suddenly grown a conscience, so I kept an extra close eye on him, but he helped pull the cot to the door without incident, with me pushing and Herc walking alongside the bed, ready to defend us. Hanson stared daggers at us from where he stood.

"Halt," Vaughn said as we reached the exit.

Before we had a chance to react the aerosol containers positioned above the door burped a puff of hot, moist air at us.

"The hell?!" Herc advanced on Vaughn.

Nonplussed as ever, Vaughn said, "It's a disinfectant. An automated system, perfectly harmless. We occasionally work with substances that require this." He inhaled theatrically. "Look, I'm breathing it in. Deodorant sprays contain more dangerous chemicals than this."

I didn't really trust him, and from the expression on my friend's face, I could tell Herc felt the same way. But we experienced no immediate ill effects and Herc gave no indication that his magic detected foul play, so we left it at that.

We rolled the cot past the succession of rooms and to the elevator bank. Vaughn pressed the call button.

"No way," said Herc.

I nodded and picked the middling up from the cot. She was wearing a hospital gown.

"Where's her stuff?" I asked.

Vaughn reached under the cot and handed us a neatly folded stack of clothes. I recognized the jeans and sweater from the auction.

"She'll need lots of fluids," Vaughn said, not unkindly. "Water's fine."

"What did you do to her?" I asked.

"We drew blood and performed some tests. We haven't harmed her, I swear."

"What for?"

Vaughn looked me in the eye. "I believe that information is outside the scope of the agreement you proposed, Mr. Brent. Goodbye."

He turned and headed back the way we came.

I huffed and puffed as I carried a grown woman up a flight of stairs. They make that sort of thing look easy in the movies. I can vouch it wasn't. Herc led the way, carrying the bundle of clothes.

The lobby was empty, the security guards gone. No one challenged us in the parking lot, either.

Herc drove us to where I'd parked my car, glancing at the woman who slept in his back seat.

"One day you're gonna tell me what this was all about, right, Conrad?"

"Believe me, you're better off not knowing." I squeezed his shoulder. "Thank you."

He didn't press further. A true friend. If he ever needed it, I'd gladly return the favor. I hoped he knew that.

He dropped us off at the Oldsmobile. I was happy to be in my enchanted car where I kept a small stash of amulets and protections. It wouldn't replace everything I had lost that day, but there was enough so I wouldn't feel naked and helpless.

I drove straight to my secret apartment in Sheepshead Bay. I parked in front of the house and carried the middling inside. This was the first time I'd ever parked my car so close to my hideout, and carrying an unconscious woman into the house wasn't a great way to maintain my low profile in the neighborhood. But I didn't have a lot of options. I needed to get to where my magical artifacts were stored in case Pharma Douche and his cohorts elected not to honor the terms of the deal I'd forced upon them.

I carried the woman into the bedroom, placed her onto the bed, and covered her with a blanket. I laid her stack of clothes on the chair next to the bed and placed a bottle of spring water on the nightstand. Then I closed the bedroom door behind me, discarded the artifacts I'd burned out with the Heart of Ur, and restocked as best I could. Finally, I cleaned and bandaged my wound and changed into a shirt that hadn't been shredded by bear claws.

I collapsed into an armchair in the living room and waited.

CHAPTER 9

NEARLY two hours had passed by the time I heard movement from the bedroom. I remained seated. I figured she'd need time to acclimate to her surroundings and get dressed before a stranger barged in. After a few minutes it became quiet again, and eventually my level of concern outweighed my politeness.

I knocked lightly, waited a few seconds, and having heard no reaction opened the door.

The woman lay atop of the bed, dressed in her jeans and sweater. The water bottle was half empty. She seemed out of it, staring absently into the ceiling. Perhaps whatever they'd used to sedate her hadn't worn off yet.

"Hello," I said. "My name is Conrad Brent."

She made no response, but her muscles tensed. I was reasonably certain she could hear and understand me.

"You're safe here," I said. "You've been through an ordeal, but you're safe now."

Still no response.

"Are you feeling all right?"

She turned her head toward me a smidgeon and mouthed something inaudible.

"Sorry?"

She added something, mouthing several words only someone who was fluent in lip reading could have deciphered. Perhaps she hadn't the strength to speak yet, which seemed odd given she was able to get up and dress herself moments earlier. She beckoned me closer.

I approached the bed and leaned in to hear her better. She twisted and drove her knee into my groin.

I grunted, doubled over in pain, and collapsed onto the edge of the bed. The woman scrambled past me and toward the door.

"Wait!" I made no move to pursue, fearing that even if I could overcome the pain my chasing after her would only serve to scare her more. "There are very dangerous people looking for you. Please, don't be hasty."

She paused in the doorway, a ball of nerves, ready to bolt the moment I made the wrong move.

I sat deeper on the bed and tried to keep my voice even and calm. "I mean you no harm."

She stared at me, then turned to survey the living room. There were tribal masks on the walls, bits of papyrus hung in picture frames, a pair of eighteenth-century grandfather clocks lined up in the corner, and all sorts of miscellanea on my desk. Items that might not predispose a stranger who grew up in the age of corny TV shows and movies to thinking I was the good guy. Ever since Robert E. Howard's Conan stories the common wisdom went: brainy magic user is the villain, muscle-bound jock with a sword large enough to compensate for something is the hero.

"I'm sure you have questions, and I can only imagine how frightened you must be. But please, this is the safest place for you right now."

"You're a liar!" She spat the words out, anger and frustration rather than fear in her voice. "I saw you. You were there when the kidnappers sold me."

I was surprised she had been conscious and had the presence of mind to remember faces from the auction. How much more terrifying the ordeal must've been for her if she had remained rational through it all!

"I was there," I admitted. "I was trying to rescue you. It was how I was able to learn where you'd be taken."

She studied my face. How could she believe me, I thought, after what she had been through?

"You're in Brooklyn," I said. "There's a few hundred dollars in the top desk drawer in the living room. You can take the money, and you're free to leave whenever you want. I won't try to stop you. All I ask is that you consider hearing me out if you decide to stay."

She stood there for a time, then ventured into the living room. I got off the bed and, wincing in pain, went to the door, to the spot she had occupied but no farther, so she'd know I wasn't trying to interfere. I watched her take the cash from the drawer and open the front door. I said nothing.

She stepped outside, leaving the front door open, and looked around. The sights and sounds of a peaceful residential street surrounded her. Through the front door I could see a grandmother pushing a stroller past the house. Across the street a teenager walked her Pomeranian. The normality of everyday life versus the insanity of abduction and the outlandish, peculiar items inside my home. The uncertainty of what had happened to her versus possible revelations I could provide.

The woman looked back to me. I remained standing at the bedroom door. The decision had to be hers.

She came back inside and stared at me across the living room, her arms folded.

"Tell me everything."

I limped to the chair, maintaining a distance between us that would make her feel more secure.

"You can see my aura, yes?"

She nodded.

"People who have auras are magic users, generally called the gifted."

I launched into an explanation of magic, of the secret history of our world, and all the things an average mundane manages to ignore. One of the most difficult things for the newly manifested gifted to accept is how all this supernatural stuff has been going on around them their entire lives without them ever noticing. Human brains are funny like that. A mundane might observe an eight-foot ogre with sickly green complexion and filter out what's supposed to be impossible, seeing only a large, bearded biker. Giants and halflings walk among the mundanes and they're accepted among them, even as they manage to land roles on TV shows like *Game of Thrones* playing dwarves or oversized knights.

It's not that the gifted are so brilliant or have some sort of Illuminati or a government agency to keep themselves hidden from the masses. Mundane brains filter reality in the way acceptable to them. They explain the unexplainable through hallucinations, déjà vu, intoxication, or even UFO sightings. The gifted need only go about our business without causing too many waves, and our secret remains intact.

I told her all this until I reached the point where I had to explain what a middling was.

"You can do magic too, but only by using artifacts imbued with power by other magic users," I said. "You lack the ability to generate such power on your own."

"I'm a half-baked sorceress?" She shifted her weight. "That's news to me."

"You see the peacock feather in the vase on that shelf? Go ahead and grab it, please. You can use it to levitate small objects."

She picked up the feather, holding it like a magic wand.

"Now what, do I have to say something in Latin?"

"Point it at any object that weighs under ten pounds and will it to fly."

"*Will* it, how?"

"You don't have to really think about it, same way as you don't have to consciously tell your hand how to scratch your nose or instruct your feet about how to position themselves in order for you to walk. It's easier to actually *do* than to wrap your mind around."

She pointed the feather at an empty wire-mesh trash bin that stood by my desk, and focused.

The trash bin wobbled on the floor as if it were being shaken by invisible hands. Then it lifted off the ground and hung about two feet up in the air.

"Holy shit!" The woman gasped, and the trash bin dropped to the ground and rolled on its side until it hit a wall. She looked around the room and at all the arcane items on my shelves. "What else can I do?"

"Slow down," I said. "First, you need a name."

She opened her mouth to speak but I held up my hand.

"Don't tell me your real name," I said. "Don't tell *anyone* your real name, ever. Names have power, but also they tie us to our mundane loved ones, and we don't want our enemies to ever find them."

She frowned at this. "Does that mean every gifted leaves their loved ones and goes into some sort of a witness protection program?"

"Not every gifted, but those who are most likely to make enemies do. People like me, who opt to join the Watch. People like you, who are abducted by villains."

The latter explanation seemed to have really hit home. I explained to her about choosing her own name from this point on. She thought it over.

"Willodean," she said. "It was my grandmother's name, and I've always liked how it sounds."

"That's good. But don't tell anyone else that second bit. The less strangers know that can connect you to your family and your real name, the better."

"Okay then … Conrad," she said.

"Discovering you're a magic user is the fun part," I said. "Here's the not-so-fun part."

I launched into an explanation of what a middling was and how everyone wanted them dead. Wanted *us* dead.

It was a difficult decision to reach: Should I tell her that I was a middling too? After so many years of keeping even my closest friends and allies in the dark, the obvious choice would have been to keep the secret. But I needed her to trust me if we were to ever find a way to cure our mutual affliction. She had been through a lot already and I didn't want to start out by lying to her. I told her everything.

It was a long conversation. We talked for several hours and it started getting dark outside. At some point we ordered takeout from a local Thai place. I continued to regale her with my story and answer her questions between bites of noodles.

She told me her story, too, and it wasn't much different from anyone else's. She had been a kindergarten teacher in South Carolina, leading a perfectly normal, comfortable life when her abilities began to manifest, and she started seeing auras, as well as all the stranger things in the world around her. It only took her a few weeks to find a group of local magic users, and it took even less time for them to realize she was a middling. She hadn't been lucky like me, hadn't learned she was different from the rest of the gifted quickly enough to take precautions. Ultimately, she didn't even know which of her new "friends" had contacted the Traveling Fair.

It's not like there's a how-to manual for emerging middlings. I wondered if perhaps we weren't quite as rare as I'd been led to believe. Rather, most of us might not have survived long enough to hide …. But, no; if middlings were more commonplace, assholes like Hanson and Vaughn wouldn't shell out millions to get their hands on one.

Willodean had a sharp and inquisitive mind and she was easy to talk to. I found myself opening up more and more, after so many years of keeping secrets. She scoffed at the superhero comparison though.

"Batman? No way. This is no mansion. I see no butler. And this,"—she pointed at the white cardboard takeout boxes on the dining table—"isn't filet mignon. There's got to be a better fictional character to describe you." She tapped her fingers on the table absentmindedly as she worked it out. "I've got it. You're a magical Rorschach from *Watchmen!*"

"Rorschach? Please. My eyes rolled so hard I just saw my own aura. I'm not nearly so cranky, and I have a sense of humor."

"I'm not stuck in this apartment with you," Willodean growled in her best imitation of Rorschach's voice. "You're stuck in here with *me!*"

We both chuckled.

Having someone to share the truth with was nice. Willodean was smart and remarkably resilient, if she could go from tension and fear to making light of her situation so quickly. And she liked comics. We were going to get along just fine.

The phone rang.

I figured it was Mose again. At some point I'd have to stop dodging his calls. But the caller ID displayed Herc's name.

"Are you feeling okay, Conrad?" he asked without preamble. He sounded off somehow. Rattled.

"Fine, I think. Why do you ask?"

"Those bastards did something to us. Whatever chemicals were in that spray they hit us with on the way out, they're messing me up."

"Shit." I felt fine, like I'd told him, but perhaps whatever-it-was worked faster on him than it did on me. "Messing you up how? Did you go to the hospital?"

"Physically, I'm all right," said Herc. "It's worse than that. It's screwing with my magic."

A knot formed in my stomach. "What do you mean?"

"My powers are failing," he said with the sort of dread you might hear in the voice of someone who was going blind.

I had lied to a good friend and exposed him to mortal danger, all so I could save a stranger and further my secret search for a cure. And now he was paying the price for my rash and ill-considered rescue plan.

"Where are you?" I grabbed a Post-it Note and a ballpoint pen from my desk. "I'll be right there."

Herc, Willodean, and I sat in his living room. It was considerably neater than mine, adorned with modernist furniture and decorated with black-and-white prints set in polished nickel frames. Herc was apparently a really good photographer, something I'd never known about him.

He wasn't in the mood to discuss his hobbies just then. He was focused on a crumpled-up ball of printer paper that sat on his carpet. He was trying and failing to levitate it with his mind.

I handed him the peacock feather Willodean had used earlier. "How about now?"

He pointed the feather and the ball of paper rose toward the ceiling. He let it drop, put down the feather, and tried again without an aid. It didn't move.

Herc cursed in frustration and kicked the ball. "Those dipshits turned me into a middling."

"Don't rush to conclusions," I said, even as I was fairly certain he was right. "I've never heard of anything that could do that." That much was true. There were rare rituals that allowed a practitioner to steal another's magic, as the Crimson Prophet had attempted to do with me, but not to extinguish it outright. The law of conservation of energy, and all that. "Have you?"

"No, but …. She's a middling," he pointed at Willodean. "They were experimenting on her. They sprayed us with something that sure as shit wasn't Old Spice, and now my powers are gone. It's Occam's razor."

I didn't have a counterargument. It seemed likely, in retrospect, that they'd exposed us to that spray on purpose. Vaughn had no problem inhaling the same stuff we did, which might mean …

"You know what else I think?" Herc asked. "That Vaughn guy was a middling, too."

"He did willingly expose himself to the spray while his boss stayed behind," I said.

"That, but also their entire attitude makes sense in hindsight," Herc said. "If your stunt fried all the magical artifacts in the building, the middling would be helpless against a pair of gifted. It's no wonder they gave up their prize without trying anything more hardcore than bluffing and threatening."

Willodean frowned at being called a prize but didn't say anything. She remembered Vaughn from the auction, but they'd drugged her again on the way to Jersey and she didn't have any recollection of what they did to her afterward. She didn't remember being rescued either, and only knew Herc was involved because I'd told her about him on the drive over.

"What about you?" Herc asked.

"Pardon?"

"Did they neuter your powers, too?" He gestured toward the crumpled paper ball. "Give it a try."

Willodean and I exchanged a quick glance. She must've wondered which way I was going to play this.

Herc had proven his friendship and loyalty. I felt I could trust him with the truth. But what would the ramifications be if I told him? Would he ever trust me again, or would he push me away at the time when he was at his most vulnerable and needed my help? On the other hand, I could continue lying to him. I hadn't avoided being discovered all these years without a bag of tricks up my sleeve. There were several different ways I could pass his litmus test without him being the wiser. But that would muddy the waters and contradict his otherwise solid deductions and make it more difficult to find the cure all three of us needed.

I made a show of focusing on the paper ball.

"This may sound like a cliché," I said, glaring at the immobile ball, "but up until today this has never happened to me before."

It was a gamble. If Herc thought Nascent Anodynes International had stolen my powers like it had his, I wouldn't have to pretend around him or risk losing his trust. On the other hand, if and when he found out the truth and realized I'd opted for the bigger lie instead of opening up to him, the ramifications of that could be far worse. Unfortunately, such a risk was old hat to me. I thought of Terrie Winter and John Smith, my closest allies at the Watch. My other friendships were built upon the unsteady foundation of lies, too. All the more reason to find the solution, find a cure, become *whole*.

"We can't tell anyone until we figure this out," said Herc. "We've both made plenty of enemies along the way and if they find out we've been crippled, it'll be open season. Not to mention the bigots who hate middlings on general principle."

Leave it up to the man who had been a middling for about five minutes to succinctly outline the problem.

"That would mean we can't sound the alarm about Vaughn," I said. "But if he has this weapon, the Watch and the other gifted need to know."

"We'll tell them if we can't crack heads quickly enough to solve it on our own." Herc's hands balled into fists. "I say we pay NAi another visit, find Vaughn, and beat him like a rented mule-shaped piñata until the secret to restoring our powers spills out."

"Because the bad guys would never expect you to do that after they sprayed you with Magic-B-Gone?" Willodean chimed in.

"They might not expect us so soon," said Herc. "And they definitely won't expect me to bring a Jeep-load of friends packing nonmagical heat. I'm gonna call in some chits." He turned to me. "Think you can manage with just your artifacts?"

"Yeah," I said, keeping a straight face. "I think I can make that work."

We rolled up to the NAi building a little before midnight. Herc was driving again, with me riding shotgun, and Willodean—who'd refused to sit things out—in the back seat.

A Ford Escalade with four guys sporting short military hairdos and armed with automatic weapons followed us. From the looks of them they were serious dudes with combat experience who wouldn't bat an eye at fighting frankenbeasts in a New Jersey office building any more than fighting insurgents in Kandahar.

Guns and magical weapons drawn, we entered the lobby. The door was unlocked and the lights were on, but the guards were gone.

It took us about ten minutes to sweep the building, from the top floors to the basement where Willodean had been kept. The place was empty.

I don't just mean there were no people there. Everything—from the massive front desk to office furniture and water coolers—had been removed. The floor and walls in the lobby were scrubbed clean; blood and gore from the pile of animal parts were gone without a trace. The building smelled heavily of bleach and some other foul chemical. Herc's paramilitary friends recognized the scent; they said it was a special solution used to destroy DNA evidence.

Anyone who's ever moved apartments knows how much time-consuming labor is involved. Our enemies' ability to disappear so thoroughly in so short a time was more impressive and scary than all the frankenanimals they had put together in their build-a-monster workshop.

"Now what?" Willodean asked. The three of us stood in the lobby of the abandoned building while Herc's friends climbed back into their Escalade. They had helped search the premises, but they were loaded for combat and not for investigation, and had uncovered nothing.

"Now we upturn heaven and earth until we find the bastards," said Herc. "They stole our powers and I will stop at nothing to get them back. Mark my words."

"They're a large corporation with offices and real estate holdings, and a paper trail longer than the Nile," I said. "They can't just pack everything up and hide in the wilderness like some lone werewolf. There are patents and tax filings and all kinds of other documents with names and addresses on them. We've got people who're good at digging into this sort of thing."

Herc nodded. "Damn right. It's time to call on the Irregulars. Like Sherlock Holmes said, 'The game's afoot.'"

I agreed with the sentiment. It was actually Shakespeare who'd first written that in *Henry V*, but I didn't bother correcting my friend. He'd been through enough that day already.

CHAPTER 10

IT took us four days to track down Marko Hanson. When we'd first met in New Jersey he'd claimed to be the one in charge of the facility, which was technically true but also a huge understatement. The snide bastard was in charge of the entire company. His name and signature were on all the paperwork, and there was plenty of paperwork to find. Nascent Anodynes International conducted business in over one hundred locations across a baker's dozen of countries. They had investors and board members they were accountable to.

Vaughn, on the other hand, was a ghost. His name appeared nowhere on the paperwork, nor on the company payrolls. The only proof of his existence was the eyewitness accounts: the big rat was often found at his master's side, whispering in Hanson's ear.

We discovered all this without magic. Working for the Watch often involved finding people, and each of us had built up a rolodex full of competent lawyers, computer hackers, private investigators, forensic accountants, and other sharks skilled at navigating the waters of modern society. Some were high-priced contractors while others were volunteers. You save someone's daughter from being eaten by monsters once, and there's no limit to how many times they'll be eager to utilize their professional skills on your behalf.

Herc and I got the ball rolling with our respective contacts, and tips came pouring in. We learned that Hanson had a high-level meeting coming up in New York City, one he couldn't blow off just to hide from us. Herc's Irregulars were going to be there—both the mundane and gifted variety—but I figured I'd bring extra magical muscle, just in case. Our enemies had demonstrated resilience and cunning before and would surely have nasty surprises in store for us.

Herc and his Irregulars arrived at the posh midtown office building, located only a few blocks from Holcomb Tower, hours in advance of when Hanson was scheduled to show up. They scoped the area and were on the lookout for any NAi advance security teams.

I had placed calls to John Smith and Terrie Winter earlier. It took some convincing to get them to lend a hand in a situation they knew nothing about that was technically outside the scope of the Watch's charter—again. Especially since I'd been ducking Mose's phone calls and he had made his displeasure known to others. I fervently hoped that capturing Hanson and neutralizing his anti-gifted bioweapon would go a long way toward pacifying my boss. Terrie had agreed to help despite her reservations. John was more difficult to convince. He said he'd think about it, and I wasn't certain whether he'd show up at the rendezvous point.

Willodean stayed behind, despite her protests. She'd moved into my Sheepshead Bay apartment while we searched for Hanson and Vaughn, and I'd slept at my studio in Midwood. She studied magic, read the texts I'd provided for her, and practiced using some of the less dangerous charms and amulets in my inventory.

I had expected my landlord to grumble about the stranger moving in downstairs, but he winked at me when I ran into him one evening. "Is about time you found nice girl," he told me with a heavy Russian accent. I had thought it prudent not to disabuse him of his notion.

When the time came to take on Hanson, again, I put my foot down. Willodean wasn't trained like Herc and I were, wasn't skilled in the use of magic, and we didn't want to risk Hanson's goons recapturing her if things went sideways. And so I was armed to the teeth but alone as I waited for Terrie and John in the coffee shop off Fifth Avenue, a few blocks from where our operation was to take place.

I watched John enter, dressed in an impeccable three-piece suit as usual. I felt happy he decided to come after all, but the emotion quickly faded as Gord and Father Mancini filed in behind him.

The Watch representatives from the Bronx and Staten Island weren't my enemies, but they weren't close friends, either. They were allies, friendly enough to stand united with me against the odd common enemy like the Cabal, but not the sort to volunteer their help on an operation like this. Their presence did not bode well.

"Guys," I said amicably, as the three of them approached my table. Gord loomed over everyone in the place as he brought up the rear.

"Conrad," said John. "Mose wishes to see you. You must come with us, now."

I glanced at the clock hanging on the wall. The numbers on its face had been replaced with stylized coffee beans. The shorter hand pointed a little shy of three beans.

"You're blowing my op. It's going to go down in less than an hour, and you don't want to leave Herc there without backup, do you?" I was certain everyone liked Herc better than they did me. "Come with me and lend a hand, or stay neutral if you want to. As soon as we're finished, we'll head to the Watchtower together, I promise."

John always played his cards close to his chest, his expressions difficult to read, but I thought he might have looked … sad. "In light of recent developments, we can't allow that to happen," he said.

"What does *that* mean?"

"I'd rather not discuss the matter here," said John.

The shop wasn't busy in the afternoon, but there were enough people around that any confrontation would carry the risk of collateral damage. Not that I seriously thought I could take any two of them, let alone all three, if I tried.

"Kindly follow us."

I reached into my pocket. Gord leaned forward and Father Mancini clutched his cross.

Very slowly and deliberately I pulled out my phone. "Whoa. Relax, guys. I just need to warn Herc—"

Gord made a fist. The phone I was holding shattered into bits of metal and plastic right in my hand.

"What the hell? I just upgraded to the new model. It was like eight hundred dollars. Why did you have to go all Darth Vader force choke on it?"

Gord glowered at me. "You will come now. No more talk."

He looked pissed. Really pissed, like someone had taken a dump in his cereal. I was pretty sure I hadn't done anything recently that would tread on his extra-large toes.

"Don't try anything, Conrad. For the Lord's sake." Father Mancini sounded upset, too.

I didn't know what this was all about. Surely, Mose couldn't have been that mad at me for staying out of touch for a few days—all of us had really long leashes; the job required it.

Could my secret have possibly been uncovered? With Herc joining the middling ranks and with our quest to locate Hansen, I wondered if some stray bit of information had found its way to my fellow guardians at the Watch. At the very least, I had a convenient excuse for having lost my powers.

Whatever it was, I'd have to do as I was told and sort things out. Even if I somehow managed to outwit the other guardians and escape, they knew where I needed to be in an hour, and I really didn't want to test them further.

I followed them outside and we piled into a Cadillac. Gord squeezed into the front seat while John and Father Mancini made me sit between them in the back, like an abductee in a cliché mobster movie.

The car turned on Broadway and crawled downtown. Manhattan streets are always congested, a problem even magic couldn't alleviate in a meaningful way. Precious minutes were wasted in bumper-to-bumper traffic.

The others ignored me and after several failed attempts to start a conversation I quit trying. It was a really uncomfortable ride.

The offices of the Watch occupied a floor in the basement of the Manhattan Municipal Building. For over a century, the forty-story building had housed many of the civil servants who ran New York City. It was designed with the approval and oversight of the Watch and located atop an ancient nexus of power. I'd asked about its nature but had never gotten a straight answer, other than an assurance that it enhanced the supernatural protections. Those protections were built into the building's architecture, from the enchanted statue of Civic Fame at the top, to the protective runes hidden behind the walls, to the blessed cornerstones at the foundation. Hanson's people had utilized the same technique in New Jersey, but their wards had been a pale shadow of the protection layers added by generations of the gifted. The building ranked among the most secure locations in the United States, along with the White House, Fort Knox, certain sections of the Smithsonian, Graceland, and Area 51.

We flashed our IDs to get past mundane security and walked several flights down, to a floor that didn't appear on the official maps or the building blueprints filed with the city. The door leading into the Watchtower was marked with the sigil of the effulgent eye. A printout was attached to the door with a bit of Scotch tape directly below it for the benefit of the mundanes. It read, *HR Archives, 1927–1939. By appointment only.* To date, no one needed city employee data from the Great Depression era badly enough to schedule an appointment.

Only a few people occupied the desks and offices on our floor—the Watch had never been keen on employing a large staff. They looked up at the four of us, recognized us, and went back to work. Our presence wasn't unusual at the office, and the rank and file were seemingly unaware that this time I was being brought in against my will.

I kept it cool, as did my peers. We marched all the way across the Watchtower to the mahogany door. I opened it and walked through. My colleagues remained behind.

The office I'd entered was well lit and consisted of an immense desk, a few filing cabinets, and a pair of waiting-room chairs for visitors. Behind the desk sat Mose himself.

He was nearly as tall as Gord, and three times as wide. He must've weighed over four hundred pounds, though virtually none of that was fat. He stared at me evenly, his ancient eyes narrowed, his bald head still, his back straight, like a bodybuilder Buddha.

Mose Humphrey looked middle aged, but he'd been around since the early 1800s. Once upon a time he'd been known as Mose the Fireboy, a volunteer firefighter in the Bowery who had arguably been New York's first superhero.

According to legend, he was eight feet tall (an exaggeration), strong as an ox (a slight understatement), a great brawler, and a snappy dresser who liked to live life as large as his own frame (accurate facts). Young Mose had loved food and women and drink, all in excess.

What the legends didn't tell you was that he was the most powerful gifted in New York City, and its sole Watch member until he'd recruited others in the 1840s and then disappeared for several decades. When he returned, he'd reclaimed control of the Watch and had remained in charge of the organization ever since. As best I could tell, he never left his office. (I had to wonder if there was a hidden shower and a toilet behind one of the wall panels.) He also seemed to have curbed his oversized appetite, subsisting on a humble diet of about 10,000 calories a day. He no longer possessed his penchant for gluttony in other ways either, prompting people to speculate whether he'd found religion or lost some ineffable bit of his soul during those missing decades.

Even at over two hundred years of age and cooped up in his underground office, no one doubted Mose's ability to outfight Gord, outspellcast Smith, and outwit me. He was a force of nature and—for all our powers and abilities—the main reason so few of the bad guys were willing to cross the path of the Watch.

"Conrad," he said, his deep voice reverberating through the room. "I've been trying to reach you."

"Yeah, I've had one of those weeks and stayed out of touch for a bit. I'm sorry about that. That's not a reason to shanghai me and jeopardize my operation, though. I've been laboring to put it together nonstop for several days—"

He raised his enormous hand, palm facing me, forcing my tirade to halt. "This won't take long. I have but a single question for you, Conrad."

I crossed my arms, then uncrossed them, conscious of signaling defensive body language. "Yes?"

"Are you a middling?"

Mose's question struck me like a thunderbolt from clear skies. Despite my usual optimism, I'd visualized a moment like this many times over the years, practiced an eloquent defense I might present if and when I was confronted, thought of tricks I might use to obfuscate the truth. But now, facing the ancient, powerful leader of the Watch in the privacy of his office, all I could manage was, "What?"

Mose stared at me impassively. "I don't like repeating myself."

"No!" I said, my voice breaking a little. I tried to infuse rage into it to hide the fear. "And I resent the implication!"

Mose studied me for several seconds. Each of them felt like eternity squared.

"I don't believe you," he said.

I felt small in his presence, not only in physical size, which was a given, but in a matter of intelligence as well. I felt certain I wouldn't be able to lie my way out of this one, felt like a first-year physics student trying to convince Einstein that gravity didn't exist.

What could have prompted this confrontation? It must've been Hanson, who'd sprayed Herc and me with his bioweapon. He or his minions must've whispered into Mose's ear in order to discredit their enemy, accidentally stumbling upon a deeper truth.

"There is a man by the name of Marko Hanson," I said. "He is in the possession of a substance that can neutralize a gifted's natural power. Several days ago, Hercules Mulligan and I were exposed to—"

"Stop."

Mose actually raised his voice, and the word felt like a command, as though he'd infused it with magic.

"I've known about you for years," he said. "I often wondered if you respected me enough to admit the truth if I ever asked you directly. Now I have my answer."

You know the cliché about the world spinning around you? I now knew exactly what that felt like—and I'd been in situations where the ground had literally spun under my feet before.

"You've thought me a middling for years and said nothing?"

"I'm not prone to ancient prejudices," said Mose. "You were good at your job. I thought your situation gave you an edge, placed a certain chip on your shoulder. You had to work three times as hard as anyone else to achieve half the result, and you didn't let that slow you down. I found that … admirable."

I was having a really hard time with the realization that Mose knew. I'd thought myself so clever, so capable of misleading enemies and allies alike, and all this time Mose had merely found it convenient to ignore my ruse.

"You've become erratic recently, Conrad. You've been putting your desire to transcend your limitations above your duties and responsibilities to the Watch. You placed your fellow members at risk in confronting the Cabal, and you were about to do so again, in pursuit of your vendetta against this Hanson fellow. This was a problem, and you needed to be reined in, but you ignored my calls. Even so, it could've been worked out. Unfortunately, someone else has also discovered your secret."

"Who?" I asked, dropping the pretense.

"Karl Mercado."

This really wasn't my day. It was difficult enough to accept that Mose knew the truth, but Karl? A prospect who'd been clueless about magic until merely months ago, who'd known me for all of a couple of weeks? How could *he* have figured this out? Had Mose claimed that Santa Claus had dropped an exposé about me down his chimney, wrapped around a lump of coal, I would have been more likely to believe that.

"I'm sure you realize by now that Karl deeply dislikes you," said Mose. "He claims he's been paying careful attention to your methods and actions, and building his case ever since he learned of the concept of middlings. When he felt certain, he didn't come to me directly, perhaps sensing I might order his silence. Instead, he first informed the other ranking members of the Watch and only then broached the subject with me."

"Whatever the others think of me, surely they wouldn't take the word of a newbie over the man they've fought side by side with for years."

"That might be so, if you could prove him wrong. But you can't. Your balancing act only works because no one is looking too closely. No one suspects a middling might be this bold."

He was right, and I was in a world of trouble.

"What are you going to do to me?" I asked.

"I must again reiterate that I hold no ill will toward middlings," said Mose. "However, a great many people do. The knowledge of your condition is going to spread quickly, and you will soon become too much of a liability, a cause for dissent among our allies, and an additional reason for our enemies to paint a target on our backs. I have no choice but to terminate you. That is, terminate your position at the Watch. I have no intention of killing you."

I clenched my jaw and stared at Mose defiantly. Above his left shoulder an old clock ticked softly. Herc and his people would be attacking Hanson any minute now, sans my backup. I'd failed to help him as thoroughly as I failed to find the cure for my condition, a goal to which I'd dedicated so many years of the life Mose had just magnanimously offered to spare.

"We'll have to make the punishment appear severe," said Mose. "We'll confiscate all the magical items in your possession, make a scene of kicking you out of this building, and banish you forever from New York City."

I flashed my ex-boss a bitter smile. "That's probably for the best. When the word spreads, the middling fan club as well as every evil punk whose head I've ever cracked will be gunning for me."

"Indeed." Mose didn't look much pleased with the situation, though with him who could really tell? "I can make arrangements to help you get out of the city. I own a cabin on a few acres of land outside of Rochester. You're welcome to stay there until you figure out what you wish to do next."

"You're literally sending me to a farm upstate? Thanks a bunch."

Mose nodded. He was offering me a kindness in his own way, but he wasn't the type to wring his hands over my fate. He often said anyone could throw a good punch, but an individual truly worth their salt would know how to take a good punch and shake it off afterward.

"I must decline your generous offer. There are loose ends I have to tie up."

"Suit yourself, so long as you leave the city in the next twenty-four hours," Mose said. "I'd advise you not to wait that long. Who knows what other ears Karl has been whispering into? For now, turn over your charms and amulets. Every single one of them. I'll know."

He watched me lay out an array of enchanted items on his desk. Mose could've let me keep a few trinkets, as means of defending myself. But if he had, that kindness would have *cost* him something, and he wasn't sentimental. Artifacts were useful, and I'd obtained most or all of them while enjoying the protection and backup of the Watch, so he felt entitled to keep the lot.

Naturally, I tried getting away with hanging on to a few choice morsels, but he somehow could sense their presence. He knew when I gave up every last magical item on my person and was left defenseless against the gifted for the second time in the span of a week.

Mose nodded toward the door.

"I wish you luck, Conrad. Don't ever come back."

CHAPTER 11

TRUE to his word, Mose orchestrated a small spectacle of my departure. Although no official announcement was made to the staff, Father Mancini confiscated the ID card that allowed me access to the building in a spot where everyone would see it. He and Gord then escorted me across the floor like a pair of rent-a-cops summoned to kick a dismissed employee off the premises. The only missing prop was the cardboard box full of my personal belongings. I got to carry out nothing of value, having been politely robbed by Mose on my way out.

Once outside I still couldn't call anyone. In this situation I would have normally called the Watchtower and had someone there connect me or procure the necessary numbers. Even if I walked into the nearest store and bought a new phone, I didn't recall anyone's number by heart—who does these days? Activating the new phone and restoring my information from backup would take way too long.

My options were to flag a cab and go uptown to where the confrontation between Herc's team and Hanson's people would almost certainly be long over, or head to Brooklyn and avail myself of my rapidly dwindling supply of magical trinkets. Despite the concern over Herc and his people eating at me, the decision was almost a no brainer.

I hopped on the Q train.

In the movies, action heroes race to their destination in fancy cars, lead foot on the pedal, tires squealing as they zigzag past slower vehicles. When it comes to places like New York or Los Angeles, that's just bullshit.

Because of red lights and traffic it takes less time to get from downtown Manhattan to south Brooklyn by train than it does by car, unless you're driving an ambulance or a police cruiser with sirens on. In real life, the action hero would be abandoning their car double-parked in the middle of the road unless they could afford to spare ten to fifteen minutes driving around looking for a parking spot.

As the word of my firing was surely spreading among the Conrad Brent fan club and I was literally in a race for my life, I spent forty minutes in a subway car sitting between a high school girl who was listening to K-pop on such high volume I could hear the nauseating songs through her headphones, and an old guy slurping ramen noodles from a Styrofoam cup. Drops of hot water from his cup sprayed my shoes. The stink of human sweat mixed with the odor of the noodles. I didn't even have a tiny screen to stare into so I could pretend my fellow passengers didn't exist.

To pass the time I made a mental list of all the people and creatures likely to go after me the moment they learned I was a middling, and no longer under the protection of the Watch. It disturbed me how quickly I came up with a dozen candidates. I could hope they'd bloody each other jostling for who'd get their chance at me first, but that was merely wishful thinking.

When the train finally pulled into the Sheepshead Bay station I squeezed past my fellow straphangers and ran to the house in the most undignified manner.

The front door was ajar. My apartment had been ravaged, like a china shop after a close encounter with a herd of bulls. Everything of value seemed to be missing.

"Conrad?"

I heard Willodean's voice and a wave of relief passed over me. At least whoever did this hadn't gotten her, too. She entered the house behind me, looking frazzled but unhurt.

"Where have you been? I've been trying to call you for the past two hours."

"An angry giant broke my phone. Long story. What happened here?"

"There were eight of them. They turned the whole place upside down looking for hidden safes or something. I asked who they were, and they said they were the cops and showed me something that looked like a warrant, but they were all gifted and they didn't seem like cops to me. They just kept packing up your stuff into boxes and loading them into a big white van. I tried to stop them, but they told me they'd throw me in jail if I"—she made air quotes with her fingers—"*interfered with official business*. When I kept making a fuss, they made me wait outside."

"Was it a tall Mercedes van with a blue stripe along the side?"

"Yes! You know them?"

"You might say that. They're the Watch cleaning crew."

Willodean pointed at my clothes and books scattered across the floor. "They appear to suck at their job."

"I wish. They're the people who show up after someone like me is done mopping the floor with the latest villain, and they mop the floors. Sometimes literally. They clean up the blood, remove the bodies, and either repair whatever structural damage the fight caused or make it look like whatever went down was mundane in nature." I thought back to the lobby of the Nascent Anodynes International building, scrubbed of monster blood and body parts, and wondered if Hanson employed a similar team. "It's also their job to comb the site for any magical items that might have been left behind. They're especially good at that."

"Why would they come here? Ah! They didn't know this was your apartment, did they?"

I summarized the events of the last few hours to her.

"What you're saying is, your boss fired you, robbed you, and sent a crew to jack all your stuff? You should complain to HR."

"They weren't even supposed to know this place existed," I said, dejected. "Mose has been three steps ahead of me on everything. I bet they tossed my other apartment, too."

"I hate to pile on the bad news, but they also towed your car."

Willodean winced when she saw the expression on my face. I'd had the Oldsmobile since my earliest days at the Watch. It was a spoil of war, a prize I'd taken from the first arcane enemy I'd ever defeated. I'd poured time and money into it until the vehicle was more badass than I was. And now the Watch had taken that, too.

"It won't make up for everything, but there's a tiny bit of good news. Before they kicked me out, your landlord came down and argued with the woman in charge of the intruders. He didn't get far, but while he kept her distracted I stole one of the artifacts."

She beamed at me as she produced a brooch from her pocket. It was a large amethyst set in gold. "This looked expensive and important. What does it do?"

I smiled, her enthusiasm infectious even at such a low moment. "It repels zombies."

Willodean's eyes widened. "Zombies are real?"

"Not the George Romero or the *Walking Dead* type. The real ones are corpses reanimated by black magic. They don't swarm and they don't eat brains. They're about as effective as large guard dogs if you keep them in a confined space, and you don't have to feed them. The animation spell lasts a few weeks, but one has to go through the trouble of procuring a fresh corpse, and few people want their valuables to stink of rotting flesh, so zombies are rare. If we ever encounter one," I hefted the brooch in my hand, "this will repel them real good."

I thought back to what she'd said. "Our cleaning crew happens to be a sausage fest. Did you say there was a woman in charge?"

Willodean nodded. "Short brunette. Bossy. Had this walking stick but she carried it around and didn't use it to lean on."

Terrie Winter. One of the few people I'd call a friend. She'd led the team of gifted who stole my stuff, presumably knowing that I would be helpless against my enemies without it. But could I blame her? Our friendship was based on a lie. I had lied and manipulated her any number of times, including recently when I'd gotten her out of the borough she'd chosen to protect during the Traveling Fair auction.

I had always sought comfort in how the ends justified the means, how I was maneuvering people into helping me for all the right reasons. But had I been, really? At the end of the day, did the universe care whether Conrad Brent had magical powers?

I had no claim on Terrie's friendship or loyalty. Even so, her direct involvement in my downfall somehow stung worse than Mose's dismissal or the others' opprobrium.

"Conrad?" Willodean's voice broke my train wreck of thought. "What should we do now?"

"First, we need to get ahold of Herc."

"I've been calling him. He isn't picking up."

"That can't be a good sign. Call him again, please, and leave a voice mail. Let him know what's been happening and to reach us at your number."

While Willodean made the call, I searched through the house hoping the cleaners might've missed something. They were good at their job; they'd taken everything remotely magical in the apartment, from the prized Atlantean shard and the heavy grandfather clocks to the scroll inside the mezuzah on the doorframe and the cross hanging above the door. They'd taken my laptop and my spare cell phone, as well as any books and notes related to the arcane. They'd found the hiding spot behind the radiator grill, and they'd broken into the safe that was deadbolted to the floor in one of my closets. The contents of the safe were gone, replaced with a folded sheet of paper that hadn't been there before. It was a note handwritten in neat cursive script.

Conrad,

I'm sorry my duty and our friendship have come at odds today. If you ever need help with anything that doesn't go against the Watch's mandate, you know where to find me.

—TERRIE

After the day of gut punches, Terrie's note felt like a cool drink of water in the desert. Not that I considered taking her up on her offer. For all his cynicism or practicality, Mose was right: I was bad news now, and I would paint a target on the back of those who might decide to help me.

I went to the kitchen and lit the note, using the fire from the gas stove.

"Whatcha burning? Evidence?" Willodean asked.

I held the paper until the flames licked my fingers, then threw the rest in the sink.

"Bridges," I said.

I had to accept that my time at the Watch had come to an end. I had to believe I'd accomplished more good than bad while I was there, but I wasn't done. I owed Herc my help, and I wasn't going to let some prick go around stealing people's magic. Hanson and his minions were going down.

We took a cab to Midwood and confirmed that my other apartment had been thoroughly searched as well. Willodean's phone rang as we were leaving. She handed it to me.

"Herc! You're on speakerphone with me and Willodean. What happened? Are you all right?"

"More or less," he said. "Could've used some assistance, for sure."

"I've had problems," I said. "I got kicked out of the Watch."

"Seriously?"

"They figured out I lost my magic and didn't want middling cooties," I said. I felt awful keeping up the pretense, lying to my last remaining friend, but I still couldn't bring myself to fess up. If there was ever a good time to tell Herc the whole truth, this definitely wasn't it.

"Damn ingrates," he said.

I told him about my unhappy trip to the Watchtower, and about the cleaners confiscating my stuff.

"We had a rough day, too," said Herc. "Hanson brought an army of bodyguards, both gifted and mundane, like he was the pope on a visit to Syria. Between how solid his defense was and you and yours standing us up, we almost aborted the op. In the end though, we went for it. We figured if we grabbed Hanson fast enough we could use him as a hostage and exfiltrate …." He paused there, and when he resumed speaking his voice was cracking. "Bottom line, my desire to regain my powers got the better of me, and we rushed in like fools."

"What happened?"

"It was a meat grinder. Lots of casualties on both sides. We had the element of surprise and two of my guys nabbed Hanson, but his crazy bodyguards seemed to have no problem risking the bastard's life to get him back. They riddled Chen and Kowal with bullets even as my boys had their hands on the target. Pretty sure Hanson caught a few flesh wounds from friendly fire, but they were able to win him back, the damn cowboys."

"I'm sorry about your friends."

"Yeah. Me, too. But it's Hanson who should be really sorry," Herc said. "He and I, we ain't done yet."

"Do you have any intel as to where we can make another run at him?"

"Better. We managed to take one of his people. We're interrogating him now."

"One of his bodyguards?"

"Nah. A Wall Street type. Man-child in a tailored suit. A VP or something-or-other at NAi. He's not gifted, but he knows what's up. Took less than ten minutes to crack him. We're taking measures to make sure he's telling the truth."

As a member of the Watch, I'd been obligated to come down hard on the people who used the sort of measures Herc was talking about. But I wasn't with the Watch anymore, and this was war. Let Mose enforce the rules. I only cared that the information we were getting was the truth, or at least true according to what the guy they were questioning knew.

"What have you learned?"

"They've been working on the bioweapon for a decade and needed some compound in a naturally occurring middling's blood to make it all come together. They got enough plasma from Willodean to neuter every gifted in New York by a comfortable margin."

"How do we reverse it?"

"The bastard doesn't know. He says their main research facility for this stuff is in Munich, spearheaded by some genius named Clarissa. He claims Clarissa isn't human but is fuzzy about what sort of being she is."

This made sense. If Clarissa were a troll or a vampire, she would appear as a somewhat unusual-looking human to a mundane. Even if he knew what she was, it would be almost impossible for his brain to process her true visage.

"Sounds like we should pay her a visit," I said. "Preferably before they realize we might know what we know and disappear that facility the same way they did their Jersey outlet."

Herc hesitated. I could hear him breathing on the other end of the line. Then he said, "I think you should go without me."

"That's not like you," I said. "What aren't you telling us?"

"I'm not going to be mobile for a few days. They got me in the side. Clean shot, bullet went right through, missed all the important bits."

"Damn it, Herc, you told me you were okay!"

"I said more or less. And I will be, in a few days. But we can't afford to wait that long."

"No, we can't. Besides, I have to get out of New York before Mose comes down on me like a ton of bricks."

"I'm coming, too," Willodean said. "I'm not sitting things out again."

"It'd be safer if you stayed with Herc."

"You keep saying you aren't safe in New York now that people know you're a middling. All the villains who attended the Traveling Fair know *I'm* a middling, too. I'm better off traveling half a world away and maybe helping you find some answers." She looked at me defiantly. "If you want me to stay behind, you'll have to make me."

"Fine," I said. "We're going to Germany. But we can't take on Hanson's security empty-handed. We'll have to make another stop first."

Half an hour later we arrived at Mordecai's Jewelers. I asked Willodean to wait outside—the fewer people who could connect the two of us while we were still in New York, the better. Two of Mordecai's men escorted me past the brightly lit showcases and the mundane customers. It wasn't until we entered the private showroom filled with arcane wares that they pulled their guns.

"Place your hands on the desk and don't move," said one of the men. They both appeared to be in their late twenties, dressed in starched polyester shirts and dark-blue silk caftans, the traditional garb worn by Hasidic Jews regardless of season or temperature. As someone who wore a trench coat year round like some clichéd noir detective because it afforded me the use of a great many pockets, I wasn't one to judge. "Be very still. If I so much as suspect you're reaching for an artifact of any sort …."

He didn't finish the thought, the implied threat hanging in the air.

The word had spread as quickly as I'd feared. Clearly these two knew I was a middling. I hadn't expected such a strong negative reaction at a place where I'd been a valued patron for many years. If they were willing to threaten me with guns, what could I expect from the rest of the gifted community?

I stood perfectly still, palms on the counter. My captors appeared nervous even as their handguns were pointed at me. They reminded me of a dog who'd finally caught the car he'd been chasing and had no idea what to do with it.

After a couple of minutes, Mordecai arrived.

"We've captured the *mikhasheifah*," said one of the youngsters. I hadn't heard the term before but didn't need three guesses to figure out what he meant.

"Aaron, Moishe, put your guns down," Mordecai ordered. "Conrad, you have my sincere apologies."

One of the men holstered his pistol, the other only lowered it a fraction.

"But he's *mikhasheifah*," he repeated. "It says in the Talmud—"

"Do not presume to quote the sacred texts, Aaron, when you aren't even old enough to study most of the ones that pertain to the higher arts," said Mordecai.

I vaguely recalled that people under the age of forty weren't allowed to study Kabbalah and read certain arcane texts in his culture.

"The sacred texts may frown upon middlings, but they grant you no authority to judge, let alone threaten one! Even in the times of the Temple, the Sanhedrin had to be assembled to pass any sort of judgment. The Almighty would never wish or expect for you to take such matters into your hands."

Aaron lowered his weapon and shifted his weight from foot to foot uncomfortably, his eyes downcast.

"Leave us," Mordecai ordered.

Reluctantly, the two young men shuffled toward the mundane part of the shop.

"I'm sorry the actions of my hot-headed staff have added to your troubles," said Mordecai.

I waved dismissively, as though having guns pointed at me now and again was par for the course. "I take it you've heard of my predicament."

Mordecai thought for a moment, perhaps choosing his words. "Like I told my men, it is not for me to pass judgment."

"You recently told me you believe me to be a good man. I'm still that same person, and I'm struggling to unravel a conspiracy that endangers all gifted."

Mordecai nodded. "A conspiracy, you say?"

I told him about Hanson and his company, and what had been done to Herc and, supposedly, me.

"I've never heard of this Nascent Anodynes International"—Mordecai said the name as though it were the title of a dirty magazine he'd found under a teenager's mattress—"but the power you describe is terrifying indeed. I've recently heard of a gifted man in Lakewood who lost his powers in the fashion you describe." He stroked his beard, contemplating. "I wonder how many more have suffered the same fate but are hiding their affliction in fear of being labeled *mikhasheifah* ...."

"An affliction. I like that term." I stepped toward one of his shelves. "The Watch took back their toys, as well as all of my toys, and my lunch money, when they threw me out. I know it's another big ask, since I might never be able to return to New York and repay you, but could you loan me a few items so that the next time someone points a gun at me I don't have to stand around and wait to be rescued by a friendly shopkeeper?"

I felt a sense of déjà vu. I was back again, asking a favor of a man who owed me nothing. Only this time I had no expensive trinket to offer him, nor the backing of a powerful organization. All I had to rely on was his friendship and charity.

"It's considered a great *mitzvah* to provide loans to the needy," said Mordecai. "But in this case, I can't offer you a loan."

My heart sank. Mordecai wasn't my only option, but he was my best shot. I knew any number of places where I could procure a handgun in Brooklyn. Then I could pay a visit to one or more of the people who were firmly in the Bad Guy section of my ledger and do to them what Mose had done to me, only less gently. But all of this would take time I didn't have, and provide additional opportunities for the more dangerous individuals on that same list to find Willodean and me.

"Instead, I will provide to you what you need as payment for your services," said Mordecai.

"Services? What do you need me to do?" I *had* told him that Mose had ordered me leave New York.

"What you're already doing, of course." Mordecai smiled. "You're working to unravel the plans of this Hanson and to protect the gifted, even as the gifted have turned their backs on you. Least I can do is to provide some of the tools you might require to achieve your goal." He pointed toward his showcases filled with expensive magical items. "Come, let's get you equipped."

I felt like a medieval knight who'd lost his horse and lance and armor to bandits and had been given a spiked club and a flimsy wooden shield in their stead. Don't get me wrong; Mordecai was more than generous. He would have likely given me the shirt off his back if that shirt had been enchanted in some useful way—but even his extensive inventory wasn't exactly filled with combat-level magic. His typical customer was far more likely to shop for good luck charms, protective wards for their homes, or the arcane equivalent of boner pills than for fireball-tossing staffs or amulets that could generate force barriers.

"How did it go?" Willodean put away her phone and eyeballed the shopping bag in my hand as well as a few pieces of jewelry I now wore.

I joined her on the bench in a pint-sized park near Mordecai's shop. "As well as I could've expected. We're now armed with more than just our winning personalities, if only barely." I opened the bag and started handing her some of the goodies. I explained what each item in our meager inventory did and how to activate it.

"If I ever need an illumination spell I could just use the flash-light app on my phone," Willodean complained, fidgeting with an enchanted ring.

"Unlike your phone, this can provide light without running out of juice for weeks at a time," I said.

"I'll keep that in mind next time I go spelunking," she retorted, but put the ring on anyway.

"Did he happen to buy you a pair of tickets to Germany?" Willodean asked. "I hope they're business class."

"No, and no," I said. "We're going to Switzerland first, and we're not flying."

CHAPTER 12

"HAVE I mentioned how multinational corporations make me nervous lately?" asked Willodean.

We stood in the shadow of an eighteenth-century three-story building a stone's throw from Wall Street. Above the façade's columns, *ABADDON, INC.* was etched in four-foot-tall letters.

"They're not like NAi," I said. "They've been around at least as long as the Watch. Mose and their CEO, Daniel Chulsky, have an understanding." I steered her away from the grand entrance and toward an unremarkable door on the side.

"The same Mose who threw you to the curb?"

"I'm betting the doortroll doesn't know about that yet."

"The who?"

"Well, I can't really call him the door*man* ...." I held the door open for Willodean.

We entered the guardroom, which was more of a corridor. It consisted of two doors—the one leading to the street and the one leading inside—and a desk. Behind the desk sat Tiny.

Tiny the troll was on the small side as trolls went. He was just under eight feet tall, his gangly feet fitting awkwardly beneath the desk. Yellowish tusks protruded from his mouth. His real name was Tinnerbin, or Tinnerdin, or something like that, and he hated being called Tiny, which is why I exclusively called him that. It's not that I hate trolls, but I dislike gatekeepers who try to lord the miniscule modicum of authority their position vests in them over their visitors.

"Halt!" rumbled Tiny. His voice was deep and impressive, but I knew his intellect was roughly equal to that of a toilet bowl. "No unauthorized entry permitted." A bit of saliva pooled on his tusk.

Willodean blanched, having never seen a troll of any size before. I waved. "Hiya, Tiny. We're on Watch business."

Tiny sneered down his pug-like nose at me. "Papers?"

"What papers?" I gave him my best indignant look. "You know me!"

"I know you, annoying loudmouth," said the troll. "I don't know *her*."

"How cute, he has a nickname for me, too," I told Willodean. "I wonder where he heard it; Tiny isn't smart enough to think up something like that on his own."

The troll stared at me. He was trying so hard to come up with a retort, steam was almost blowing from his flat ears. Inspiration must not have struck because he merely repeated himself. "Papers?"

"She's new," I said. "No papers yet, but she's with me."

The troll considered this, processing information slower than a twentieth-century computer. "No unauthorized entry permitted," he said again.

"Look, we're in a hurry," I said. "Do you want me to call Mr. Chulsky down here and have him sort this out? I'm sure he'll be thrilled to have his day interrupted by an obstinate troll." I held out my hand toward Willodean and she passed me her cell phone. I hefted it as a visual aid, even though I'd never spoken with Tiny's boss nor did I have his number.

Tiny's train of thought moved slowly, like a line of lemmings toward a cliff. No doubt he was confused by my use of "obstinate," but he must've been used to just skipping the bigger words. Ever so slowly, the implied threat permeated his mind, or maybe his two brain cells finally found each other and sent a jolt of electricity through the vast emptiness of his synapses. Either way, he grunted something unintelligible and hit the button under his desk, opening the inner door for us.

"Thanks," I said. "See you around." Then I walked past him with Willodean in tow.

We entered a large vestibule with several dozen identical doors positioned at even intervals along the two walls. A placard on each door listed a city. We walked past Tokyo, Abu Dhabi, Marrakesh, Prague, and Los Angeles and stopped in front of the one that read Bern.

"Portals?" Willodean asked.

"Sort of," I said. "This building exists outside of regular space. Don't ask me how it works; smarter people than me have lost their marbles trying to figure it out. The short of it is, you can walk into the same building from any one of these cities, say hello to our friend Tiny back there, and then step through the door of your choice. Beats flying business class."

Willodean sized up the door. "Well, I've always wanted to try a real-life *Star Trek* teleporter," she said.

I thought the *Stargate* comparison would be more accurate but chose not to argue. I opened the door. The corridor on the other side of it looked identical to ours.

"After you."

"Switzerland is known for several things," I said as we walked the picturesque streets of Bern. It was late evening, as we had jumped through a bunch of time zones, and the streets were bathed in the warm electric lights from lamp posts and windows. The air was crisp and considerably cooler than back in New York. "Chocolate, watches, and cheese are top of the list. But there are also the banks, and then there are vampires. Would it surprise you to hear that the last two are related?"

"I've recently worn whatever part of my brain is responsible for being surprised to a nub," said Willodean. "Still, the notion of vampire bankers intrigues me."

"It's a natural fit," I said. "The concept of compound interest could only have been invented by an immoral, immortal bloodsucker that doesn't get out much."

"What are they like? I hope they're suave and sophisticated like Lestat, and not mopey sparkling perverts like Edward."

"They're more *Wolf of Wall Street* than *Twilight*," I said. "You'll see for yourself in just a few minutes."

Willodean stopped abruptly. I took half a step before I caught myself and also stopped. "Problem?"

"Yes, as a matter of fact. I don't so much mind seeing a Swiss vampire at night, but I'd like to know *why* I'm doing it. You've been very forthcoming about magic and monsters and playing tour guide to the wizarding world for me, and I appreciate that. But you make a terrible team player. You have a plan of action, and that's good. But have you considered actually sharing it before you drag me to visit some stranger's coffin?"

I thought about the way I'd manipulated Herc and deceived Terrie and John in recent weeks, of all the bluster and misdirection I'd been so proud of wielding expertly over the years.

"You're absolutely right. I've been guarding secrets for so long, I've become used to keeping my own counsel. Decisive action over thorough planning and all that. It's not easy to break old habits, and I'm sure I will screw this up again—I apologize in advance for that. But I promise to try my best, and to listen when you catch me reverting to my usual ways."

Willodean seemed at least partially mollified. "All right," she said, "why don't you start now?"

"Right. We know where our next lead is, and we need to move on it quickly because Hanson must realize we've captured someone who has that information, and we also know how quickly his people can sweep evidence under the table based on what we saw in New Jersey. Ergo, we must put together a force powerful enough to overcome whatever defenses and protections Nascent Anodynes has in place, one that's geographically close enough to strike sooner than they might expect."

"I see," Willodean said. "But we also don't have any money, or magic, or influence to pay them with, so it's not like you can pick up the phone and order a dozen mercenaries from the Foreign Legion."

"Exactly. We need someone powerful enough to help us take on NAi, whom we can actually convince to help us."

"And that happens to be a vampire? Count Swiss Chocula?"

"Vampires, plural. But yes."

"How are you going to convince them to help us?"

"I'll do what I do best. I'm going to bluff."

At first glance the offices of Bracher & Schurter, GmbH, seemed like those of any other hedge fund. They occupied the middle floor of a five-story building in downtown Bern. An attractive secretary walked us through an open office setup where traders barricaded themselves behind walls of monitors, with heaps of printouts vying for real estate on their desks against empty cans of energy drinks and candy bar wrappers.

We were directed toward a grouping of very comfortable armchairs and offered tiny cups of strong, black coffee.

"Mr. Bracher is on a conference call," the secretary said in accented English, "but he will see you as soon as he can."

The waiting area was near a small number of offices along the wall; the door with bronze lettering that read JULIEN BRACHER was closed.

Willodean and I sipped coffee and watched the traders work. After a few minutes, little details that differentiated this place from a typical finance operation became easier to notice.

The office was bustling with activity even though it was around midnight local time. Heavy velvet drapes covered all windows. The traders, who were staring intently into their screens, appeared sickly and pale, and looked more like stereotypical computer hackers than bankers. To our left, a pair of them were arguing passionately about something in German. Spittle flew from the mouth of the shorter portly trader as he waved a printout filled with complex mathematical equations. His thin, gangly interlocutor had looped fingers into the elasticated straps of his suspenders. He sighed theatrically and rolled his eyes at the shorter guy's arguments, then launched into a tirade that, I'd swear, sounded like what Sheldon Cooper would say if Sheldon Cooper spoke German.

"They're … nerds!" Willodean stared at the traders like she was watching a nature documentary. "Vampire nerds. Who would've thunk it. Is that one actually wearing a pocket protector?"

"It makes sense when you think about it," I said. "They're smart, a bit antisocial, and they don't get out much."

"And they like counting things," Willodean said, delighted at her deduction. "Which makes them good at math."

"Ah, you've read the Chinese legends about vampires suffering from the compulsion to count grains of rice?" I asked, impressed.

"Rice?" Willodean gave me side eye. "No. I've watched Count von Count on *Sesame Street*." She raised her finger and spoke in a deeper voice. "One arithmomania …. Ah, ah, ah!"

I watched several of the traders pile into Bracher's office, undoubtedly summoned ahead of our meeting. Once his entourage was in place, the comely secretary invited us in.

Julian Bracher seemed an unremarkable man. He was of average height, average build, and his short brown hair was combed to cover an encroaching bald spot. Thick-lensed, horn-rimmed glasses that were a few years out of fashion sat a tiny bit askew covering much of his face. He seemed the sort of person to whom one might not be inclined to give a second glance, which was exactly how he liked it.

Bracher was seven hundred years old, and among the wealthiest beings in the world. He made safe, long-term investments and hid the gains in a web of private companies, anonymous bank accounts, and proxy real estate holdings. He tended to adapt to whatever the humans were up to, using his influence only in extraordinary circumstances. As far as I knew, the last time he'd flexed his financial muscle it had been to keep the Nazis out of Switzerland.

The old vampire sat behind his desk, with a semicircle of his advisors standing behind him. I recognized his junior partner, Kurt Schurter, whom I'd briefly crossed paths with a few years ago previously in New York. He stood at Bracher's right hand.

"Mr. Brent." Bracher spoke with the quiet assurance of a person who never had to raise their voice to command the attention of the room. "To what do we owe the pleasure?"

I launched into my pitch, explaining who Marko Hanson was, and what Nascent Anodynes had developed. I made what I thought was an eloquent case as to why having a shadowy group being able to turn gifted into middlings was a bad idea for everyone, and how Bracher might help.

"Correct me if I'm wrong," Bracher said, having listened patiently until I ran out of steam. "You were recently dismissed from the Watch. You're in exile, devoid of your equipment and influence, no longer supported by your organization's power structure, yet you insist on carrying on your private war against this Herr Hanson. And you're asking me to finance the next stage of this war. Why would I do that? You say this new magic that strips the power from the gifted is a paradigm shift, but we vampires aren't gifted; this thing they've developed will not work against my people."

"You have to live in the same world as the rest of us. When word of Hanson's weapon gets out there will be panic, uncertainty, conflict. Surely those things aren't good for business?"

The vampires who stood behind their boss chuckled. Bracher looked at me with the patience of a kindergarten teacher who had just caught a kid drawing on a wall with a crayon.

"Spoken like a man who doesn't understand business," he said. "We've navigated countless human calamities, from wars and plagues to the industrial revolution. Change is always good for business, if you learn to ride the wave of change rather than allowing it to sweep you under."

Sensing my argument wasn't appealing to its audience, I changed tactics. "You say the Watch took away my equipment and influence, and that's true. But they couldn't take away everything. I still have what's in here." I pointed at my temple. "I know all sorts of things, some of which could prove useful to you."

Bracher's expression turned to mild amusement. "Do enlighten us as to the nature of this useful information."

"For one thing, I know amassing wealth isn't your only goal. For centuries you've been working on making society at large friendlier to vampires. You've invested heavily in underground subway systems, you've financed fiction and films that rehabilitate your image, such as *Interview with the Vampire* and *Twilight*. The world may never forgive you for the latter. But your greatest undertaking has been to increase the price of silver so as to remove it from everyday use."

Bracher's face remained unreadable but his cohorts weren't as stoic. They exchanged glances and shifted nervously as a mere human laid bare their secret agenda.

I turned to Willodean. "Did you know the reason vampires couldn't be seen in mirrors was because early mirrors were backed with a reflective layer of silver? Modern mirrors use aluminum instead, eliminating an obvious method of detection."

Having remained quiet thus far, Willodean nodded. She seemed fascinated with my revelations, even if they had little direct bearing on our situation.

"Early film was exposed using silver in the emulsion fluid to create photographs. But later cameras, not to mention digital ones, have steered away from this method. The more expensive silver becomes, the less likely a vampire is to become inconvenienced by its presence."

"It's a fine theory," said Bracher. "Even supposing it's true, how are your deductions of any use to us?"

"My deductions may not be useful on their own, but they allow me to conclude that an alchemical formula for converting silver into platinum would be of sufficient interest." This really got their attention. I pressed on. "Using this process, you can not only further increase your wealth, but make a significant dent in the world's silver supply."

The vampires behind Bracher seemed more enthused at this news than Comic-Con attendees at the sight of Nathan Fillion. A couple of them were typing furiously into their tablets while others watched over their shoulders and whispered to each other excitedly.

Bracher's expression hadn't changed. He studied Willodean and me from behind those thick glasses. "Alchemical formulae are complicated, even for experienced practitioners. How have you retained this treasure even as you lost the rest?"

"Modern technology," I said. "I uploaded the scan of the page containing the formula to a private online account."

"Zat's a risky move," said Kurt Schurter. While Bracher's English was almost unaccented, Schurter sounded like a Hollywood cliché of a German mad scientist. "Zere haf been reports of Zilicon Valley companies using image recognition programs to find and copy zensitive arcane data schtored on zeir zervers."

This was news to me. Next time I decided to store sensitive data online, I'd have to remember to take a picture of it next to a cute kitten or something and hope that would fool the algorithms. "All the more reason to download the file soon, delete it from the internet, and hand it over to your fine selves," I said.

One of the vampires handed his tablet to Bracher and whispered into his ear. Bracher nodded several times as he listened and read the screen. He looked up at me.

"The numbers don't add up," he said. "If there were a viable way to convert silver in the manner you're describing, someone would be using it. Yet there's no evidence of any significant dip in the world supply. I must conclude the process is flawed in some way—if it exists at all." He raised his eyebrow at me.

He was right, of course. The formula worked, but it turned a kilogram of silver into something like ten grams of platinum, resulting in a giant net loss for the user. Not that I was willing to admit it.

"Damn it, Bracher, I'm a doctor, not an alchemist. Also, I'm not even a doctor. All I know is that the process works."

Several of the vampires snickered, but Bracher clearly wasn't a *Star Trek* fan. He shook his head. "I'm sorry, Herr Brent. I don't feel embarking on this course of action on your behalf would be prudent. As you say in English, the ends don't justify the means."

I thanked Bracher for his time and soon we were headed downstairs.

Willodean waited until we left the building, then glared at me. "What the hell was that? I figured you'd pull several more rabbits out of your hat before giving up."

"Bracher wasn't likely to be swayed, especially not once he made up his mind," I said. "But he was never the one I had hoped to convince."

Willodean chewed her lip as she worked it out. "Schurter?" she asked.

I nodded, pleased at her deduction. "I've met Schurter before. He's much younger and a bit more impulsive than Bracher. Eager to make his own mark on the world, and considerably more enamored with alchemy than his senior partner. I'm willing to bet if we walk slowly, he'll catch up to us and propose a side deal."

I wasn't wrong. Schurter's messenger showed up before we reached the corner. The junior partner asked for a meeting after sunset on the following day and offered to put us up in a hotel until then. That latter part was thoughtful of him; we could sure use the rest.

We checked into the hotel and ordered room service. The two of us sat on the couch in the spacious suite we'd been provided, hungry and exhausted by the ordeals of the day. Despite the devastating losses I had suffered, I felt so comfortable just sitting in silence next to Willodean. It felt *right*.

Willodean was smart, beautiful, and driven. And there was a lot more connecting us than the shared misfortune of being middlings. She made the same kind of snarky jokes I did, and she laughed at mine. I found it so easy to open up to her, even though I usually had a difficult time opening up to anyone.

In retrospect, I should have realized earlier that I was developing feelings for her. But I was damaged goods; I'd spent so much time and effort walling myself off from others, that I must've hidden the fact even from myself.

I half turned toward her. She turned too, and our eyes locked. She smiled at me.

What a fool I had been, bottling my emotions, suppressing them like that, when there was no telling how much time we might have, and what dangers awaited us in the days ahead.

I leaned in to kiss her.

Willodean yelped in surprise and pushed me back.

She jumped from the couch and stared at me, wide-eyed.

"I … I'm sorry," I stammered. "I thought …" I let the words trail off, not knowing quite how to finish that sentence.

Some of the tension sapped from Willodean's shoulders and she sat in the armchair, several steps away from the couch we had shared.

"I'm sorry, too, but I can't," she said. "There is … was …" She took a bit of time to compose herself. "You told me not to reveal too many personal details back in your apartment, remember?"

I nodded. I could tell where this was going. "There's someone else, right?"

"There was," she said, her voice brittle like thin ice. "The day I was abducted, I was with my fiancé. He knew nothing at all about magic and he wasn't ... one of us."

I could tell she didn't want to say this man *wasn't gifted*, even if that was by no means an insult.

"He tried to fight the men who came for me, and they killed him." Tears welled in her eyes. "They killed Greg."

I sat up, but she leaned back in her armchair, apprehensive in the way she had been when I'd first introduced myself back in our apartment. So I remained seated and tried to appear relaxed and nonthreatening. "I'm so sorry," I said.

"I want to make them pay for what they did to him," she said. "Hanson, Anodyne, the Traveling Fair. I will do whatever is in my power to avenge him."

I nodded. There wasn't much I could say. I had been feeling sorry for myself and for walling off my emotions, while she was carrying this terrible burden, grieving for the man she so clearly loved.

Willodean blinked tears from her eyes. "I like you, Conrad, but I'm nowhere near ready for another romantic relationship. I might never be ready. Can you respect that? Or are you one of those guys who thinks a platonic friendship between a man and a woman isn't possible?"

"I can respect it," I told her. And I believed I could. Better to squash those feelings before they bloomed into something that left me pining irrationally for a woman who wasn't available. "But you shouldn't have to grieve alone. Do you want to tell me about Greg?"

She did. The food came and we ate it, and we kept talking into the night.

CHAPTER 13

WE got a good day's sleep and met with Schurter after sunset the following evening. I had been correct in estimating his level of interest, but the deal we eventually struck contained two surprises. First, Schurter insisted on coming along in person. He admitted to being a bit of an adrenaline junkie but also wanted firsthand access to Nascent Anodynes's files in addition to the alchemical formula. He was so eager for it, I almost felt bad about knowingly cheating him. Almost.

The second surprise had been the muscle he'd hired on our behalf. I'd expected a team of mercenaries. Instead, he had called one guy who appeared to be in his thirties, with a bushy mustache and weathered, suntanned face that made him look a bit like a young Tom Selleck. The suntan also made it clear he wasn't a vampire like Schurter. Willodean and I both expressed doubts about a single operative, no matter how talented, being sufficient for our needs. A quick demonstration had convinced us that the Legion was not only sufficient, but worth every Swiss franc our patron was paying him. He proved a viable stand-in for a team.

We drove from Bern to Munich in Schurter's Porsche SUV with tinted windows. The vampire blasted ABBA songs from the car's fancy speakers the entire way. The rest of us were glad for the trip to be over. We parked in some industrial suburb, down the block from our target, and the Legion climbed out.

The Munich facility was a fortress. Whereas the New Jersey facility had relied largely on anonymity to keep out interlopers, in Munich the high concrete walls topped off with barbed wire, the armed guards along the perimeter, and the lack of a welcome mat at the gates sent a strong keep-away message.

The Legion walked right up to the gates. The two guards stationed there watched him approach along the well-illuminated sidewalk but didn't appear overly concerned by the sole pedestrian. The arcane protections our enemies were certainly using to scan him wouldn't reveal anything out of the ordinary, either. He walked right up to the guardhouse next to the gate and did his thing.

In the blink of an eye there were a dozen identical men clustered around the spot where the Legion had stood. Before the guards could react, each of the legionnaires—that's what he had called his copies, having scoffed at Willodean's use of the term "clones"—drew a taser. Some fired at the guards; others forced open the gates and ran inside. We watched through the open gates as the legionnaires continued to split until there were three dozen armed men running rampant inside the facility's walls.

We could hear gunfire and screams all the way from where the Porsche was parked. The Legion had charged extra to use the taser after I'd insisted on minimizing the loss of life. It seemed the guards didn't share my pacifist notions. I hoped the Legion would maintain his restraint as he took them out.

Eventually, the sounds of struggle subsided, and a lone legionnaire peeked out from behind the gates to wave us in. Schurter drove the Porsche through the gates and toward the building.

"The building is clear," the legionnaire said.

We rushed in past several guards, who were twitching—but alive—on the ground. Inside, one of the legionnaires lay dead, bleeding from several bullet wounds to the gut.

Willodean gasped and stumbled. She turned toward the body, even though it was clearly beyond help.

Another legionnaire stopped her by resting a hand on her shoulder. "It's only a paper cut," he said. "They'd have to kill half a dozen of me before it became a flesh wound."

We searched the facility quickly, paying special attention to computers and paper records of any kind. We weren't having much luck. If a paper trail existed here, it was buried deep within a mountain of other data. Too deep for us to discover in a smash-and-grab.

"I rounded up what few employees I could find," said a legionnaire.

There were a handful of the staff gathered in the conference room. They sat on the floor while several legionnaires towered over them with tasers. They looked frightened and miserable, and didn't seem at all like they knew why they were being ambushed. Which also meant they probably weren't high enough up the corporate food chain to tell us anything useful.

"Where's Clarissa?" I asked.

No one volunteered an answer, but the eyes of at least one man widened with recognition. I grabbed him by his lab coat and lifted him up.

"Where is she?" I asked again. "Speak, or I will feed you to him." I pointed at a legionnaire.

The poor man shook with fear but wouldn't speak.

"Allow me," said Schurter. He got very close to our prisoner and held his chin as the man tried to turn away. In moments, the man had stopped blinking and his pupils had grown large. Whatever geas or hypnosis the vampire was using seemed to be working, as far as I could tell. Gifted and middlings were immune to this power.

"Answer ze nice man's question," said Schurter.

"Clarissa quit months ago." The man seemed to be speaking against his will. It was as though he was fighting and losing an internal battle. "She left the country."

"Vere to?" asked Schurter.

"I don't know!" Tears rolled down the man's cheeks. He couldn't lie under Schurter's control, but he couldn't help it if he truly didn't have the answer.

"What manner of creature is Clarissa?" I asked.

Before he could respond, we heard more gunfire and the legionnaires in the room screamed in pain. Their synchronized voices were creepy as hell.

The nearest legionnaire turned to us and the look on his face was that of genuine fear. "It's the Cabal," he whispered. "You didn't tell me we'd be fighting against the Cabal!"

Schurter stared at me, agape. "Vat haf you done, you zuicidal fool?"

"I had no idea the Cabal had any involvement with Hanson's company," I said.

"Ve haf to get out of here!" Schurter opened the nearest window and peeked out.

"We're surrounded," said a legionnaire. "I think they were waiting to attack until you three were inside."

"Where are they spread thinnest?" I asked. "We'll try to break through."

Instead of responding, the legionnaires winked out of existence.

I turned to Schurter. "Does that mean he—?"

The vampire morphed in front of my eyes, shedding his clothing and growing thick, gray fur. He turned into a huge bat—it was easily the size of a house cat—and flew out the window, his wings flapping loudly.

I had thought that ability had been a myth—with vampires it wasn't easy to tell what attributes were true and which were embellishments. The newfound knowledge did little to improve my current situation. I turned to Willodean.

"You gonna disappear, too?" she asked.

"I'm not that kind of guy," I said, putting on a brave face and wishing my various means of disappearing weren't in Mose's possession.

"We should probably run, then," she suggested.

We made it out of the conference room and down the corridor before running into several well-armed Cabal mages.

We were handcuffed, checked for magical artifacts, and led downstairs. On the way out of the building we briefly saw the Legion, who had been surrounded by several Cabal gifted. They hadn't handcuffed him, though they didn't look particularly chummy, either. The bastard must've surrendered without a fight once he realized who he was facing. To be honest, I couldn't really blame him. The Cabal was a dominant force among the gifted in Europe, and he surely wouldn't have signed on to this mission had he known of their involvement.

Had I known of their involvement, I would have played this thing differently, too.

We were unceremoniously shoved into the back of a van, and it drove off. Our guards either didn't speak English or chose to ignore us. They wouldn't respond to any of my questions or snide comments. This reminded me of being taken to the Watchtower just a couple of days earlier. I hoped not to make being abducted by humorless goons a habit.

Willodean remained quiet. I'd noticed her tendency to fade into the background in certain interactions with others, be they friends or enemies. At first, I'd thought it was fear or timidity, or perhaps social anxiety, but I hadn't given her enough credit. Over time, I realized it was wisdom and control: she paid careful attention and assessed all the details, then acted only when she could do so effectively and with sufficient knowledge of the situation. It was an admirable quality, really, even if I didn't follow suit. My response to being taken prisoner by armed ruffians was generally to egg them on.

The van stopped in front of an ugly one-story building. The sign by the entrance read *LEICHENHAUS*, which meant nothing to me until I saw a smaller sign in English. It read: THE MORGUE.

For once, the grim reality of our circumstances got even me to shut the hell up.

They led us past some offices and into the bowels of the morgue. The cavernous basement contained a wall of chrome pullout drawer units for bodies like you see on TV, and metal examination tables. Some of the tables were occupied with corpses. They were stiff, ugly shells whose spirits must've been evicted from their mortal coils with extreme prejudice. They hardly resembled the embalmed bodies with a ton of makeup applied that one might see at an open-casket funeral. Most of them were human, but there was also a giant, his feet dangling from the metal slab.

I shivered. It wasn't just the sight of death; it was cold down in the basement, perhaps to slow the decomposition process.

We were led to the far end of the basement where a steel cage the size of a minivan was built into the corner. Runes and other arcane symbols had been drawn on the ground and walls around the cage to thwart any spellcasting. Our captors shoved us inside, locked the door behind us, and left without a word.

Inside the cage there were low benches along two of the walls, and a small metal toilet in the corner which offered no privacy of any kind. There were two additional occupants, sitting morosely on opposite benches. Both were gifted, according to their auras.

An overweight man in his late forties hugged himself for warmth and fidgeted on the edge of the bench, his T-shirt and khakis insufficient for our chilly prison. He looked up at us, the expression on his face conveying as much misery as I felt.

The woman sat still, her hands hidden in the pockets of her oversized red hoodie, the hood covering her face. The hood shifted slightly as she looked at us. Then she began to cackle.

Her laughter was a strange sound, more bitter amusement than merriment. We watched with apprehension as she got it out of her system. Then she rose from the bench, stepped toward us, and pulled back her hood.

"Of all the prisons in all the towns in all the world, you had to get yourself thrown into mine," said Moira O'Leary.

I was at a loss for words again, which was becoming a problem. Snarky comebacks and pop culture quotes were kind of *my* brand.

The shock on my face must've been obvious because Willodean broke with her stay-silent-and-study-the-situation thing. "Who is this woman, Conrad?"

"She's the Cabal agent I had the displeasure of crossing paths with recently. She works for the people who abducted us, and she's probably here as part of some convoluted plan to extract information from us. Anything else would be too much of a coincidence. I don't believe in coincidences. And I don't trust *her*."

"As well you shouldn't," called out the flabby man from the other bench. "She robbed me of my hoodie!"

"Shut up, Dale," Moira told him. She stared daggers at me and her jaw flexed. "You can think what you want, but the irony is rich, considering I'm in this frozen hellhole because of you! I was already in a heap of trouble for failing to complete my mission, but when my superiors found out you were a mudlark, it was from the dog house to the big house for me." She paused, and her eyes went wide as she stared at Willodean. "Wait a sec. Could it be … ? You're that other mudlark, the one he rescued, aren't you?"

Willodean took a step back. Moira was staring at her with the intensity of a wolf about to pounce on a hare. Dale sat up straight and watched us with great interest now that Moira had identified both of us as middlings.

"Do you expect me to feel pity for you?" I asked. "You went after innocent people. You deserve to be imprisoned for that."

Moira snorted. "Do you know what this place is? It's not the sort of jail where you can get out early for good behavior. Ending up in this cell is the last stop on the journey over there." She pointed toward the corpses atop the examination tables. "You think I deserve the death penalty? Does your mudlark friend? Huh?" She paused, letting her words sink in. "If we don't get out of here, we're all done for."

"And here it is," I said. "I don't know what your endgame is, but I'm not planning a prison break with you."

"I already knew you were an idealist," said Moira, "but I hadn't realized you were also a fool." She stomped back to her bench.

An uncomfortable silence followed. Willodean broke it by walking over to the man and sitting on the bench next to him.

"Hi. You're Dale, right?"

He nodded, eying her warily.

"How long have you been here, Dale?"

"Since yesterday afternoon."

"And what about her?" Willodean pointed at Moira.

"I don't know. She was already here when they brought me in."

"That means she's been here since before we talked to the vampires," Willodean said to me. "Since before we even left New York. The only person who knew we'd be coming here back then was Herc. You don't seriously think he betrayed us to the Cabal, do you?"

"You have a point," I grumbled. "Then again, maybe this total stranger you got this information from is in cahoots with Moira. Maybe the Cabal has a powerful clairvoyant, or perhaps they anticipated an attack on the Nascent Anodynes facility as soon as Herc's people abducted one of their executives."

Moira rose from her bench. "Did you say Nascent Anodynes?"

"What of it?" I asked.

Her eyes narrowed, and she stared at me in silence for a time. She must've been deciding how much to tell us, and how much of that would be lies.

"When I returned from New York," she finally said, "my prospects weren't good. I needed a big win, something to get back into the Cabal's good graces. I went to an oracle in Brussels and paid him an outrageous sum to tell me how to do that. He told me I had to find someone named Clarissa who used to be an employee at Nascent Anodynes. I was caught breaking into the building where she supposedly worked."

Willodean and I exchanged glances. Finding Moira here was still a hell of a coincidence, but if she was after the same target as we were, it made a little more sense.

"How would finding this Clarissa person help you?" Willodean asked.

The ramifications of the bioweapon falling into the hands of the Cabal were even scarier than this prison.

"The oracle said she had something of great value, and that I'd recognize it," said Moira. "He tends to be rather vague on the details, but always accurate."

I nodded, thinking back to the oracle of Eighty-Sixth Street and her maddening prophecies.

"What do you know about the partnership between the Cabal and Nascent Anodynes International?" I asked.

"Partnership? Pfft. They pay protection money, like everyone else. I just didn't expect the place to be so well guarded, or they never would've captured me."

I blinked. Could it be that the Cabal goons had been responding to an alarm set off by the NAi guards? Could it be that they didn't know who Willodean and I were? If so, someone would be coming to interrogate us, and it was even money on which of the two villainous outfits that someone would be from. Either way, our circumstances would only get worse once they figured out our identities.

Moira was thinking things through as well. "I gather you were captured trying to break into Nascent Anodynes's offices, too? Which means my pals over there"—she motioned toward the guards at the other end of the morgue—"don't know your true identities, or your value. Yet." She smiled in the way that made me think of a hyena from *The Lion King*, and batted her eyes. "Why Conrad, you could be my ticket out of here. I could shout for the guards, tell them who you are. Surely my masters at the Cabal would reward me for such information."

"You've got nothing," I said. "They've already captured us. They'll figure out who we are soon enough. Your only chance at survival is to escape; same as ours."

Moira's smile widened, and I realized how neatly she'd manipulated me into suggesting an escape, minutes after rejecting the idea of working with her at all. "I'll help you escape," she said. "On one condition. You have to take me to Clarissa."

I gaped at her.

"Spare me the dumbfounded look," said Moira. "If you were trying to break into the same building as me then you must be after the same thing. Otherwise, as you put it, all this is too much of a coincidence."

"You're right," I admitted. "But we don't know where Clarissa is."

"I do," said Dale.

All three of us focused our attention on him. He'd sat through our verbal sparring so quietly, we'd damn near forgot he was there at all. Except he *was* there, listening to our every word. So he knew we were middlings. He could try the desperate gambit of alerting the guards, too.

"Let me guess," said Moira. "You got caught looking for her, too?"

"No," said Dale. "I used to work for Nascent Anodynes. I've been there for a few months, and I met Clarissa before she left the company. I know where she went afterward. If you get me out of here, I'll take you to her."

I studied Dale and he looked back at us earnestly. He didn't strike me as an evil henchman type, nor as a rogue like Moira.

"What's your story?" I asked Dale. "Why are you here?"

"I didn't do anything wrong." He raised his voice. "I'm innocent!"

"Said every person in prison, ever," replied Moira.

"It's true." Dale looked miserable. "Look, I wasn't going to say anything, but it sounds like you two, of all people, would understand my plight." He looked around and lowered his voice, even though the guards were all the way on the other end of the cavernous basement, clustered around an electric space heater by the door. "They captured me because I'm a middling, too."

Dale looked terrified and uncomfortable, yet somehow hopeful, like he'd found kindred spirits. If he was lying, it was an Oscar-worthy performance.

"Oh, great," said Moira. "What did I ever do to deserve getting stuck in the middle of a mudlark convention? I must've eaten a lot of puppies in my past life."

"What, you don't think attacking innocent people is enough to generate some bad karma points?" I asked.

"Settle down." Willodean inserted herself between Moira and me. "Yes, the coincidence is suspicious to say the least, but now is not the time to focus on that."

Moira switched her attention to Dale. "Why were you working at Nascent Anodynes, mudlark?"

Before I had the chance to stop him, Dale blurted out: "I was looking for a cure, like them. Clarissa's research seemed promising."

"Interesting." Moira sidled up to Dale on the bench and wrapped her arm around his shoulders. "The eggheads at Anodynes are working on a cure for your kind?"

"Not exactly," said Dale. He leaned away from Moira, uncomfortable with her sudden interest in him. "They're developing a weapon to turn someone like you into someone like me."

And there it was. This fool has just told a desperate, dangerous Cabal operative about the most powerful weapon ever developed against the gifted.

Moira smiled again, looking like the hyena that had swallowed the cat that swallowed the canary. "Marvelous," she said. "All of you mudlark Pinocchios have been dreaming of becoming real boys and girls. Far be it from me to stomp on that particular fantasy. You take me to Clarissa, help me get her weapon—and if there's a cure—I'll be more than happy to let you all have a taste."

I opened my mouth to argue and immediately shut it closed. We couldn't get out of this prison on our own. Moreover, stripped of weapons and protections we were all at Moira's mercy. The immediate concern was to escape before the lot of us joined the stiffs on the examination tables. As to preventing the unscrupulous, unhinged mercenary from getting her hands on the bioweapon? I'd burn that bridge when I got to it.

"Deal," I said.

Willodean shivered from the cold and wrapped her arms around her torso. "Now that we're all friends, can we please get out of here?"

"This prison is designed to hold the gifted," said Moira. She pointed at the runes and sigils surrounding our cage. "Those protections are there to stunt one's magic, but they're not strong enough to shut it off entirely. Also, this cage is meant to hold one or two people at a time, not four." She stomped her foot on the concrete floor in frustration. "Four gifted might overpower the protections and the guards and make a break for it, but since all three of you are useless mudlarks, I have no earthly idea how to escape."

"Why did you promise to get us out, then?" I asked, raising my voice.

"I said I'd help you escape, not mastermind the whole thing," said Moira.

"Magic isn't the only skill one might use," said Dale as he eyed the door of the cage. "I'm pretty sure I could pick that lock." He smiled ruefully as he showed us a small bit of copper wire.

It was a suspiciously convenient skill set for Dale the supposed mild-mannered NAi employee to possess, but I felt just then wasn't the right time to question it.

"They didn't bother searching us thoroughly," I said. "I have a little something that can counter some of the effects of those arcane protections." I dug a stone amulet out of my pocket.

The Cabal wasn't as incompetent as this sounded. After all, what's the point of searching the gifted? Why confiscate the knife when the equivalent of the gun—their most dangerous weapon—is their own power?

"Now we're getting somewhere," said Moira. "All we have to do is figure out how to stop the guards from killing us the moment they notice us trying to get out of the cage."

"I have an idea," Willodean said. "Moira, you seem like the sort of person who would dabble in black magic."

"Thank you," said Moira.

"Umm, okay." Willodean went on. "Do you know any necromancy?"

CHAPTER 14

IT was a good thing the guards thought us nothing more than arcane thieves. They weren't paying attention to the goings-on inside the cage so long as we didn't do anything obvious to attract their attention. Instead, they had congregated by the space heater near the entrance to the morgue, where the cadaver-filled examination tables and other miscellanea partially obstructed their view. So, none of them batted an eye when we pretended to huddle for warmth, blocking their view of Moira who sat down cross-legged on the floor of the cage and chanted an ancient incantation. The words, if one might call them that, sounded like they scraped her throat raw before oozing out between her teeth.

Moira touched the skin at my ankle with her icy-cold fingers. Her other hand rested on Willodean's foot, just above her shoe. She was drawing on our life forces to help power and sustain her spell against the Cabal's wards. The sensation of being slowly drained like a cell phone battery was not painful, exactly, but deeply uncomfortable in ways I had a difficult time categorizing. Sort of like sandpaper pressed against a festering wound on one's soul.

I winced, and Dale gave me a sympathetic look. He appeared thankful that Moira only had two hands, thus sparing him the experience.

Moira finished her spell and let go of us. She remained seated, her eyes closed, her face sweaty despite the meat-locker climate of the morgue. As unpleasant as it had felt for me, the spell must've been ten times worse on the caster.

While Moira recovered, the rest of us stared through the bars. For nearly a minute nothing happened. I was beginning to think the spell had failed until one of the cadavers twitched.

"It begins," Moira said in a voice that would instantly get her a super villain role at a Hollywood audition.

"You're up," I told Dale.

Dale moseyed over to the door and ministered to the lock. His chubby fingers handled the piece of wire he was using with the dexterity of a concert pianist caressing the ivories of his Steinway. And although he was working fast, the guards surely would've noticed had they not been otherwise occupied.

The cadavers were moving.

Some of the dead were sitting up on their examination tables, others sliding off and struggling to their feet. At first they all seemed sluggish, like someone rudely woken from a pleasant dream by an alarm, flailing in the dark for the snooze button. But they were waking up fast, their movements becoming coordinated, dangerous, feral.

The guards were on their feet, too. One was shouting into his cell phone, no doubt calling for reinforcements. The second pulled a pistol and aimed it toward the cadavers, his hand shaking. The third was casting a spell.

Several of the dead stalked toward the guards. The gun-toting guard took a step forward and shot the advancing cadaver in the head at nearly point-blank range. The thunderous shot reverberated through the brisk air. The dude must've seen some of those zombie movies and TV shows that shuffle onto the pop-culture landscape with all the tenacity and charisma of the undead they portray. Everyone who watches that crap knows you must destroy the brain to put down the zombie. Unfortunately for the guard, the cadaver had not watched the same films.

The walking corpse surged forward, ignoring the neat little bullet hole in his head, and grabbed for the guard's throat.

Real zombies don't bite, and the magic that animates them has nothing to do with what's left of their rotting gray matter. They hate all living things, and they kick and punch and tear, their rage fueled by black magic.

The guards fought for their lives against a dozen enraged stiffs who couldn't be killed and couldn't feel pain because they were already dead. As much as I despised the Cabal, I couldn't help but feel a modicum of pity for them.

"All done!" Dale pushed door of the cage open.

"Wait!" Moira held up her hand. "Let my pets clear the field."

The guards lasted a minute, tops. The spellcaster managed to cast a force barrier, which held until the undead giant kicked at it several times with his size twenty-two feet. Then the three humans disappeared under the pile of rampaging zombies who literally tore them apart.

I couldn't bear to watch, so I focused on my fellow inmates instead. Willodean turned away from the grisly scene and threw up into the metal toilet in the corner of the cage. Moira's face was pressed against the bars, and she observed the action with the enthusiasm of a pugilist aficionado at a prize fight. Dale was fidgeting with his bit of wire, visibly struggling to ignore the screams coming from across the morgue.

When the screams finally stopped, Moira nodded in satisfaction. "Time to boogie."

We emerged from the cage and walked toward the dead.

"I sure hope this works," Willodean muttered. She hung close enough where only I heard.

"Hey, it's your plan," I whispered back. "But don't worry. It'll work."

We approached the roaming cadavers. Moira strolled confidently in the front with Willodean and me a few steps back, and Dale cowering behind us. The nearest zombies turned and watched us, immobile for a few seconds like wild animals deciding whether to attack or flee. But that was my imagination assigning a thought process that wasn't actually present. The malevolent magic animating these bodies allowed a singular course of action. The nearby dead started toward us, and even those by the entrance were switching their focus to their new targets.

"Now's good," I said.

Willodean unclasped a brooch she was wearing over her heart and held it out toward the zombies. The amethyst set in gold glinted under the fluorescent lighting of the morgue.

It was the single artifact she'd managed to save while my house was being tossed by the Watch cleaning crew. The artifact I'd thought mostly useless given its niche purpose. Willodean had hung on to it and found a useful way to harness its power.

The zombies shrank back from the brooch enchanted to repel them, scrambling to keep their distance. I caught a whiff of their scent, gagged, and wished the brooch's power had a greater range.

We made a beeline toward the exit, but when we had nearly reached it, Moira turned toward a metal shelving unit a dozen steps off to the side of the front entrance. Intent on her target, she seemed unconcerned to be leaving us and the protection of the brooch behind. Willodean paused, first eyeing the door, then the zombies that seemed ready to pounce on Moira as soon as she stepped outside of the invisible zone protected by the brooch.

Willodean had mere seconds to decide, but I already knew we were in for a detour. She wasn't the type to leave even a Cabal sorceress to fend for herself in this sort of predicament. She followed Moira, the brooch held high. I walked alongside her. Dale muttered something under his breath and hurried along after us, keeping as close to the brooch as he could get without bumping into us from behind.

Moira didn't slow down or acknowledge Willodean's help in any way. She rifled through the shelves until she found a bundle the size and shape of a large umbrella. She unwrapped the cloth and drew a short sword with a somewhat-curved blade and an elaborate gilded guard from its scabbard. I guessed it was a saber.

"A cutlass?" said Dale. I almost slapped my forehead; I should've recognized the sword design immediately. "Are you going to look for an eye patch and a parrot next?"

"This is Kindness," said Moira. She hefted the cutlass. "They took her from me on the way in, and I sure as hell wasn't going to leave her here on the way out."

"Kindness?" asked Dale.

Moira nodded, without taking her eyes off the cutlass. "Every worthwhile blade should have a name."

"It's because she kills people with it," said Willodean. "It would be clever, if it weren't terrifying."

"Thanks," said Moira. "I think I like her, Conrad. She gets me." She gently slid the cutlass back into its scabbard and fastened it to her hip. "I found that joke on the internet," she said in a tone that dared us to belittle her accomplishment. She glared at Dale. "It seemed appropriate."

Dale raised his palms. "Far be it for me to argue with a sword-wielding necromancer," he said.

"I hate to break up the getting to know each other session," I said, "but we should scram before the reinforcements show up."

For once, I got no argument from any of them.

We stepped into the cool Munich night, which felt downright toasty to all of us after the hours spent in the ice box. Moira took the lead, striding purposefully down the street, and we followed. I squashed my feelings about the situation as best I could. She was the one with magic, and she seemed to know where she was headed.

My faith in her temporary leadership was shaken when she led us into a small twenty-four-hour kebab shop located a ten-minute walk away from the morgue. I was about to make a snide comment, but the smell of grilling meat assaulted my senses and I realized how hungry I was. From the looks of the others, they felt the same way.

Moira slid a few Euro banknotes to the young Middle Eastern guy manning the counter. He didn't seem to mind the sword at her hip; he must've seen far stranger, working the graveyard shift. He grinned at Moira and piled rectangular paper containers filled with chicken skewers and French fries onto the plastic tray. My stomach rumbled, and I was almost prepared to forgive Moira all her past sins because she'd bought food for all of us.

We squeezed onto the plastic benches around the table and attacked the food with great vigor under the overly bright neon lights.

For a few minutes, no one talked. The fast food was greasy and salty in all the right ways, and most importantly, hot. We made such an unlikely group: a Cabal sorceress, an ex-Watch operative, a known middling, and … whatever the hell Dale was. His story didn't quite add up. He claimed to have worked for Nascent Anodynes but also to be a middling, and he just happened to be a skilled lock picker. What was his deal, anyhow? I noticed Moira watching Dale and was certain she must be thinking the same thing.

"You," Moira poked Dale on his forearm. She spoke while chewing, her words barely intelligible. "Talk."

Dale looked at her with the expression of a canary watching the house cat from inside its cage.

"Can I have my hoodie back, please?" he asked.

"No." Moira wiped her mouth with the sleeve of the red hoodie. "You told me you know where Clarissa is holed up. I saved your neck. Now, talk."

I bristled at Moira taking singular credit for the escape, but a debate on the subject didn't seem worthwhile. Willodean didn't argue the point, either. She was too busy eating, but she glanced at the brooch she wore upon hearing the rogue's words, and rolled her eyes.

Dale took a few moments, whether to gather his courage or to decide on what lie to feed us, I couldn't say. Finally, he acquiesced. "She's in Ukraine. Chernobyl. She said something about a sanctuary."

I cursed under my breath. He surely meant *the* Sanctuary.

"Well, shit," said Moira.

"Problem?" asked Willodean, noting the look on my face.

I looked around, unused to discussing such matters in public places. We were the only customers in the shop, and the guy behind the counter was focused on the soccer match playing on the small TV behind the counter.

"After the nuclear plant accident made the land around Chernobyl unsafe for humans in the 1980s, a group of magical creatures moved in," I explained. "Unaffected by radiation, they built a community in a place where they didn't have to worry about being harassed by humans. More and more creatures flocked to this so-called Sanctuary, and we have no idea how many live there now. Once the radiation levels began to subside, humans attempted to return to the area. The inhabitants of the Sanctuary took it upon themselves to keep their territory, by whatever means necessary. Any human found on their land is killed on sight."

"Vampires, morgues, and nuclear power plants," said Willodean. "This isn't the tour of Europe I'd dreamed about taking someday."

"You're still willing to go?" I asked her. "I wouldn't blame you if you choose to sit this one out."

"I'm going," Willodean said firmly. "We've talked about this."

"Not me," said Dale. "That doesn't sound like a nice place at all. I think I'll stick around in Germany, where only the Cabal is trying to kill me. You can even keep my hoodie."

"Oh, you're coming with us, sunshine," said Moira. "You're coming with, and staying with, until I have Clarissa's weapon in my own fair hands. That way, if you've lied to us and sent us on a wild goose chase to one of the most dangerous places in Europe, I can kill you myself." Her palm rested on the hilt of Kindness.

Dale swallowed hard.

"What manner of creature is Clarissa?" I asked, for the second time that day. Our failed assault on the NAi building felt like forever ago.

"She's a goblin," said Dale.

"Now I *know* you're lying!" Moira was loud enough that the worker glanced away from his TV screen.

Dale turned pale and looked like he would rather be back in the Cabal prison than having this conversation. "It's true," he muttered.

"Goblins aren't generally known for their intellectual prowess," I explained to Willodean.

"He's sugarcoating," said Moira. "They're plain dumb. It would take some sort of goblin Einstein to learn high school chemistry, let alone become a scientist."

"That sounds like racist nonsense to me," said Willodean. "What, only humans can be smart? Seems like what Europeans would say about the rest of the world, just a century ago."

Moira rolled her eyes. "Millennials and their ideas. Goblins aren't the same as humans. Their brains are demonstrably smaller."

"Ah, so that must mean the giants and trolls are always smarter than us humans, then?"

"Look, your point is well taken, Willodean," I interjected. "We know Clarissa is smart, and we know she's a goblin, according to Dale. Let's assume those facts are accurate, unless proven otherwise, shall we? And speaking of trolls, there's an Abaddon branch in Kyiv, so I think I know where we're going next."

The sun was rising by the time we got back to Bern and entered the Abaddon building. Tiny the doortroll frowned at us from behind his desk.

"We're back," I said, forcing cheer into my voice.

Tiny's frown deepened, which I didn't think was even possible.

"Loudmouth," he rumbled. "*I know.*"

"Huh? Know what?"

"You got thrown out of the Watch. That means you can't come through here anymore." At that thought his frown turned upside down, and he treated us to the view of his tusks. "Begone!"

"Nonsense," I said. "That's what Mose and I want people to think. I'm undercover."

Tiny wasn't impressed. He pointed at the door with his clawed, oversized finger.

"I demand passage on behalf of the Cabal," said Moira.

Tiny focused on her and thought for several seconds, which was pretty quick for him, then said, "Papers?"

I was astounded by that development. Abaddon had a similar arrangement with the Cabal as it had with the Watch? It made a certain amount of sense, given the Cabal's influence in Europe, I supposed. I wondered if Mose knew. For a moment, I made a mental note to tell him, before remembering that I was no longer a part of the Watch.

Moira held up Kindness, still sheathed. "That's all the papers I ever need, troll." Then she strolled toward the other door.

Tiny rose to his full height and leaped over the desk. He towered over Moira, his wide muscular frame blocking most of the corridor. He roared, "You may not pass!"

I leaned toward Willodean and muttered, "Where's a Balrog when you need him?"

Moira looked up at the doortroll and grinned in that special way I'd come to recognize as a precursor for trouble. She returned her cutlass to her hip and raised her hands, palms out. "In that case …" Then she hit the troll below the belt with several quick strikes, like a boxer unloading on a punching bag.

Troll anatomy must be similar enough to our own, because Tiny *oophed*, clutched at his genitals, and curled into the fetal position. Moira stepped over him and headed for the interior door.

I wasn't sure how quickly a troll might recover, and I didn't want to find out. "Come on," I told my companions, and rushed after Moira.

"So sorry," Willodean told Tiny as she followed me.

Dale brought up the rear. He scraped against the wall to try and avoid any contact with the troll.

We found the door labeled *Kyiv* and stepped through.

CHAPTER 15

TO think that only days ago I'd complained about getting my boots dirty minutes away from Belt Parkway. As we trekked through the wild underbrush and beneath the imposing, gnarled branches of a Slavic forest near the border between Ukraine and Belarus, I would have gladly traded each hour spent hiking here for a day sauntering on the shore of the Atlantic.

We had procured a rental car in Kyiv, a little European sedan that looked new and clean but ran like its engine had been salvaged from a Soviet Union-era jalopy. We followed internet maps on Dale's cell phone—Willodean's didn't work in Europe, and Moira's had fallen victim to her scuffle with the Cabal when she'd been captured—to navigate our way across Ukraine.

The ride would have been uncomfortable, what with Dale sulking and my mistrust of Moira. However, Willodean peppered the Cabal sorceress with questions about the nature of magic, the gifted societies in Europe, and the Cabal itself. It reminded me how new she was to the secret world we shared, how limited her exposure to it had been.

Willodean's apparent naïveté had been disarming, and Moira's responses progressed from brief and grudging to detailed and illuminating. I listened in fascination to her worldview and thoughts on magic, and on middlings in particular.

Moira harbored no ill will toward the likes of us, yet she didn't have any particular aversion to the genocidal policies the gifted practiced in regard to middlings. It was just part of the world she knew; no different, I imagined, from ordinary German citizens in the 1930s going about their lives as the trains shuttled rounded-up Jews, homosexuals, and dissidents to concentration camps. To my mind, her tacit acceptance of the practice made her no less complicit than those citizens.

As we passed Chernobyl and approached the Belarus border, the paved highways turned into dirt roads, and ours was the only vehicle in the area. Soon enough, we parked the rental car on the side of the road and headed into the forest on foot.

Hours later we were tired and grumpy, and very possibly lost. Even Willodean ceased her questioning as the day went on, and the only soundtrack to our journey was the chirping of birds, the rustling of leaves, and intermittent complaints from Dale.

"This seems like the sort of place where there would be bears," he said, eyeing the thick vegetation to his left. "Large, hungry bears."

"Bears are the least dangerous thing around here. You—"

Moira cut off her response and ceased moving. She held up her fist, signaling for us to stop. Then she crouched behind a patch of bushes, and we followed.

At first, I heard nothing out of the ordinary. But soon there were distant voices, and then a trio of creatures walked past us so closely I could smell the strange musk off of them. A troll led the way, a bit smaller than Tiny but still a tall and broad-shouldered brute. Behind him was a pair of humanoids I couldn't classify, with large saucer-like eyes, sharp Roman noses, and lipless mouths that were located farther down the face from the nose than where humans would have them. It made those beings look unsettling. All three carried burlap sacks filled with who knows what. They chatted casually in a melodic language I didn't recognize at all—could've equally likely been Elvish or Ukrainian—as they headed off. They weren't alert, so we were fortunate to avoid detection. We remained still until their voices could no longer be heard.

"Guess we're in the right place, then," said Willodean.

Moira pointed in the direction the trio had gone. "We should head that way."

"Isn't it more of a fifty-fifty?" Willodean asked. "They could be walking to or from the Sanctuary."

"Less likely they'd be carrying stuff away from their base," I said. "It's not like they've established trade with nearby human villages and are bringing produce to market."

"Whatever direction you pick, let's go," said Dale. "I can feel myself getting cancer."

"The radiation levels are low enough by now that spending a few days in the area is safe. Don't buy a summer home here, though," I said.

Dale grumbled something about me not being an expert on radiation as he followed along.

Twenty minutes later, we reached a village of a few dozen houses, each surrounded by fields and gardens, spread out across the clearing. A cluster of several larger buildings, including a church, stood at its center. I could see several gnomes and a Chewbacca-lookalike covered in goat fur tending the fields.

"The Sanctuary," said Dale.

Moira gave him a dirty look. "Thanks for mansplaining that. The rest of us thought this was Cardiff."

Willodean stepped between the two of them. "What's the plan, then?"

"Maybe—" I began to speak, but Moira cut me off, asserting her authority as the leader of our little expedition.

"We wait until dusk," she said. "We find a good vantage point and see if we can spot the goblin. If not, we figure out where one of those gnomes lives, and we make the pipsqueak take us to her."

"Gnomes know how to keep secrets," I said. "I speak from personal experience."

"And I know how to make creatures talk. But, if you want to try and intimidate that thing instead," Moira pointed at Chewbacca, "be my guest."

I'd read somewhere that farmers tend to get up very early in the morning and go to bed early. This seemed to hold true with the residents of the Sanctuary. As we waited for it to get dark, we saw a variety of creatures farming, working, and otherwise milling about in the village. Some we recognized, and some we didn't. There were no goblins, though.

The Sanctuary appeared idyllic, or at least peaceful. A sleepy little village hidden away from the rest of the world, where the residents could be left truly alone. It wasn't for everyone; I'd take the excitement and bustle of living in a large city over the tedium of watching crops grow in a live-action version of *Farmville* any day of the week. But I imagined for many of these beings an existence away from humans was practically paradise.

At dusk, a half-dozen gnomes packed themselves into a single house, so we chose another target, a house near the edge of the clearing that appeared to be occupied by a lone satyr.

Once it became dark the mosquitos came out in full force, as if we needed an extra incentive to finally get moving. We crept toward the house, past the vegetable patches, and onto the wooden porch. The layer of faded green paint was peeling and cracking in places, but the porch was otherwise tidy and cleanly swept. Fireflies glowed in the distance and a chorus of various insects provided the soundtrack to our heist.

"Pick that lock, Dale," Willodean whispered.

Dale tried the handle and the door opened with a soft squeak. The concept of leaving the front door unlocked was so foreign to me as a New Yorker that it surprised me more than some of the previously unfamiliar cryptozoology specimens we'd observed in the Sanctuary during the day.

We snuck into the house. It was illuminated by a few candles and looked ordinary. Its original inhabitants must've left in a hurry after the nuclear plant accident in 1986. Decorative plates, knickknacks, and photographs rested on shelves. There was even an Orthodox Christian icon in a carved wooden display case. The new occupant seemed to ignore all that stuff rather than add personal touches of his own.

We found the satyr in the kitchen, cooking something that smelled less than appetizing in a shallow pot. By the time he realized someone was in his home, we were practically on top of him.

The satyr took in the sight of the four of us and emitted a strange sound, somewhere between a squeal and a bleat. He looked to be middle aged, his pointy beard mostly black with only a handful of gray hairs, wrinkles beginning to encroach around the eyes and lips on his elongated face.

"*Shhh*," said Moira. She held up Kindness meaningfully as an incentive for the goat-man to comply.

He babbled something that sounded like a question.

"English?" I asked.

"*Ni*," the satyr shook his head.

Moira frowned. "*Deutsch? Francais?*"

The satyr stared at her with his hircine eyes and shook his head again.

"*Advas koine?*" asked Dale. When the satyr didn't respond he said, "No Greek, either. The satyrs used to be the sophisticates of the ancient world, and often polyglots. This one doesn't do his species credit."

I didn't know many satyrs, but a couple I'd met in New York were socialites and insufferable know-it-alls when they weren't busy chasing tail. Giacomo Casanova, the Marquis de Sade, Freddie Mercury and Steven Tyler were all satyrs. The trembling creature with stupefied eyes standing in front of us bore little resemblance to those bon vivants.

Willodean tried another tack. "Clarissa," she said, pronouncing the name clearly. She pointed at the wall, roughly toward the center of the village. "Clarissa?"

The satyr's eyes narrowed. He bared his teeth in a very unherbivore-like fashion and babbled a string of sentences that sounded more like threats than directions.

"I don't speak goat," said Moira, "but based solely on his tone, I don't like the things he's insinuating about Conrad's mum."

"Please," I said. "Leave sarcasm to those capable of wielding it at above kindergarten level."

The satyr was becoming more agitated and bolder, despite the blade being pointed at him.

"I was hoping to conserve my magic, especially since the three of you are useless in that department, but we haven't got time for this." Moira laid her palm on the satyr's forehead and whispered an incantation.

143

The fight went out of the satyr. His muscles relaxed. He remained standing, but slouched, his arms dangling, his head tilted. Drool pooled at the corner of his mouth.

"What's she doing?" asked Willodean.

"She's trying to fish the information we need from his head," I said.

I hated every moment of what I was witnessing. A sorceress was using dark magic to invade another being's mind. This was exactly the sort of thing the Watch had been created to prevent. And yes, the satyr was a magical creature, so technically outside of the Watch's purview, but he wasn't gifted; he was *of* magic but couldn't wield it, couldn't defend himself against Moira's power.

Most of all, I hated myself for being a part of it, hated standing there silently and allowing this travesty to go on. How much evil would I condone for the sake of expediency? I'd always felt that the ends-justify-the-means argument was ethically and intellectually dishonest. And yet, I'd broken rules and bent ethics on a daily basis in service of protecting my secret, and doing what I felt was right. Were Moira's actions truly worse than my own?

"What did she mean about conserving her magic?" asked Willodean. "Don't the gifted have a lifetime supply?"

"There are limits," I said, never taking my eyes off Moira and the satyr. "Some gifted are very strong, like Herc, and can do a lot. Others barely have the spark."

"Is there a measuring scale? Can Moira figure out, through trial and error, how many fireballs she can cast before she runs out of juice and needs to recharge by eating a magic mushroom?"

"No," I said. "I've always found the notion of quantifying magic like that in books and video games frustrating. Magic is no different from a person's other attributes, like strength and stamina. If I arm wrestle the Rock, you can be pretty sure he'll beat me. But he won't know in advance how many miles he can run or how many pushups he might do before collapsing of exhaustion. The strength of one's magic can be estimated but not quantified, just like their physical strength."

"Unless you're a middling, in which case you can absolutely quantify that number," said Willodean bitterly. "It's nice and round and can't divide by it."

"No wonder the goat-man went aggressive on us," Moira said, grinning. "This one has a thing for Clarissa." Her face was covered in a sheen of sweat. Rifling through a being's thoughts was more difficult magic than throwing fireballs or putting up shields. "I guess it's true that satyrs will chase anything in a skirt."

"That's none of our business," I said. "Do you know where she is, or not?"

"Yeah. It's not far," she said, as though quantifying distance were a constant. *Not far* could mean different things in a sprawling metropolis and in this one-horse town, that horse probably being a centaur.

Moira released the hold on the satyr and he curled into a ball right on the floor of the kitchen, babbling something incomprehensible. His hoofs scraped against a cabinet, leaving jagged scratches in the laminate veneer. The Cabal sorceress raised her cutlass.

I grabbed Moira's hand as I inserted myself between her and the satyr. "What the hell are you doing?"

"We've got what we needed from him," she said.

"So?"

"So, we cut the loose ends. You want him raising the alarm?"

"We can tie him up and gag him, but we aren't killing innocents. We're not the Cabal. It's not how we do things."

Moira glowered at me, but she relaxed her hand, and once I let go, she sheathed Kindness.

"Why do you like taking unnecessary risks so much, Conrad? This is real life, not some Hollywood movie. Dull-eyed couch potatoes aren't judging your moral character by the number of cats you save. I mean, this pathetic thing's not even a person."

Willodean snorted. "You mean the same way middlings aren't people?" She rested her hands on her hips and stared at Moira.

Moira wouldn't meet her gaze. "Fine," she said. "Tie him up. But don't forget who's in charge here, and who's the only one of us with magic."

"Yes, mistress," deadpanned Dale. He struck such a fine balance, the rest of us couldn't be sure whether he was mocking Moira or not. She didn't bother to challenge him, especially since he proceeded to rummage through the kitchen drawers for rope.

Dale sat the satyr in a chair and tied him up. He gagged the poor creature with a towel and secured the ball of cloth with sealing tape.

His movements were sure and efficient, as though he tied people up all the time.

After he was done, Moira tested the knots. "Not bad," she said. "Looks like somebody's bondage fetish is paying off."

Rather than take the bait, Dale stared at her noncommittally.

"Let's get on with it," Moira said.

We left the gift-wrapped satyr and followed Moira past a handful of houses until we reached the destination she'd plundered from the satyr's mind.

This house was larger and better-kept. There were solar panels on the roof, and a few of the windows were illuminated with electrical light. Once again, the door was unlocked. We walked right in and followed the sound of soft classical music to a spacious living room.

A woman was reclining in a puffy armchair under a floor lamp and reading a thick book. An LP record player in the corner was piping in the sort of music they might use in a Grey Poupon commercial. When she heard us come in, she set the open book face down on one of the plush arms of her chair and got up slowly.

For a moment we all studied each other. She was large for a goblin at nearly five feet tall. She was thin and gangly like an awkward tween entering puberty. Her face placed her likely age into the forties, a spiderweb of wrinkles emanating from around her eyes. Her cheeks were pockmarked, and her ears slightly elongated. She was dressed in a calf-length, floral-pattern dress, red marigolds and yellow daffodils contrasting against her slab-gray skin. Even to the gifted, she might have passed as human from a distance.

I took a small step forward. "Clarissa, I presume?"

She nodded as she continued studying the four of us. Her gaze lingered on Moira's scabbard. "I'm afraid you have me at a disadvantage, sir." Her voice sounded like that of a much older woman, but it was cultured and clear.

"Oh good, this one speaks English," said Moira.

"My name is Conrad Brent, and I'm with the Watch." I didn't figure she needed the details of my recent misfortunes. "My associates and I have come here to ask for your help."

"You shouldn't be here," Clarissa said. "It isn't safe for you to be here."

"Couldn't agree with you more," said Dale. "If you tell these nice people what they want to know, we can be on our way."

"Marko Hanson and his company are using the bioweapon you developed to strip the gifted of their powers," I said.

Clarissa looked as though someone had slapped her. She stared past us with sad eyes.

"We need an antidote."

Clarissa sighed deeply. "I have regrets," she said, slowly. "Much like Nobel with dynamite, or Oppenheimer with the bomb. I wish I could take it all back." She looked up and stared directly at me. "But I can't. There's nothing I can do for you."

"Can't, or don't want to?" I raised my voice. "My friend, a good man, has lost his magic because of what you did. Countless others are threatened with the same fate, and all of it is your fault."

Clarissa didn't flinch at my anger, but her shoulders slumped. "At first the work was theoretical. I sought to unlock the gifted gene, to allow everyone to become more than they were. It wasn't clear as to whether this goal could even be accomplished through science .... But then there was an accidental breakthrough. Instead of turning on the gifted gene, I seemed to have found a way to turn it *off*. I was so excited, so focused on the thrill of discovery that I didn't stop to consider the implications."

Her eyes were focused now, her small frame tense.

"By the time my team and I were approaching the clinical trial stage, we were told it would be a deterrent, a means of stopping the gifted from abusing their power, a weapon of last resort .... Any student of history should have seen right through such propaganda, but I was willing to delude myself because the research was so intellectually fascinating. It was only after my team and I had succeeded in creating the drug that we were asked to work on the means of making it airborne or delivering it through the water supply. They wanted it mixed with the influenza virus to try and make it contagious. I couldn't be a part of that anymore, so I got out, went into this self-imposed exile—"

Clarissa's tale was interrupted by Moira's slow, sarcastic clapping.

"That is one long, boring soliloquy, goblin. These saps probably sympathize with your tragic story, but I grow tired of it. Give me the formula, the research, whatever you have on this weapon, and I'll let you live."

Clarissa focused on Moira. She still appeared intense, but her face showed no anger or fear akin to what the satyr had displayed earlier.

"No," she said. "Even if I wanted to comply, I couldn't. I've destroyed my notes and files, anything that could help someone else duplicate my work."

"What about an antidote?" Willodean stepped forward. "Our goals are different from hers. We don't want to replicate your weapon. We want to counter its effects."

"I'm sorry," Clarissa told her. "There's no antidote. At least not that I've discovered—I worked on that in my last months at Nascent Anodynes, but I made no significant progress."

My heart sank. I thought of Herc. As much as I hated being a middling, having the true power of a gifted once and losing it must be a thousand times worse.

"You may have deleted your notes," said Moira, "but I can take the knowledge from your mind."

Clarissa crossed her arms. "Do you have a PhD in genomics? If not, good luck parsing the information in my head. It's not a straightforward task, like fishing out a name or a passcode."

I expected Moira to be annoyed, to lash out at Clarissa, but instead she grinned savagely.

"I like your spirit, goblin. Guess I'll just bring you back with me instead and have other eggheads interrogate you until you give up the goods."

My mind was in overdrive. Clarissa had no reason to lie to us about the antidote, and while my mission appeared to be a failure, I wasn't going to let Moira abduct the scientist so the Cabal could torture her for information. But Moira was still the only one of us with magic, and I had no charms or amulets I could use to stop her. My best bet was to play along for now, to bide my time until an opening presented itself.

"I'm not going anywhere with you," said Clarissa. "Do you think I would have come to this secluded place had I been willing to allow what I'd created to spread? How did you find me, anyway? I told no one of my destination."

"Your coworker knew about it," said Willodean.

"Coworker?"

Willodean pointed at Dale.

"I've never seen this man before in my life."

All of us turned toward Dale, who smiled sheepishly and held up an index finger.

"I can expl—"

There was a loud crash. Inhabitants of the Sanctuary forced their way inside Clarissa's home.

CHAPTER 16

FOUR supernatural creatures rushed us, angrily shouting something I couldn't decipher. Two of them were wood spirits of some sort, slender androgynous creatures covered in green moss, each slightly taller than Clarissa. They held spiked clubs with their unnaturally long fingers. A hairless humanoid with bronze skin and red eyes wielded a garden hoe. A wide-shouldered, thick-muscled minotaur with a war hammer brought up the rear.

Dale dove out of the way, a club missing his head by a few inches. I threw a nearby stool at our assailants, then rushed to the kitchen and pulled a pair of serrated knives from the rack. The blades looked like they were probably no good for anything but slicing bread. Willodean followed, grabbing another four-legged stool and holding it legs out toward the attackers for lack of a better weapon.

Moira unsheathed Kindness with her right hand, drew an arcane symbol in the air with her left, and spoke words of power as she placed herself between the attackers and the rest of us.

With the mossy green dudes nearly within arm's reach, she spread the fingers on her left hand, palm out, and summoned a sonic boom that knocked all four intruders off their feet. It shook the rest of the house and could probably be heard throughout the settlement, but it seemed the time for subterfuge was over, anyhow.

Before the creatures could recover their wits, Moira stepped forward and kicked one of the wood spirits hard in the face. Its head snapped back and its body hit the floor with a *thud*. She slashed at the second with her cutlass, rending a long gash from its breast down to its belly. Dark-red blood poured from the wound and matted the green fur.

The bald bronze guy who looked like a life-size Oscar statuette came at Moira from the side, but I stepped forward, grabbed hold of his hoe, and yanked hard. Oscar and I played tug-of-war for half a second, then I let go and he lost his footing, crashing into the wall behind him. Decorative plates teetered and rattled on the shelf above his head. One fell over and broke into porcelain pieces next to him. I closed the distance before Oscar could recover his wits and punched him in the face, trying not to think of what would happen to my fist if his skin were actually made of metal. But, despite the metal-looking exterior, Oscar seemed to possess a glass jaw. He went down after one good swing and whimpered on the floor amidst the ceramic shards.

When I turned, Moira was fighting the minotaur. He was considerably taller than her, and his heavy hammer outmatched her cutlass, so Moira got in close enough for a slow-dance, where he couldn't deliver a proper swing, and aimed a cut at him.

The minotaur's huge fist closed around her wrist and most of her lower arm, and twisted. Moira grunted but held on to Kindness. As the minotaur attempted to lift her up by her wrist, she kneed him several times in the groin.

The minotaur roared but didn't double over. He lifted her until her neck was level with his face, then he lowered his head, his sharp curved horns aimed at her flesh.

With a loud *thud*, Dale shoved a spiked club he'd picked up off the floor into the back of the minotaur's head, nearly driving its horns into Moira's face. The great beast buckled to his knees, then fell face down. A trickle of blood oozed from where the sharp metal spike stood embedded in the base of his skull.

Moira uttered a string of obscenities as she climbed out from under the fallen minotaur.

Dale bent down and pressed his fingers to the creature's neck, checking the pulse. "He'll live," he said flatly. Once again, I couldn't read Dale's tone: did he speak with relief or regret?

The entire fight had taken ten, maybe fifteen seconds. Our foes lay on the ground, still or moaning softly. There was shouting outside. Somewhere, a bell rang.

"We have to get out of here," I said.

Moira stared past me and cursed.

I wheeled around to find no one behind me. The back door of the house was ajar. Clarissa was gone.

"She couldn't have gone far," Moira said.

"Are you mad? We have to leave, now!" Willodean shouted.

The voices outside were multiplying and getting closer.

Moira grunted in frustration and punched the wall. Another decorate plate plunged to its doom. "Fine. Let's go."

I lifted the hammer. It was too heavy and would slow me down too much. I picked up one of the spiked clubs instead and kicked the other one toward Dale. He looked at it as though it were something distasteful and made no move to collect it. Willodean walked over and claimed the club.

Moira headed for the back door and we followed. Outside, there was no sign of Clarissa. The moon and stars provided enough illumination to get by. As we headed away from the house and toward the forest, we saw a group of at least two dozen beings gathering at the center of the village. More were trickling in from the nearby houses. Some among them were literally carrying pitch-forks and torches.

The satyr was there, surrounded by others and telling them something, gesticulating wildly. He must've freed himself minutes after we'd left to have raised the alarm so quickly.

One of the creatures at the edge of the crowd spotted us, pointed, and shouted a warning. The varied mob of beings surged toward us.

We ran as fast as we could, but more of the Sanctuary residents were exiting their homes, and a group of them headed to intercept us. It was a race to the edge of the forest, and we were losing.

I ran as fast as I could. Willodean nearly kept up, only a few steps behind me. Surprisingly, the overweight Dale kept pace with me and wasn't even panting. Moira was a sprinter—she kept increasing the distance between us and reached the edge of the clearing three dozen paces ahead of the group. She barely beat our pursuers, who rushed from the side to block our path.

Two ogres and a werewolf stood between us and the clearing. The wolf was shapeshifting in front of our eyes, her hands and feet growing sharp claws, her face elongating, and her carnivorous teeth protruding from her jaw. Thick, coarse fur emerged to protect her soft skin. The ogres brandished what looked like *shashkas*—Cossack cavalry sabers. From their stances and grips, it seemed they were well versed in how to use their weapons.

Moira stopped, looked back, hesitated.

I knew better than to count on her. She was faster than us; she had her magic and her cutlass. Her odds of survival were exponentially higher without being saddled with a trio of middlings.

So, it was up to us: two American city slickers armed with clubs and an enigmatic empty-handed European. I didn't love those odds one bit, but every second wasted allowed the rest of our pursuers to get closer. We had to make it through.

I raised my club and stepped forward.

Moira rushed the ogres from behind, her cutlass in hand. She shouted a battle cry, drawing their attention away from us. The werewolf, now fully transformed, came at her on all fours, but Moira cast a spell with her free hand, throwing the shapeshifter aside so hard that her lupine bones crunched loudly against the trunk of a birch tree.

Then Moira took on the ogres, slashing at them with Kindness, landing a few shallow cuts on their feet and arms even as they did their best to parry the attacks.

I closed the distance and swung as hard as I could at an ogre's back, holding the club with both hands. He fell face down into the dirt, and Moira's sword thrust would have ended him had the other ogre not managed to block the killing blow with his *shashka*.

The remaining ogre fought fiercely, and it took us several precious seconds to force him to retreat. By then, at least a dozen more pursuers were only a few steps away.

The rest of the mob advanced toward us. There were trolls and orcs and creatures unknown, united in their apparent desire to punish the intruders. Behind them, illuminated by torches, moved an elephantine shape with several appendages swaying like thick pythons above its body.

"Sweet Jesus, what is that?" asked Willodean.

Moira stared at the monstrous shape in the distance, her eyes widening. Her expression was one I'd never seen on her face before: abject fear. She turned without a word and sprinted away from the village.

I didn't need or want to know what it was. The menagerie of magical creatures out for our blood was scary enough for me.

"Come on!" I shouted, and followed her.

Willodean and Dale, who'd hung a few steps back, out of the reach of ogre blades, rushed toward the forest, the mob at their heels.

We were only a handful of steps past the tree line when Willodean tripped on a tree root, which extended up from the ground and had been hidden in grass and fallen leaves. She screamed, and before the rest of us had the chance to react, half a dozen pursuers were on top of her. Several of them set to restrain her while others continued their hunt.

I turned back, but Dale grabbed hold of me and pulled me away. "There's nothing you can do for her now!" he shouted. I struggled, but he was surprisingly strong and practically carried me into the thick brush. "We have to lose them first," he whispered into my ear as he manhandled me through the brambles. Somewhere along the way, I lost the club I'd been clutching. Sharp shrubs prickled my face and I closed my eyes for fear of being blinded, letting Dale lead me deeper into the woods.

We fought past the shrubs and were able to run again, leaving our pursuers—and Willodean, poor Willodean!—farther and farther behind. Dale moved through the dark vegetation with the grace and certainty of a forest spirit, and I had no choice but to follow.

Gradually the sounds of pursuit became muted, then completely lost in the cacophony of owls hooting, insects chirping, the rustling of leaves, and other sounds of the forest at night. Only then did Dale stop.

I leaned with my back against a tree and slid downward, my shoulder blades scraping against the bark, until I was sitting. I panted heavily, my chest on fire from the exertion. Dale loomed over me awkwardly.

"You're bleeding a bit," he said, pointing at the side of my neck, and passed me a crumpled-up paper napkin.

I dabbed my neck, soaking up blood, then pressed a clean bit of tissue to the cut to stem the flow. "Just a scratch. A stray branch got me."

Dale handed me a thin flask. "Disinfect it."

If my face was as grimy as my hands, that was probably a good idea. I opened the flask and poured some of its contents on my neck. I winced as it stung something awful. Then I took a solid swig and coughed violently. The stuff burned my tongue and throat worse than it had stung my cut.

"What is this?"

"Absinthe," said Dale. He took the flask back and chugged it like it was a can of beer. "Ahh. This is the good stuff. Takes getting used to."

I made no reply and for several minutes we were both silent, listening to the forest. When the pain in my chest and neck had subsided to tolerable levels, I climbed to my feet.

"You know where we are?"

Dale nodded.

"Which way is the village?"

Dale waved. "Over there." He pointed in the opposite direction and added, "The car is this way. We should hurry. I suspect Moira won't wait for us if she gets there first."

"I'm going back," I said.

Dale tilted his head. "Come again?"

"I'm going back for Willodean."

"You've got to be kidding me. The poor girl is probably dead by now. And if she isn't, what exactly do you think you'll be able to do for her?"

"She's alive. They were restraining her back there—when they could've murdered her on the spot. Which means there's a chance to get her out. There's also still a chance, however remote, to get some useful information out of Clarissa. I have to try—"

Dale grabbed me by the shoulders and got in my face, close enough that I could smell the absinthe on his breath.

"You're insane, man. Did you not see the hatred in their eyes? Do you not understand what true, deep hatred is really like? They will kill her back at the village. They would kill you, too. Some of them would probably eat you."

I couldn't argue with his assessment, but it didn't matter. This wasn't about logic or strategy; it was about doing what was right in spite of caution and reason. I would walk toward the danger and face impossible odds for a chance to save an innocent person. It's what I'd done for years. It's what the Watch—aside from its politics and its problems—had always been designed to do. We were a bunch of crazy adrenaline junkies, each guided by their own internal moral compass. We weren't too different from cops and firefighters and soldiers—ordinary people voluntarily taking up dangerous vocations for the benefit of those around them. And while the Watch had kicked me out, they couldn't strip away the character traits that had made me join in the first place: bravery bordering on a death wish, a hint of insanity, and a level of overconfidence matching that of the Most Interesting Man in the World blitzed on Red Bull.

"I'm going," I told Dale firmly. "Don't worry. I've been in worse predicaments."

Off the top of my head, I couldn't think of any.

The Sanctuary was abuzz with activity, like a disturbed anthill. Beings of all kinds milled about. Their torches and flashlights provided ample illumination. Willodean was nowhere to be seen, which meant she was indoors somewhere—I refused to consider the possibility that I had been wrong and that our pursuers had dispensed mob justice to her in the forest.

The church building at the center of the village appeared to be the local hub. Sanctuary residents were going in and out, and many more were hanging around in front of the place than near any of the other structures. There was a good chance that was where they had brought their captive.

I had no invisibility charm, no force shield, no magic, no weapons of any kind—even the club I'd claimed had been lost. I had no allies—Moira had run off, and I'd said my goodbyes to Dale in the forest after he'd accepted that there was no talking me out of going back. Worst of all, I had no time; I couldn't wait for an opportunity to present itself because I couldn't be sure what they were doing to Willodean or how much time she had left. So I did what I had done so many times during my years with the Watch: I walked toward the threat armed with nothing more than my wits and protected only with the cloak of bluster.

I calmly approached the nearest group of beings, not breaking my stride even as they readied their weapons, bared their fangs, and protracted their claws. I stopped just out of arm's reach, smiled in their snarling faces, and said, "Take me to your leader."

They seemed thrown by my demeanor and pretend confidence. They exchanged words, then a pair of burly specimens, each at least a head taller than me, grabbed me and searched me roughly for weapons or hidden threats. They twisted my arms behind my back. Pain shot through my ligaments. But they hadn't used those sharp blades and fangs and claws—not for the moment at least.

An orc said something to me and pointed toward the church. Although he was speaking another language, the meaning was clear enough. I headed in that direction, flanked by my two captors, with the rest of their motley group following close behind.

It was only a few minutes' walk, but it felt longer. More and more creatures joined the procession, ogling me unkindly as I was led toward the church like it was my personal Golgotha. When we got there, all but a couple of them remained outside. Even my captors hadn't gone in, shoving me through the wide doorway instead.

The nave was cleared of pews. Only a few remained, lining the walls under the multitude of candles that illuminated the space. Orthodox icons featuring haloed old men who oversaw the repurposed space in silent opprobrium. A handful of the Sanctuary residents important enough to be there sat on the pews. But it was the thing directly in front of me that made me stumble and almost lose my footing. From across the nave, a three-headed dragon stared at me with six serpentine eyes.

The dragon's tail curled in the altar area, but its body extended well toward the center of the relatively small church. It was the size and shape of an elephant with three python-like necks, thick as a man's torso, terminating in serpentine-like heads. Each head hissed lightly as the creature breathed. A pair of vestigial bat-like wings, too small to lift even a fraction of its mass, protruded from the dragon's back. The barbed tip of its tail twitched and thumped against the ground as if it belonged to an irritated, oversized cat.

From what I'd read, dragons were among the few supernatural species who possessed powerful magic, well beyond the capabilities of human practitioners. They were insular and malevolent, fueling the myths and legends that cemented their stereotype. Also, according to those same books, they were long extinct.

The dragon stared at me with its unblinking, very much extant eyes. I supposed I couldn't expect the scholars to get every little detail right.

"You have trespassed upon the Sanctuary, biped vermin."

The dragon's deep voice boomed, loud enough to dredge up flashbacks of New York dance clubs, where one's ears wouldn't stop ringing for hours afterward. Yet none of its three mouths moved.

"Excuse me," I said. "If you're going to project your thoughts into my mind, do you have to be so loud about it?"

The dragon ignored me, shouting its thoughts at a consistently deafening volume. "The penalty for such trespass is death."

The creatures sitting along the pews stirred and made various noises and motions of approval. It seemed the dragon was projecting not only to me, but all those within—well, not earshot, but to whomever was in the room, at least.

"That seems rather extreme," I said. "Why don't we talk about this, like civilized beings?"

The dragon took a step forward, advancing a good five feet toward me. His heads uncoiled through the air like lunging cobras, stopping close enough that I could almost touch them. Each head was a bit larger than my own. One of them opened its mouth and hissed, a forked tongue protruding between razor-sharp fangs.

"Civilized? Your kind is anything but. You bring destruction and chaos and misery as you spread to all corners of the world! You poison the water, pollute the air, and pave over the fields. You kill or drive off every sentient being in your path until there's nothing left but the infestation of humans breeding in their skyscraper nests, living in their own filth and squalor like so much vermin."

I tried to speak but the big guy was working himself up into a fervor.

"I have gathered the dispossessed, the world's children unto me here in the Sanctuary, in the place humans have damaged so thoroughly that they could no longer live here safely. I have gathered them to live in peace under my protection, but here you are, breaking into their homes and hurting them for no crime other than rushing over to defend their own. Is that what you choose to call civilized?"

"This is all a huge misunderstanding," I said. "We didn't want to bother you at all, or to disrespect your way of life. We—"

"Did you not assault one among our number in his home? Did you not violate his mind against his will? Did you not abuse him and tie him up?"

The dragon had a point. We were 100 percent at fault when it came to that poor satyr. I wondered whether we might have done better by approaching the Sanctuary respectfully and asking for an audience, but from everything I'd heard and read about the place, that strategy would not have paid off, either. I was also pretty certain that the dragon had no interest in educating me on the finer points of how terrible human beings were in general and our group of adventurers in particular. He was putting on a show for his followers, so if I wanted any chance of saving Willodean, I'd need to make the great lizard look good to his audience.

"We did," I said. "It was wrong of us, and I am here to accept fault and beg forgiveness for our actions."

This took some wind out of the dragon's sails. His heads pulled back, and he considered my words for a long moment.

"Remorse?" he projected in a scandalized tone, as though I'd suggested something unseemly. "Where was your remorse when the good citizens of the Sanctuary came to apprehend you? You could have begged forgiveness then, but instead your cohorts have set upon them, wounding several of our bravest!"

"There was a misunderstanding," I said. "They charged us with weapons drawn, didn't give us an opportunity to talk. We retreated to avoid any further injuries on either side. It is out of respect that I have returned to apologize, and to plead our case."

It's difficult to maintain righteous indignation when the other party is humbly admitting fault. Even for a dragon.

"What could you possibly say to excuse your behavior, biped?" There was an undertone of anger to his thoughts that I didn't like one bit. "Be succinct."

"We had no choice but to come here. Lives are at stake. Our entire society may be in danger, in ways that could affect not only humans but the supernatural races living alongside us as well. And all we wanted was information, answers that could only be found here."

I launched into an explanation of our mission. I expected the dragon to interrupt, to badger me, but he allowed me to state my case.

"We're middlings," I concluded. "If anyone understands the persecution and unfair treatment some of you have experienced at the hands of the gifted, it's me and the woman you've captured. But whereas I've learned to live in their society, like so many of your brothers and sisters who live among the humans, my friend is an innocent, who only recently learned of magic and of her unfortunate place at the bottom of the hierarchy she never suspected existed. I implore you to judge me however you will, based on what I've told you, but to let her go."

One of the dragon heads twisted to face a yeti-like creature in the corner and nodded to him. He disappeared into one of the rooms adjacent to the nave and returned with Willodean.

Her mouth was gagged with cloth, her arms and feet bound by rope. She appeared terrified, but otherwise unharmed. The yeti half pushed, half carried her until she stood alongside me. In the pews, the various beings discussed among themselves what I had revealed. I figured the dragon would ask their counsel. He did not.

"You've all heard this biped's words," the dragon projected. "The so-called reasons to invade our Sanctuary and to harass our kind. 'The ends justify the means' is the most human of arguments, flawed and filled with hubris." The snake heads loomed over us and muscles in the three thick necks tensed. "I care not if these are middlings, gifted, or some other subspecies of vermin. The two of them are equally guilty of the crime of being human."

The dragon's huge body moved forward until it dominated the center of the room.

"When you discover a termite infestation within your walls, you do not negotiate with them. If there are cockroaches in your kitchen, you don't try to sort out which are guilty and which are innocent. You're not required to show compassion to the fleas who live in your fur or mosquitos that land on your skin. All those creatures are vermin, and there's only one appropriate course of action when you encounter vermin. They must be exterminated."

All three of the snakehead maws opened and flickers of blue flame ignited within their throats.

I tried to speak, but the dragon's magic constricted my throat. The damn reptile wanted his soliloquy to be the last thing his followers heard before he fried us to a crisp.

I'd thought I could talk my way out of this predicament as I had done so many times before. That I could find something the residents of the Sanctuary needed, something they wanted, some way to connect with them that would allow us to open a dialogue. But I'd thought I'd be dealing with the sort of beings we'd encountered throughout the Sanctuary. I hadn't been prepared for the dragon.

He was making an example of us. There was no negotiating, no logic. His narrative for the Sanctuary was that humans were a terrible blight, not to be reasoned with regardless of circumstances. It was how the worst of the gifted viewed the magical creatures of the Sanctuary, and how many of those same gifted viewed the middlings. The dragon wasn't at all interested in rising above his enemies, in taking the moral high ground. He desired the same thing so many human leaders wanted over the centuries: to consolidate his own power by binding the residents of the Sanctuary with ties of common hatred against outsiders. And now Willodean and I would be sacrificed in service of his goal.

The dragon exhaled three streams of blue welding-torch flame.

I shoved Willodean to the side, hoping to buy her a few more milliseconds of life. The gesture was futile, but I acted upon instinct rather than logic.

The flame shot toward us and broke against an invisible barrier.

Someone had erected a force shield that not only blocked the fire but also some of the dragon's magic. I looked to Willodean to see if she had somehow managed to access her gift and erect the barrier.

She was looking back at me in a way that left no doubt she'd been wondering the same thing about me.

As surprised as we both were, it was the dragon who was really peeved. His three heads hissed like a boiling teapot, inhaled mouthfuls of air, and breathed out hotter, more voluminous jets of flame.

The shield held.

"I'm afraid these two are with me."

The voice came from behind us. The dragon's heads twisted in unison to focus on the speaker. We turned to find Dale standing in the doorway.

It was definitely Dale, except something about him had changed. Gone was the neurotic, cautious persona who would meet your eyes with reluctance and always look away first. This new Dale's demeanor was stately, his back straight; he appeared charismatic and entirely comfortable in his own skin, like some big-name Hollywood star.

"You!" the dragon projected. There was hatred and fear in his voice. Whereas his hatred toward us had felt theatrical and bordering on disdain, there was something much deeper and more personal this time.

Dale saluted the dragon. "It's good to see you again, Zmey Gorynych," he said. "You look well."

The dragon shook with anger. His tail twitched like that of an irritated cat, knocking into the walls at the back of the church.

"Good to see me? The last time we met, your kind drove mine out of Ireland. I swore an oath to kill you!"

Dale smiled. "You were a bad lizard," he said. "Patrick and I had no choice but to show your brood the door. As to your foolish oath, I'm willing to let bygones be bygones and write that off to youthful exuberance." Dale walked forward until he stood alongside me. He motioned with his hand and the ropes binding Willodean fell to the ground. "You're not young anymore, Zmey. You seem to have matured, and your behavior has improved somewhat. You've got a pretty good thing going here, with this Sanctuary of yours. You can have it. But these two are under my protection. I'm going to take them and go."

The dragon emitted a low rumble, a physical sound rather than a mental projection this time. Its heads coiled like snakes preparing to strike. Various magical creatures at the pews were on their feet, some brandishing weapons, others baring claws and fangs.

Dale watched them in amusement. "Or," he said, "you could give in to your anger, and try and live up to your oath."

Dale held up a finger. All around us, residents of the Sanctuary were lifting up into the air, twisting and turning in confusion as though the gravity in the church had been turned off. The dragon remained on his four feet. The three of us were stationary as well. But the others floated in the air like flakes in a souvenir snow globe.

"Do you believe challenging me might be a good idea?" Dale asked. "Take your time and really think about it. They say three heads are better than one."

The dragon stared at Dale, and at his helpless followers. His tongues flicked in and out of his mouths. Then he slumped and the rumbling in his belly subsided from the volume of a car engine lacking a muffler to barely audible.

"Go," he projected. "Go, and never return."

Dale's smile widened. "I'd say I won't, but we're both too long-lived to make and keep such promises." He waved, and each of the dragon's underlings glided gently toward the floor. All of them landed without injury. "Until next time, Zmey—don't eat anyone I wouldn't eat."

Then Dale waved again, and the world blurred.

CHAPTER 17

I blinked rapidly to get rid of the strange sensation. When I'd managed to focus again, the three of us were in a lavishly decorated room. Rugs and paintings hung on the walls above mahogany bookshelves filled with old tomes. Willodean and I sat on a large, comfortable couch that dominated the center of the room. Dale occupied one of two plush armchairs that faced the couch from across an antique coffee table, atop which sat a decanter with amber liquid and a bowl of fruit. Dale patiently waited for us to acclimate to our surroundings.

"Why, Dale," I said, "I'm beginning to suspect you're not a middling at all."

"My name is Dolus." He reached for the decanter and filled three thumb-sized crystal glasses. "And once upon a time I really was a middling."

Willodean picked up her glass with a trembling hand and downed it like a shot. She placed the empty glass back onto the coffee table. "So ... what are you now?" she asked.

"Now I'm a god."

Dolus said this matter-of-factly. He refilled Willodean's glass, then lifted his own and took a small sip.

Willodean let out a nervous laugh. She looked to me for support, but I was too busy processing what Dale—no, Dolus—had said. His claim might have been hyperbolic, but he was easily the most powerful gifted I'd ever encountered.

"God?" Willodean asked. "Like, old man, long white beard, lives on a cloud?"

"*A* god," Dolus said. "Not *the* God. There are a handful of us around."

Dolus seemed to be enjoying our confusion, drinking it in along with his fine liqueur. I didn't care. My mind was racing, sorting out the implications of his words.

"You say you were a middling. How did you gain your powers?" I asked.

A mischievous smile spread on Dolus's lips. "Yes, you've arrived at the heart of the problem. You've been searching for a way to get your hands on some magic for a long time, haven't you? You just didn't have enough of the puzzle pieces to figure it out, but you're putting them together now, aren't you?"

He was giving me a little too much credit. If there was a connection, I hadn't grasped it.

Willodean drank her second glass, slower this time. "Where are we?" she asked.

"Paris," Dolus said. "They say Rome is the eternal city, but if you're going to live for centuries and not become dreadfully bored, you could hardly pick a finer place than here."

Willodean got up, walked to the window, and lifted the velvet drape to peek outside. "You've teleported us halfway across Europe with a thought?"

Through the window, the many lights of the nighttime city twinkled.

"This seemed like a fine venue for our conversation." Dolus took another sip. "It has good booze."

Willodean let the drape fall back into place. "Why didn't you use your magic sooner? Why freeze in a prison cell? Why trek through the radioactive mud in Chernobyl?"

"I wanted to learn more about our mutual friend," Dolus told her, pointing at me. "I've been following Conrad's exploits for some time, but that's not the same as witnessing how a person behaves firsthand, seeing what decisions they'd make under pressure."

I thought back to how we'd met, the improbability of those events. "You engineered this whole thing, didn't you? Not only did you get yourself captured by the Cabal, but you somehow managed to nab Moira as well?"

"Close, but no cigar. Speaking of ...." A thick cigar appeared out of thin air in Dolus's hand. It was already lit, and he took a drag. "Moira had been incarcerated through no fault of mine, and when I learned of your showing up in the same city to attempt a break-in, it was a simple matter to anonymously alert the Cabal and get us all into the same cell."

Willodean glared at Dolus, her fists clenched. "You betrayed us to the Cabal?"

Dolus raised up his palms in a placating gesture. "You were trying to find Clarissa, and I helped you do exactly that. No one at NAi knew where she had absconded to. Had I not intervened, your mission would have been a dead end."

If looks could kill, Willodean's glare would have reduced the cigar-smoking self-declared god to ashes. "This entire time you watched and laughed as we fought for our lives and as we hurt those poor monsters who were trying to protect their village."

"Spare me the indignation," Dolus said. "I pointed you in Clarissa's direction. The three of you made all the decisions as to how to approach her."

"It's the appearance of free will," I said. "You'd nudged us in the direction you wanted, but it was subtle enough to make us think we made our own choices."

"Again, god with a lowercase 'g'—free will isn't really my jam. But you're right about the nudging. I'm a trickster god. Subtly manipulating the events around us is what trickster gods *do*."

"Trickster god?" Willodean and I asked in unison.

Dolus clearly thrived on surprising us, and thrived nearly as much on making us hang on his every word and wait for an explanation. He let out a few perfectly formed smoke circles and watched them dissipate under an expensive chandelier.

"Loki. Coyote. Anansi. Crow. Those are some of the trickster gods you may have heard of. Then there's Prometheus himself. I used to be his apprentice, you know, when I was young. Most of us keep a lower profile, of course. Trickster gods aren't the most powerful of deities, but we make up for that in cunning. Isn't that right, Conrad?"

I stared at Dolus in confusion. I was a trickster to be sure, but what did I know of gods and mythology? What little I knew about Loki came from the Marvel comic books, and about Anansi from the Neil Gaiman novels. And wasn't Prometheus a titan? Was there even a difference?

There was a soft chime. Dolus took his phone out of his pocket and glanced at the screen, then put the gadget away.

"I'm a bit disappointed you still haven't figured it out," said Dolus. "Why have I taken an interest in you? It's been a long and trying few days, I suppose. I have an urgent matter to take care of in Bulgaria, and the two of you could do with some rest. Why don't we resume this conversation in the morning?"

Dolus snuffed his cigar with a thought and finished the contents of his glass. He rose from his armchair and stretched.

My eyes widened as a farfetched idea was born of the puzzle pieces and bread crumbs Dolus had laid out for us.

He grinned. "Ah, here we go. I can practically see the thought bubble over your head, and it reads 'holy crap' in Comic Sans."

"Say it." My voice broke, and I cleared my throat. "I want to hear you say it."

Dolus made a show of looking around, as though he were checking to make sure he couldn't be overheard, and leaning toward us conspiratorially. In a stage whisper, he declared: "Middlings are god larvae."

Then he vanished.

What does one do when they find out they might be a god?

Willodean and I talked about it, of course. How it was impossible: neither of us felt divine. Yet, it made a certain amount of sense. If middlings could somehow become gods, they were dangerous. And if they were dangerous, then the powers that be—humans, the gifted, and perhaps other gods—would want to eliminate them. That would explain the anti-middling sentiments, even if most of those who hated us knew as little about the truth as we had until that day.

Without Dolus there to feed us tantalizing bits of information, the conversation died down sooner than one might expect. We were simply too exhausted to grapple with the implications.

We explored Dolus's spacious apartment and found a kitchen with a fully stocked fridge. We helped ourselves to some cold cuts and slices of a baguette that sat on the counter. The baguette was crunchy and fresh, way too fresh considering Dolus had been traveling with us for the past several days. I suspected he'd conjured up the food for us before he left, like a good host. Either that, or ... I imagined Dolus standing in the checkout line of some Parisian twenty-four-hour supermarket and flipping through the pages of a tabloid out of sheer boredom, and grinned.

Sated, we took turns partaking of the hot shower. I washed off sweat and grime, barely managing to keep my eyes open. By the time I'd put on my dirty clothes and reemerged from the bathroom, Willodean had retired into one of the guest bedrooms. I claimed another, and fell asleep atop the duvet.

I woke to the heavenly smell of fried bacon. I rubbed my eyes, rolled off the bed, and glanced out the window. The sun was up pretty high; it must've been close to noon. People and cars moved along a busy narrow street underneath Baroque buildings old enough to have witnessed the reign of the Bourbon kings. Contrary to what they show in every dumb American romantic comedy ever to feature Paris, I couldn't see the Eiffel Tower from the window. Pity, that.

I followed the smell back to the kitchen. I figured Willodean had gotten up before me and was making breakfast. Instead, I found Dolus in front of the stove, wearing a flower-patterned apron over a dress shirt and slacks. He had a pair of skillets going, frying bacon and making a big omelet.

"Food will be ready in a couple of minutes," he said without turning around.

"I'll go wake up Willodean."

"No. Let her rest awhile. The two of us need to talk."

I waited for him to say something more, but he didn't. I watched him cook.

"How was Bulgaria?" I asked.

"A bit hectic. I'll be heading back there after breakfast."

He heaped bacon and eggs onto a pair of plates and set them onto the table next to the tall pitcher of orange juice.

"Why did you join the Watch?" he asked.

The question caught me off guard. With all the revelation bombs he'd dropped the night before, the last thing I wanted to talk about was me. But he was the host and he'd made me bacon, so the least I could do was to politely answer his query.

"Ever since I learned what I was, I wanted to find a cure. I wanted to find a way to tap into my magic like the rest of the gifted, and I had to conduct my research carefully, so as not to alert anyone to my middling status. The Watch deals with all the weird stuff in the city; I figured getting involved would be my best chance to learn—"

"That's bullshit," Dolus said mildly.

"Say what?"

"As much as you cared about your predicament, there were many better ways to seek information than spending your days chasing down rogue magicians and hunting vampires. You could've learned so much more had you traveled the world. Instead, you remained in New York and did your thing as you waited for the solution to come to you."

"It was because of my position with the Watch that I learned about Willodean and was able to rescue her," I pointed out. "It's what ultimately led me to meet you. My strategy worked, even if it took a while."

Dolus chewed a strip of bacon as he studied me.

"It takes a certain kind of person to become a protector," he said. "From the dawn of time there were people who would guard their tribe's cave armed with nothing more than a sharpened rock, and there were those who wouldn't. You, Conrad, are a protector, through and through. I watched you talk Moira out of killing the satyr, even if that act of mercy could—and did—bite you in the ass. I watched you go back for Willodean and then shield her with your body when Zmey was about to fry you both."

I thought back to the other day, when Dale had been trying to talk me out of going back to the Sanctuary, and when I'd been thinking the same thing about this protector business. I was the sort of person who would always run toward danger. Whether this was bravery or stupidity was a matter of opinion.

"Gods are no different from mortals in this regard. A few are good, some bad, most are a little bit of both, depending on their mood and circumstances. For many, it's difficult to see people, or even gifted, as their equals. Even those who start out with the best of intentions—their morals become dulled over the passage of centuries. We need to pad our ranks with those who possess the deeply ingrained instinct to protect the weak, just like the gifted need the Watch and other, similar groups, for their society to properly coexist with the mundanes."

I took a bite of the omelet and it was, of course, heavenly. I chewed as I thought things over.

"So you want me to join whatever passes for the Watch among the gods, then?"

Dolus nodded and ate more bacon.

I put down the fork and looked him in the eye. "Do you want that badly enough to set aside your trickster act and answer some questions straight? To explain the relationship between middlings and gods in plain terms?"

Dolus cocked his head. "Why else would we be having this conversation?"

I stared at him until he continued.

"Gods are basically the same as the gifted, but a hundred times more powerful. A gifted will not recognize a god, just like a regular human will not recognize a gifted, thinking them one of their own, but gods and certain other high-level beings will recognize each other by our auras, same as the gifted. When I see the shade of another god's aura I can tell their specialty; whether they're a trickster god like me, a god of love, one of the elementals, or some other flavor of deity."

"And all of these gods evolve from middlings, somehow?" I prodded.

"A middling can ascend to godhood by drinking ambrosia," said Dolus. "But there can be … complications." He patted his mouth

170

with a cloth napkin. "Possible side effects include horrible disfigurement, mental breakdown, and death."

A forkful of omelet hung halfway to my lips.

"Death?"

"There are risks, but you're a perfect candidate. The longer it's been since the middling has manifested, the better the chances of ascending successfully. Prolonged experience using magic indirectly—artifacts, charms, and such—is also an excellent way to prepare for ascension and to hedge your bets."

"That's good and well, but unlike Han Solo, I'd prefer to know the odds."

"Let's see." Dolus made a show of running some mental calculations. "Your odds of surviving the ascension are easily thirty-to-one or better." He glanced toward the guest bedrooms. "Your newbie friend's on the other hand, are only about three-to-one."

"Is that why you wanted to talk to me about this alone?"

"*Mmm-hmm.*" Dolus chowed down on bacon at a rate that made me assume gods did not suffer from clogged arteries. "Among other reasons." He chased the bacon with orange juice. "I would have preferred for her not to be here at all, but after you went back for her in the Sanctuary, I figured there was no dissuading you."

"Why are you so adamantly against her?" I asked. "She may be green, but it's not like she pissed in your cereal."

"She's bad news," Dolus said. "Her aura shade is tinged with black."

"Meaning?" I asked.

Dolus set down the plate and stared me in the eye. "If she ever ascends, she'll be a goddess of death."

"From your somber expression I gather that's not a good thing. But remember, I learned about this god business like five minutes ago. Could you stop being a god of Magic 8-Balls for once and explain this in terms a mortal can understand?"

"The death gods are among the most powerful," Dolus said. "But they're almost never among the good guys. They're mercurial and quick to anger. They shed their humanity with relative ease and live by their own code of ethics, which is typically not something you or I would find palatable."

I scratched my head. "Are you saying Willodean is going to turn into a souped-up version of Moira?"

Dolus considered this. "That's actually a rather apt comparison."

I digested this information while eating my omelet. "You're prejudging her based on what she may or may not ever become," I said. "But you don't know her like I do. She's tough, resilient, and resourceful. Exactly the sort of person I'd recruit into the Watch, much as you're looking to recruit me into whatever team of good-guy gods you've got going."

"Your judgment is clouded by your loyalty," Dolus countered. He pushed back his plate and wiped his hands on his apron. "Nevertheless, the choice is yours. I'm looking for allies, not blind followers. Relay to her as little or as much of our conversation as you will. She can even have some of the omelet."

I followed his example, pushing back my plate.

"All right," I said. "Lay it on me."

"Beg pardon?" Dolus said.

"I'm in. I've read the warning label and accept the terms and conditions. Let me have the ambrosia; I'll take two and call you in the morning."

He chuckled softly.

"What?" I asked. "Did you mix it into the orange juice?"

"I don't have any," he said. "Ambrosia is the most valuable substance on Earth. It is said to be made by celestials so vastly powerful, I'm little more than an ant to them. There are never more than a handful of vials out there, and they're jealously guarded, well-hidden, or both."

I sighed. "And here I thought becoming a god would be easy. Surely, you didn't tell me all this just so you could go Soup Nazi on me with 'no ambrosia for you!' Right?"

"I don't have any ambrosia," Dolus reiterated. "But I know where you might be able to steal some."

CHAPTER 18

WILLODEAN emerged from her bedroom minutes after Dolus had left, making me wonder if he was using magic to keep her asleep so we could have our private chat. My brain was spinning in neutral, trying to process what the trickster god had told me and to edit his information into a version I'd be willing to present to my fellow middling.

She nodded at me, stretched lazily, and headed for the table where she filled a tall glass with orange juice and downed nearly half of it in one shot. She was wearing a thick cotton robe she must've found somewhere in the apartment. For all the trauma and excitement of the last few days, she appeared at ease, utterly comfortable in a stranger's home. I thought back to how quickly she had gotten hold of herself when she woke up in my apartment in Brooklyn. Was this admirable adaptability somehow an aspect of her potential as a goddess of death?

My stupid brain served up an unhelpful image of a grinning Willodean, dressed in a black hooded robe and carrying a toy scythe at the New York Comic Con. I shook the thought loose, but it was difficult for me to associate this cheerful young woman with death in any manner beyond her cosplaying as Lady Death at some convention.

Despite Dolus's warnings and, perhaps, despite common sense, I decided I'd tell her everything. After so many years of hiding my true self, of lying to my closest friends and allies, it was surprising how refreshing it felt to be honest with her. I didn't want that feeling to stop.

But was it the honesty that appealed to me, or how I felt about Willodean herself? I wondered how long it might take her to get over her dead fiancé, and guiltily banished that thought, too.

"What's up, Conrad?" She piled a helping of omelet onto a plate. "You look like you're a million miles away."

"Dolus stopped by for a chat," I told her. "For about a minute before he teleported back to Bulgaria. He took the time out of his day to make us breakfast and tell me how to become a god."

I relayed our conversation, holding nothing back. When I got to the end and revealed the owners of the priceless vial of godhood, the way Willodean's face hardened finally matched her godly aspect. Not that I could blame her.

"The Traveling Fair has ambrosia," she said. "I'm glad, actually. I've been dying to kick those assholes where it hurts." Her fist clenched. "Right in their wallets."

"Dolus said they only have one portion ..." I trailed off awkwardly.

Willodean's eyes widened as she caught my meaning. Then she laughed. "All yours, buddy. I heard the part about my odds of surviving that medicine loud and clear. Being a deity is appealing, but I don't mind waiting a few years until I have a considerably better shot of ascending to godhood than descending six feet under, you know?"

I was mildly surprised. But then, Willodean was still new to all of this and the injustice of middling-hood hadn't quite grated on her the way it had me. After so many years of being a middling, I was ready for an upgrade, and if I skipped the step of becoming a full-fledged gifted and advanced to whatever the next level up might be—it was difficult to think of myself in terms of potential divinity—then all the better.

"All right then, where do they keep the ambrosia, and how do we go about taking it from them?" Willodean asked.

"There is a ship in the Mediterranean," I said. "Dolus told me they store some of their most valuable items in its cargo bay, relying more on secrecy than brute force to keep their treasures safe. I suspect there are plenty of nasty surprises on board, but there's no way to tell as it's warded up the wazoo. Can't peek in. We'll have to get onto the boat to see what's what."

"A Mediterranean cruise, you say? You take me to the nicest places, Conrad."

"If you like that, you'll really like the parting gifts Dolus left us with."

In the living room, a pile of amulets, charms, and other enchanted trinkets gleamed atop the coffee table. It was a veritable arsenal, comparable to my own collection back home before it had been depleted through my series of recent misadventures and its remnants confiscated by the Watch.

Willodean didn't have the experience to understand the power and abilities of each enchanted trinket, but she could clearly sense the magic emanating from the hoard. She whistled appreciatively as she rifled through them, picking up a large citrine gemstone and holding it against the light.

"Careful with that. It literally summons a swarm of bees."

Willodean placed the citrine back on the table with such exaggerated care it might as well have been a live grenade. "All of this asks a question. Why does a god with enough built-in power to teleport himself and his plus-ones halfway across Europe need all this stuff?"

"I suspect we aren't the first middlings he's shepherded toward godhood and recruited onto Team Dolus," I said.

"Makes you wonder what other teams are out there, and whether Team Dolus is the one you want to be drafted by," she said.

"It's not like he's asking us to sign a contract in blood. So far, he's the only one helping, and if—and when—he asks for some help in return down the line ... I'd like to assume that ascending to godhood won't adversely affect my judgment or morals."

Her fingers absentmindedly brushed across the stack of treasures on the coffee table. "You know what happens when you assume ...."

"I'll still have you to act as my personal Jiminy Cricket."

She nodded. "And in return, I'll need you to charge up all my magical gadgets while I do the middling thing. I think we have a deal, Mr. Trickster God."

"Sure," I said. "All that leaves is the easy part. Get onto the heavily guarded secret boat, find the ambrosia, drink it, and survive the ascension."

"Nothing to it." Willodean touched the citrine with the tip of her fingernail. "Not when we have magical weaponized bees."

I wandered the apartment until I found a landline, connected to a heavy brass contraption that looked like it was older than Alexander Graham Bell himself. I wrestled with the rotary dial, inputting the many digits of an international number.

The phone rang half a dozen times until someone finally picked up with a greeting that sounded like half-groan and half-growl.

"Herc? It's me, Conrad."

"Man, it's good to hear from you, even if it is the middle of the night." The grogginess in his voice abated to somewhat acceptable levels as he spoke. "It's been days. What's going on?"

"Sorry I couldn't check in sooner. Not a lot of working cell towers in Chernobyl, you know."

"What, you're in Russia now? Have you found an antidote?"

"I'll forgive your egregious geographical blunder on account of the late hour," I said. "But no, not yet." Since I hadn't told him the truth there was no good way of explaining Dolus and the whole god business. I felt a sharp pang of regret over keeping Herc in the dark. I thought back to how good it had felt to be honest with Willodean and almost told Herc everything, but this was definitely not a conversation to be had by phone. Sooner or later, I'd have to read him in, and I really hoped he'd be in a forgiving mood then. For now, I merely said, "I'm making some progress. Hope to have an update soon."

"You better. Things are going straight to shit here."

I had a good reason to be vague in my report, but I couldn't allow Herc the same luxury. "Care to elaborate?"

"The middling affliction is spreading, Conrad. There are two dozen cases I know of in New York City, and a couple of them are among the members of the Watch. Word's gotten out, and most of the gifted are staying off the streets because they think this thing is contagious. Meantime, all the nasty magical nonhumans who aren't affected by this got the memo and think Christmas came early. They're rampaging in the streets and neither the Watch nor my plucky band of vigilantes have been able to keep up. It's not a good look."

"Well, shit," I said. Having spent years in the Watch, the desire to get back and to protect the streets of Brooklyn was almost overwhelming. "What about Hanson?"

"He's gone to ground. After a bunch of gifted became afflicted, the Watch finally took our warnings about him and Nasty Anodynes seriously. Mose's crew raided some of their properties and interrogated some of their people, but, far as I know, they didn't find anything to connect those guys to the outbreak."

"Be careful, Herc. If people know you've been hit by whatever-this-is, they might turn on you, be it out of fear that you might spread the contagion or out of sheer panic and desperation."

I wished I could tell him that I spoke from many years of experience thinking about such things, researching the history and psychology of the anti-middling movements.

"A couple of idiots have already tried," said Herc. "Even without magic of my own, I'm more than a match for them." He was defiant, but I could hear the weariness in his voice.

"What about your wound?" More guilt panged in my gut for not opening with that, but our troubles ran deep.

"All better," he said. "Had Finegold patch me up."

Bob Finegold was one of Herc's Irregulars, an ex-army doctor equally adept at inflicting arcane damage and at healing it. It was good to hear that Herc's people were rallying around him despite his diminished status within the gifted society.

"Good luck, buddy. I'll be in touch again, soon."

"Yeah," said Herc. "Best of luck to you, too."

I hung up the phone and stared immobile at the antique device. I worried about my friends back home. Did gods experience worry

177

and shame in the same manner as mortals? Would I want it to be otherwise? I wanted to ascend, but wasn't prepared to let go of my humanity. I had to wait a full minute before I was in the frame of mind to make my second call.

This time the call was answered almost immediately. "*Ja?*"

"Schurter, you son of a bitch," I shouted into the antique transmitter. "I ought to drive a wooden stake through your traitorous heart!"

Kurt Schurter's voice remained perfectly calm. "I'm glad you're alive, Herr Brent. Having said zat, I must reiterate that I never betrayed you. It was logical for me to retreat, which I did. Later, I had a reliable broker discreetly reach out to ze Cabal, to see if it might be possible to bargain for your lives. Zey rebuked her offer, but she later found out ze two of you had escaped. If anything, I should be cross wiz you for embroiling me in a conflict against ze Cabal. But, I believe you Americans like to zay, 'all's well zat ends well,' isn't zat right?"

I had to give it to Schurter; he was a cold and calculating bloodsucker. A banker, through and through. I had to dial it down and talk to him in terms he would appreciate.

"You hired subpar help. Instead of a qualified team of hardened mercenaries who might've held their own against the Cabal, you got that one dude with a superpower, who gave up faster than the French at the sight of a German tank. Your incompetence has cost me dearly, and for that I'm going to have to make you pay."

"Zere's no need for threats. Ve—"

"You misunderstand, Kurt. I'm not threatening to harm you. I want you to pay actual money. I have to put together another team to go after what I'm looking for, and this time I won't make the mistake of letting someone else do the hiring. I'd like you to finance it, as reparations for what happened in Munich."

"I zee." Schurter thought it over for a few moments. "Does zat mean you'll provide ze information you promised me as payment, if zis new assault you're planning is successful?"

"That bargaining chip is off the table," I said firmly. "You make things right, and perhaps we can negotiate for the formula in the future." I was pleased with myself since I'd never possessed the method of converting silver into platinum in the first place. This way I never had to deliver, and the Swiss vampires would continue to believe I possessed valuable information, which could come in handy someday.

The line was silent for nearly half a minute this time. Finally, Schurter asked, "How much do you need?"

With a sigh of relief, I named a number and we began to haggle.

The cargo ship *Medea* was registered in Cyprus and belonged to a shell corporation owned by the Traveling Fair. Of course, I couldn't help but give it the nickname the *Traveling Ferry*.

The *Medea* floated in the Mediterranean, at the edge of France's territorial waters. It utilized concealing and warding spells that made the ship difficult to detect, as well as a cutting-edge mix of magic and technology to keep the ship off satellites and most forms of radar and sonar.

Mostly, though, its owners relied on anonymity. No one would bother a dingy-looking dinghy, or guess at the sort of cargo it carried.

But Dolus knew and, thanks to him, so did I. Time was of the essence, and I counted on being able to get past their defenses in a single brute force attack. The irony of how similar this situation was to us walking into a trap in Munich was not lost on me, but I hardly had a choice.

I had hired a dozen gifted mercenaries, handpicked for their skill as well as lack of any known affiliation with the Cabal. It wasn't easy to find highly qualified goons with no links to the Cabal in Europe, but for the kind of money I'd extorted from Kurt Schurter, I was able to track some down.

Willodean and I took an ordinary train from Paris to Nice, and we had our new underlings meet us there. We rented four speedboats, and I bought special charms that would temporarily silence the sound of their motors. By nightfall we were prepared to become pirates.

Silent as sailing ships, the motorboats approached the *Medea* like a pack of wolves stalking a lone stag. The four boats came to a stop alongside the much larger vessel. Two of our mercenaries used their magic to fly upward and connect grappling hooks to the sides of the boat. We climbed the hull, and the first two climbers were at the top by the time the alarm sounded.

Medea's horn issued a loud and piercing moan into the night. The ship's defenders were rousing. Soon the sounds of magic and projectile weapons discharging and bouncing against force shields filled the night.

We had the element of surprise on our side. The mercenaries incapacitated the handful of sailors stationed on the ship as Willodean and I raced toward the cargo hold. There we found a cavernous hangar filled with wooden and metal crates extending into the horizon, like the scene from the huge government warehouse at the end of that Indiana Jones film.

"They wouldn't keep it here," said Willodean. "Too many of their own people have access to the cargo hold."

I nodded. "Captain's quarters?"

"Most likely."

We went up a level, wands in hand, pausing only long enough to ask one of the captured sailors where the captain's quarters were, and had nearly made it to the captain's private cabin when portals began opening all over the ship. Armed men and women poured through.

It had been less than three minutes since the alarm had sounded. The Traveling Fair security had excellent response times.

I tried the captain's door. It was locked. "So much for a smash-and-grab," I said.

Willodean pointed her wand at the lock. I backed off. She blasted the lock and half the door caved in. I kicked through the rest.

The captain was a man in his fifties; backed up against the cabin's opposite wall, he was holding in both hands the largest pistol I'd ever seen, aimed at the entrance. I noticed these details in a fraction of the second after I came through, right as he pressed the trigger and fired twice at my midsection.

It felt as though a horse had kicked me in the stomach. I staggered back and slid down onto the thin blue carpet that covered the cabin. I saw the captain shift the pistol and train it on Willodean who was just coming through the door.

Despite the pain and shock, I never dropped the wand I was holding. I pointed it at the captain and fired.

A ball of yellow-hot plasma engulfed the captain's hands and left a jagged, melting hole in the wall to his side. The pistol he had been holding became a chunky puddle of molten metal on the ground. The captain's right arm up to the elbow was missing. His left hand was burned off at the wrist. His right shoulder and side were charred. The stench of burned flesh and singed hair filled the cabin.

His bullets had gone through my force shield and other protections as if the defenses weren't there. That required some insanely powerful magic, but also left him vulnerable to a counterattack. Had I aimed ever so slightly to the right, the man's head and torso would've been disintegrated.

All this happened during the amount of time it took Willodean to make a single step into the cabin.

She assessed the situation almost as quickly and stepped toward the captain.

"If you want to live, tell me where the ambrosia is."

The captain made no reply. He stared at what was left of his arms in shock.

Pain and nausea were making it difficult for me to focus. My gaze drifted downward. Instead of blue, the carpet under me was wet and brownish.

I was sitting in a pool of my own blood.

Outside the sounds of battle were abating. Our dozen mercenaries stood no chance against the army of defenders that had come through the portals.

Willodean pressed a flat bronze charm against the captain's forehead.

"The ambrosia. Where?"

It was the sort of magic I abhorred. The sort Moira had used against the poor satyr in the Ukraine. I'd had to come to terms with the fact that we may have to resort to it to find ambrosia. Willodean remembered her treatment at the hands of the Fair too well to be as concerned with the ethics of ripping information from an unwilling mind as I had been.

A humorless grin spread on her face. "The safe, then. Combination?"

There were footsteps outside. Willodean activated the citrine gemstone and tossed it out the door. There was a buzzing sound followed by screams.

I watched her rip a panel off one of the walls and unlock a hidden safe. My vision was blurry and I had a difficult time breathing, as though my lungs were filled with water. I coughed up some blood.

Willodean held a small vial that looked more like a test tube, the sort phlebotomists use to draw and store blood. It was filled with a viscous amber liquid that glowed warmly.

She held it out toward me and I tried to take it, except my arm refused to move.

Then I died.

CHAPTER 19

BEING dead wasn't anything like what religion or pop culture would have you believe. St. Peter wasn't waiting for me at the Pearly Gates. I didn't float out of my body to passively observe what happened next. There wasn't any white light for me to drift toward.

Instead, I felt submerged. Not in water, but in indescribable darkness. There was no pain and no emotion. I couldn't feel my body or any external stimuli. But I could still think. I could reason without the curse—or benefit—of the chemical reactions happening inside my brain. Somehow, I knew with absolute certainty that I was dead. Yet I didn't feel any fear or anxiety; just a sense of cold logic and understanding that hadn't been comparable to anything I'd experienced while I was alive. I decided it was an unpleasant sensation, though I couldn't quite put into words as to why. I realize that my opinions on the subject were formed from a very short and singular sample, but based on that, I didn't much care for death. I wouldn't recommend it.

Then something changed.

I felt a pull—still not toward the white light—but a pull in a *direction* in the place that didn't appear to have any directions at all. Like I'd been hooked and was being reeled in by an unseen fisherman.

Then I wasn't dead anymore.

I've had general anesthesia a few times. Each instance of waking up from it had felt like climbing up from a very deep pit, like coming back from the nether realm, very different from awaking from any sort of natural sleep. Coming back to life felt like that, only worse.

The first sensation I could feel again was pain. It was sharp and persistent, and varied. Like an orchestra of a hundred different hurts, some small, some gargantuan, resuming its never-ending symphony. It made me decide that I couldn't genuinely recommend the being alive thing, either.

Then my brain got off its posterior and went back to work manufacturing and releasing chemicals. I felt anxiety and fear and all the fun emotions that comprise the grand total of human experience.

Finally, the rest of my body caught up. I was able to twitch a little, and eventually to open my eyes.

Willodean was crouched over me, her hands over my stomach. Her bearing was different, her expression serene. She looked regal, more assured somehow, and far more calm than either of us had any right to be. An empty vial lay on the blue carpet next to her.

I tried to sit up and she looked me in the eyes and smiled. Her eyes glowed the warm amber color of ambrosia.

Before I had a chance to process this, men burst into the cabin, waving guns and enchanted weapons, and demanding our surrender. Willodean looked at them and her gaze stopped them in their tracks. She refocused on me. Whatever she was doing was better than morphine. The pain had gone away, and I was feeling euphoric in a way not quite similar to the effect of pain-killer drugs. My head was clear, for one.

Willodean frowned and waved her right hand past her ear, as though trying to banish an especially annoying gnat. The glow in her eyes intensified and she stood up and spread her arms.

I had to assume she was simultaneously ministering to me and warding off a magical attack. If so, she was doing the latter so well that I couldn't feel any ill effects from it.

With no warning at all we were outside, on the deck of the ship and in the midst of at least fifty enemy soldiers. Willodean spun around, and an invisible force shoved them all backward and kept shoving until they were tumbling into the sea like chess pieces being knocked from the board. A handful of our mercenaries, disarmed and tied, remained unaffected by the supernatural force at Willodean's command.

She pointed toward our people and they were gone. Teleported somewhere safe, I presumed. Her face remained impassive, but her outstretched hand trembled.

Although the foot soldiers were gone from the deck, their masters were continuing wave after wave of remote magical attacks. I could feel the faintest echo of them now, which meant Willodean was tiring. I racked my brain for a way to help her, to contribute, but could think of nothing useful. I was no more capable than a three-year-old who might wish to help his mother defend against a gang of bandits.

There was a sound that vaguely reminded me of thunder, and a pair of air-to-surface guided missiles, each longer than my arm, nearly slammed into the ship right on top of us. Willodean stopped them and they hung suspended a few feet above the deck like bullets in front of Neo's palm in *The Matrix*. But instead of making the bullets fall helplessly to the ground, Willodean appeared to struggle against the missiles, strain finally showing on her face.

I managed to find my voice and croaked, "Get us out of here."

Her amber eyes grew wide, as though the idea I'd suggested was outlandish. Then the thought appeared to register and, in no time at all, we were back in Dolus's apartment.

After orienting myself for a moment, I opened my mouth to make a snarky comment, but before I had a chance to, the amber light dimmed in Willodean's eyes and she collapsed to the floor.

I placed Willodean on the couch and covered her with a blanket. She appeared to be sleeping peacefully, breathing lightly and without discomfort. But all attempts to wake her were utterly unsuccessful. By morning, Willodean remained unconscious.

I hadn't slept a wink, getting increasingly worried about my friend. Whatever awesome superpowers she'd acquired, comas were serious business. In soap operas, people fell into comas and emerged from them with the frequency and consequences of a midafternoon nap. In real life they were serious business that, at a minimum, required urgent medical attention. I entertained the thought of taking her to a hospital, but doubted mundane doctors would be able to diagnose, let alone treat, what ailed her. Dolus was nowhere to be found. I kept hoping this was normal, some sort of a cocoon period as she completed the transformation from a middling caterpillar to a divine butterfly. So, I waited.

At some point I went to the bathroom, took off my shirt, and studied myself in the mirror. There was no trace of the bullet wounds. No scar tissue or even an inflammation. I felt absolutely fine. It was as though I hadn't been shot by the equivalent of a handheld cannon mere hours ago, as though my body had not undergone the physical and psychological stress of the last few days. I wasn't even tired or sleepy. It was as if I had just spent a couple of weeks on an extended Caribbean vacation.

Having a god around was turning out to be rather nifty.

That was the upside. The downside that I had to come to terms with was that Willodean had just ascended using what might've been the only dose of ambrosia in existence. Ambrosia that should've been mine.

I didn't blame Willodean, not one bit. She'd made the correct decision under the enormous pressure of a life-and-death situation, which had resulted in the desired outcome of "life." I'd been dying. Dead, actually. She'd risked drinking ambrosia despite Dolus's warnings about the side effects, and had saved us both. She'd won that particular round of Russian roulette.

Or had she?

I couldn't wake her up. I couldn't reach Dolus and, to the best of my knowledge, there weren't any other gods around who could tell me if my friend was in trouble or if this sort of sleep pattern was normal for a god. Meantime, the clock was ticking and—for all I knew—Willodean was dying. My desperate hope that Willodean would recover on her own was fleeing fast.

I needed help and the only place I could think to turn was the Watchtower. Sure, they'd kicked me out, but with the middling affliction running rampant I had a viable excuse for why my powers weren't working. Mose knew the truth, but he seemed more concerned with appearances than with my true nature. Perhaps a plausible explanation for his subordinates would be enough to let me back in from the cold. And if it wasn't, perhaps they'd help Willodean anyway. I could think of no better plan.

Navigating the streets of Paris with an unconscious woman slumped over my shoulder didn't seem like the best idea, so I found a medical supply shop nearby and bought a wheelchair. I jostled Willodean into the chair and strapped her in; she didn't even stir. I pushed the chair outside and down the street, feeling like a character in *Weekend at Bernie's*.

I didn't bother with a cab. The Abaddon, Inc. Paris branch was located less than ten blocks away.

Tiny was not happy to see me.

To be fair, the doortroll never appeared happy to see me. But our recent encounters had been even less congenial than usual. Last time we'd come through, Moira had literally used his family jewels as a punching bag. That's a difficult thing to get over for a male of any species.

When he saw me push the wheelchair into the guardroom Tiny didn't even bother with his usual request for papers. He stood up slowly, stretching to his eight-foot height as he rounded the desk, stepping toward us with the deliberate grace of an apex predator.

"I come in peace!" I said.

Tiny kept coming. There was a low rumble coming from his chest, akin to the warning growl of a large dog.

"Can we please talk about this like civilized beings?"

Tiny sidestepped the wheelchair and was now face-to-face (or, rather, chest-to-face) with me. His growl intensified and he bared his teeth. Even with our height difference, I could smell Doritos on his breath.

He was making it difficult for me to try and be the bigger man. In every possible way. So I quit trying.

"Hang on, friend. I think I have a breath mint here somewhere."

He roared and raised an oversized fist.

The speaker atop Tiny's desk crackled and he whirled to face it, almost slugging me with his elbow.

"Tinnerbin, I'd like to see Mr. Brent in my office, please. Would you be so kind as to show him in?"

The doortroll's ears flattened against his head and his shoulders slumped. I could swear I was watching an oversized puppy caught by his master in the act of chewing a loafer. Then he gave me a distinctly un-puppylike look. It was the look of a cat who wasn't allowed to eat the canary, complete with the promise to definitely eat the canary later, when the humans weren't around. He sullenly nodded toward the door.

"Elevator's to your left. Take it all the way up," he said.

"Thanks, Tiny," I said as I pushed the wheelchair past him. "Always a pleasure to see you, though not so much to smell you."

I could hear him growling all the way from the elevator.

At the top floor of the Abaddon building the elevator opened directly into Daniel Chulsky's office.

The office itself was spartan; a single desk with a laptop and a chair stood to the side. There was no other furniture, not even a seat for a visitor. What the room lacked in adornments, it made up for in the view. Three of the four walls were giant glass panes, displaying three different panoramas. On my left was nighttime Tokyo, lit with neon advertisements and innumerable office windows where the lights remained on day and night. On my right, rain fell on late afternoon London, Big Ben peeking out from a cloud of fog across the Thames. Straight ahead, the familiar tangle of Manhattan skyscrapers was illuminated by the sun approaching its zenith over the Hudson River.

Chulsky was standing in front of that middle window, watching yellow cabs and black town cars jostle for dominance of the roads below. He was a little under six feet tall and wore a bespoke three-piece suit. His short black hair had been coiffed and jelled until it had became a solid object. He didn't turn around when we entered.

"Nice view," I said.

"It's one of the top perks of the job," he replied.

I flipped the brake on the wheelchair, ensured that it was secure by the office's one solid wall, walked over and stood next to the CEO of Abaddon, Inc.

"Your New York building is not nearly so tall as to offer this vantage point," I said.

A reflection of Chulsky's smile flashed in the glass. "It's bigger on the inside."

We watched the sun shine over Manhattan Island.

"If it were anyone else, I'd figure there was a drone with a high-resolution camera, and these"—I waved toward the glass panes—"were state-of-the-art projector screens."

This got Chulsky to finally turn and look me up and down. "This is what I like about you, Mr. Brent. You're always fishing for information, always trying to figure out exactly how the world works. You remind me of the young Mose."

I swallowed my remark about us looking roughly the same age. When you rub shoulders with vampires and gods it's a good idea never to make assumptions about their age or power level based solely on appearance.

"There's no camera, and these are genuine windows," Chulsky went on to say. "I'm sure you believe we have this capability, given how frequently you avail yourself of our portals."

"Yeah, sorry about that. I've had a pressing need to travel recently, and I seem to have misplaced my bus pass."

"It's all right," Chulsky said. "I don't mind it as much as our longsuffering friend Tinnerbin. You've been put in a tough spot since—how do I put this delicately—your 'bus pass' has been revoked permanently by your superiors. You've done what you do best in response: utilize whatever resources you can get your hands on to achieve your goals. Yes?"

"The rumors of my firing have been greatly exaggerated," I lied. "In fact, I'm on my way to see Mose right now." That part was true.

Chulsky adjusted his tie. "I see. While I do wish you luck in mending whatever rift exists between you and your boss, I'd also like to propose an alternative. Come work for Abaddon. I could use an operative of your"—he paused, seeking the right word—"tenacity."

I was genuinely surprised by the offer. Between Dolus wanting me as an apprentice and Chulsky attempting to hire me I was beginning to wonder if my prospects as a middling were quite as grim as I had once imagined. At this rate, I'd be getting job offers from the vampires and maybe even the Cabal any day now.

"I'm flattered," I said. "But I don't even know what it is you people do here."

"It's a great mystery you'd become privy to if you joined us," said Chulsky. "All I can say for now is that I'm certain you would approve."

I looked past him at the unconscious Willodean slumped in the wheelchair.

"As tempting as that sounds, this isn't a really good time for me. I've got a lot on my plate these days, most of it inedible, and fate keeps piling on more slop."

The CEO frowned. "I see. What about some freelance work, then? I understand that you do that. After you eat your peas and clear your plate, of course."

"I'm open to that possibility," I said, careful not to overcommit.

"In that case, I'll be in touch," said Chulsky. "Today's bus ride home is on me. After that, and until we reach some sort of a mutually beneficial arrangement, try not to abuse our transit system. Are we clear?"

In other words, no more free rides unless and until I helped an enigmatic corporation with an ominous-sounding name to do whatever it was they did.

"Crystal." I headed back toward Willodean and the elevator. "I don't suppose you know how to wake up Sleeping Beauty here?"

Chulsky gave me an inscrutable look. "I know many more things than I'm at liberty to act upon, Mr. Brent." He hesitated, then added, "You're on the right track. Speak to Mose."

Chulsky turned toward the window. I mashed the button and the elevator doors slid open.

I pushed the wheelchair ahead of me as I walked toward the Watchtower. The gusts of humid New York air, the susurrus of morning crowds emerging from the underground train stations to fill the nearby office buildings, the smell of coffee emanating from innumerable food carts that lined the streets, all felt familiar in the exhilarating manner of a homecoming. I was in New York City where I belonged, and no man or gifted or god was going to chase me away again. They'd have to kill me first. Again.

At the base of the Manhattan Municipal Building stood a one-man welcoming committee. Karl Mercado frowned at me so hard, his face would surely get stuck that way.

"You've been told not to come back, middling," he said. "I'm here to reiterate that message."

The damn fool was going to fight me in the middle of the street, right in front of all those people. Loaded with Dolus's charms and talismans I was certain I could take him, but how was that going to help things?

I let go of the chair and raised my hands, palms up.

"Peace, Karl. Can we just talk for a minute?"

He didn't say anything, but the tension in his muscles and face subsided ever so slightly, to where I was pretty sure he wasn't going to try and fry me with a fireball. At least not yet.

"Why do you hate me so much?"

He tensed again, and I rushed my words before our interpersonal cold war got its chance to heat up.

"I mean, I got you out of the insane asylum, I taught you magic, and I welcomed you into the Watch. I know you're a good person because I've seen you *do* good. I've seen you risk your life to protect people. But you seem to have developed an allergic reaction to me, and I don't understand why. If I've done you wrong somehow, please tell me so I can make things right."

I could see Karl struggling with his own temper. He closed his eyes and, were I a mind reader, I'm certain I would've heard him mentally count to ten. He seemed to have gotten a grip, because when he spoke again it sounded more like frustration than anger.

"You genuinely don't get it, do you?"

I kept my hands up. "I really don't."

Around us, the human river continued to flow, everyone minding their own business and not making unnecessary eye contact. You've got to love New Yorkers.

"You're abrasive and annoying," Karl said. "You turn everything into a joke, and your jokes usually suck. But those are just minor character flaws that I could forgive in somebody else. Here's what I can't forgive. You may think I'm a good guy, but I don't feel the same way about you."

He leveled a finger at me.

"You're not a good person, Conrad. You got off on the authority the Watch granted you, and you used it to wheel and deal and collect your precious artifacts. You do an occasional good deed but only for selfish reasons. You're a transactional person, the what-have-you-done-for-me-lately type. I despised those before I had magic, and I despise them now."

He stepped closer to me as he spoke, and I slowly lowered my hands. Now, to an outside observer, it looked like we were having a normal conversation, even if he was beating me up pretty good verbally.

"I almost bought into your lies," he said. "Early on I admired you and I wanted to be like you. What a crock of shit! You were nothing but an insidious middling masquerading as a gifted, and you didn't care whose life you put at risk. All those times you let me fend for myself—with that horrid bug, or with the Crimson Prophet? It's not that you wanted to force me to learn, it's that you wouldn't risk using up one of your expensive toys to keep me out of danger. I got wise to this fact even before I knew the reason, so I got myself reassigned to another mentor because I didn't feel safe around you anymore. I don't even want to think about how many other recruits you threw between yourself and whatever danger you were facing over the years."

I had manipulated, and I had lied, but I had never intentionally endangered those around me to save my own skin. It stung to hear Karl's assessment all the more because he believed that.

"I can't prove to you what's in my heart," I said. "It pains me to hear these things, but even if your opinion of me is so low, you must admit I've never been the enemy of the Watch."

Karl crossed his arms and grumbled something that almost sounded like assent.

I pointed at Willodean. "This woman needs Mose's help. She also might be the key to solving the middling affliction. You've heard of gifted all over the city losing their powers, yes?"

"Father Mancini is among them." Karl's eyes narrowed. "Perhaps he caught whatever is causing it from you."

"Don't be ridiculous. You and I have worked together for weeks. If I was a middling, and if that was a contagious condition, you would've lost your powers long before the priest did."

His frown found a way to deepen, but he was listening.

"It's true that Mose cast me out. But I need his help—and he very well may need mine. I'm coming to see him with no tricks, no subterfuge. No ulterior motive. I just want him to help Willodean. Then if he wants me gone, I'll go. If you acknowledge that I'm no enemy of the Watch, why stand in my way?"

Karl looked at Willodean, then at me again.

"I'm not asking you to change your mind about me. I'm only asking you to do the right thing."

Slowly, grudgingly, Karl stepped aside. I pushed the chair toward the ramp leading into the building.

"If I ever learn this was some kind of trick—" Karl called after us.

I turned. "No tricks. I swear it."

I could feel his gaze burning into my back all the way up the handicap ramp.

All eyes were on us when I entered the Watchtower, but no one confronted me on the way to Mose's office. I searched their faces for sympathy, searched the room for Terrie, but neither was to be found.

Mose sat behind his desk as though he'd never moved since I'd left his office the last time, when he told me to never return.

"Mose," I said wearily.

"Conrad." He nodded. "Close the door behind you and let's talk."

I told him about our misadventures in Europe and Willodean's ascension. There was no point in hiding any of the details. Those details could prove important if he were able and willing to help, and if he weren't, I was screwed anyway. Mose listened, implacable, as I spoke of vampires and dragons, of gods and ambrosia. He didn't seem surprised by any of it.

"What makes you think this woman can solve our problem?" he asked. "Even a god can't turn a middling into a gifted at will, or Dolus wouldn't have sent you to plunder a ship."

"She's the most powerful being I've ever encountered. Dolus said a goddess of death was stronger than a trickster god, so I figure that statement included him, despite his years of experience. And she's on our side. If anyone can help us take down Hanson and reverse engineer his concoction, it's her."

"Raw power is not always helpful." Mose absentmindedly scratched his sizable chin. "Believe me when I say she is dangerous. The wisest course of action may be to smother her in her sleep."

I clenched my fists. "You'll have to get through me, first."

"Relax, Conrad. I'm advising you, not taking unilateral action."

"Some advice!"

"When Dolus warned you not to let her drink the ambrosia, he was right. It's a miracle she survived her apotheosis at all, and was able to perform so much magic immediately afterward. This means her potential is indeed enormous, but it's also the reason for her coma. Her brain couldn't handle the changes ambrosia was making and reacted by shutting down."

"Does this mean she needs a few weeks of rest and she'll be good as new?"

Mose sighed. "I wish it were so. She's now a pint-sized barrel trying to contain a gallon of magic. And, being a goddess of death, the magic she's holding isn't balloons and unicorns. When she wakes up—*if* she wakes up, there's a considerable chance of her becoming a far greater threat than the one we're facing now."

I looked at her, so helpless and calm in her sleep. It was difficult to see the danger Mose was suggesting.

"Willodean isn't some power-hungry monster. She only drank the ambrosia because there was no other choice. She saved my life, as well as the lives of the mercenaries we recruited for the mission. She deserves a chance to wake up and to try and learn to control her gift. I owe her that."

Mose nodded. "I respect loyalty. I just hope we don't all live to regret your decision."

"Real talk, can you help her wake up and heal, or not?"

"I can," said the big man.

"What's it gonna cost me?"

Just a few minutes prior to this Karl had called me a transactional person, but I thought Mose was more so. Authority was a heavy burden on one's shoulders; it meant making the difficult, ruthless decisions. It also meant demanding a high price if it was to the benefit of the Watch. I just couldn't think of much I could give or do for Mose at this point.

"Nothing," he said. "I will share the burden of this choice with you because you've proven to be a good judge of character in the past. Perhaps she'll save us all, in the end. Consider this a payment for your years of service to the Watch. Leave her with me. Even with my help it may take some time for her to recover."

"How do I know you won't smother her with a pillow?" I asked. Even before I finished speaking the words I regretted them, regretted the damage I might have just done to the mending of the relationship Mose and I had just taken the first cautious steps toward.

If he were offended, Mose didn't show it. "You're the one who came to me seeking help," he said. "If you don't trust me to provide this help, you're welcome to take your friend elsewhere."

When I came out of Mose's office, everyone was watching me with apprehension, as though I were a subway rat who somehow wandered inside the train car. My one-time colleagues eyed me in the same fashion, clearly hoping that any minute now I'd notice the open door and leave on my own.

I strolled into the supply closet and picked up a burner cell phone and a couple hundred dollars in petty cash. No one tried to stop me. The fact that I'd walked into Mose's office after being banished from the city and then walked out under my own power was sufficient proof that—at least for the moment—I was no longer the pariah I'd once been.

Outside, I dialed Herc.

"I'm back in New York. Where are you at?"

CHAPTER 20

WHILE I'd been gone, New York had become a war zone.

The news of the middling affliction had spread like wildfire among the gifted. Many had left town rather than risk losing their powers. Those who couldn't afford to leave were holed up in their homes and businesses, behind whatever wards and layers of protection they could muster.

The city had been left to the monsters.

Ghouls and vampires, changelings and supernatural predators of all kinds owned the streets. The Watch didn't have the resources to stop them all, and whenever they tried they rapidly lost some of their most powerful practitioners to the affliction.

Father Mancini had been the first victim. He'd lost his powers the day after Willodean and I left for Europe. Two days later, John Smith had suffered the same fate. It was unclear whether Terrie or Karl still had their powers; they continued to patrol their respective boroughs, but it was possible that they'd taken a page from my playbook and were relying on artifacts to stay in the fight. Only Gord definitely retained his abilities, protected by the giant blood in his veins. Among the ordinary gifted, some stepped up to protect their fellow New Yorkers, and many lost their powers in the process, too.

Emboldened by the chaos, nonhuman troublemakers from all over the continent had burrowed their way into the Big Apple.

Although the regular folks couldn't perceive the supernatural causes behind bodies that had been exsanguinated or ripped to shreds by claws, the corpses themselves were evident, as was the property damage. The cops were out in full force and dying in great numbers. Although they were completely unprepared for the threats they had to face, they stood between those threats and the citizens of the city anyway.

The media covered the unprecedented crime wave the only way they knew how. They wrote of serial killers and gang initiations. Monsters rampaging in the open were reported as either disturbed lone gunmen or terrorists. Clashes of magic were said to be drug syndicates battling over turf. Based on their own agenda, the talking heads on the news blamed the violence on immigrants, domestic militia groups, cartels, radicalized socialists, or gun-toting conservatives. The embattled mayor was entreating the governor to declare martial law and send in the National Guard.

Although the state's militia was as ill equipped to handle the problem as the police, an alternate militia rose up to challenge the monsters.

The newly minted middlings, as well as a number of gifted who retained their powers, had banded around Hercules Mulligan and his small group of loyalists who'd first sounded the alarm about the affliction and who kept uncovering and attacking Nascent Anodynes International operations all over the Northeast.

"We've interrogated the NAi people we captured," Herc told me when we first reconnected and he got the chance to update me in greater detail. "We know for sure they've been arming some of the monsters with the affliction bioagent, and we know they've been encouraging the worst of the worst to come to New York City. I just wish I understood what their end game will be in all of this. Hanson has thoroughly gone to ground. We've been taking out his people and dismantling his infrastructure, but it's like cutting the heads off the hydra. New ones pop up faster than we can take them down."

In return, I told him about Europe and explained about Willodean. He knew her to be a natural-born middling and I skipped over the bit where she only drank the ambrosia because I was too dead to do it myself. I kept searching for the right moment to tell him more, to tell him everything, but I was so thoroughly caught in the web of my own lies that I suspected the right time to tell my friend the truth in a way that would let me keep him as a friend would never come at all.

Instead, I volunteered. "I can't sit on my hands while I wait for Willodean to wake up. What can I do to help?"

The next three days were a blur. There were short breaks for food and naps—never quite enough for either—but the rest of the time we stomped on monsters.

Herc figured out that the new middlings were perfectly good for the job if you armed them with enough magical items. Basically, each of them was a version of me, but without a dark secret to hide and with the full support and backing of the local community of other gifted.

The militia representatives talked to all the artifact shops in the city and got them to help out. Mordecai's Jewelers in Borough Park and Kings Games in Midwood both loaned most of their inventories to the group. Herc recruited a large pool of volunteers to recharge these artifacts after each mission. Middlings took point in combat while anyone who had powers of their own was generally kept in reserve.

And then there were the original Irregulars. I recognized many of them: Zach Shephard, a champion kickboxer who used magic to enhance his martial skills. Aysha Rehm, who was as good at discovering old and forgotten spells in archives and libraries as she was at using them. Bob Finegold, reprising his role as a field medic. All of them had to cope and adjust to the loss of their own magic, yet they remained an effective fighting force and a group I was proud to be a part of.

By all accounts, Herc was a better middling than I had ever been. In a matter of days, he'd created a support system more effective than I'd managed to cultivate through my go-it-alone attitude. He was able to turn popular opinion in favor of middlings, who were suddenly out in the open, defending both the gifted and mundane residents of the city.

Although New York still felt like the lawless Wild West of the cowboy movies to me, Herc's militia began to turn back the tide. It wasn't easy, and we lost a lot of good people, but ultimately the monsters learned that, once again, their actions would not go unpunished. Even many media outlets began to grudgingly report that the crime wave was finally abating, though some continued to gleefully cover the worst of it to further their agendas.

On my fourth day with the Irregulars, several of us were facing off against a pack of werewolves in Central Park.

Mercifully, the battlefield wasn't a packed city street this time. New Yorkers had long known to stay out of Central Park after dark, and since the "crime wave" had started, the verdant heart of Manhattan was mostly abandoned during the day, too. We'd been tracking the pack since before dawn and had them surrounded. A semicircle of two middlings and three mundane monster hunters squared off against four snarling, oversized lupines. We herded them to the bank of the Harlem Meer in the northeast corner of the park where water reduced their fight-or-flight instinct to the fight option. Despite our strategic advantage and greater numbers, the fight was likely to be close to even.

Willodean suddenly stood between us and the werewolves. There was no portal, she simply appeared in a blink of an eye, her feet planted firmly in the dewy grass. I gasped at the sight of her awake, relief surging through me. I felt like an immense weight I'd been carrying for days had been lifted from my shoulders. She winked at us and turned her attention to the monsters.

The pack was no longer in the mood for a fight. After one sniff at her, the wolves shrank back and whimpered like Chihuahuas facing off against a Great Dane. She extended her hand toward the beasts and they began to change. Their fur fell off in clumps. Their elongated muzzles retracted into their skulls. Within a minute, we faced not four fierce beasts but three men and a woman who shivered, harmless and naked, on the moist lawn. They repeatedly tried shifting back into lupine form, but those attempts were for naught.

"I have trapped the wolf aspects in the deepest recesses of your mind," said Willodean. "It will be a long time before you can call upon them again."

The shifters looked far more terrified at this development than they were of us.

"Go," she told them. "Leave this city for good. Tell your friends: New York is under my protection. Challenge me, and they too will lose what is dearest to them."

The four neutered shifters shuffled past us in their birthday suits, their heads hung low.

"Willodean!" I stepped toward the goddess. She was literally glowing, her aura effervescent with an amber energy that looked like ambrosia itself and surrounded her like a full-body halo. I recalled Dolus saying that that he could tell apart the shades of gods' auras, but seeing one that was distinguishable by regular gifted or middlings was a first for me. "You look well."

"I feel better." She smiled as she kept curling and uncurling a strand of hair with her left index finger. "In fact, I feel like I just downed five cappuccinos and chased them with a Red Bull."

Was this the side effect Mose had talked about? It didn't seem so bad. "Mose warned that you might struggle with containing all the magic you have now. Are you feeling any effects of that?"

Willodean pondered this, still fiddling with the strand of hair by her shoulder. "I feel like a professional athlete who hasn't had her morning exercise routine yet. Like I just need to burn some of this energy off, and I have some ideas as to how I might do that." She smiled at my fellows-in-arms coquettishly. "Boys and girls, I'm going to borrow Conrad. Hope you don't mind!"

Zach and Aysha, who could perceive Willodean's unusual aura, were mostly awed by her presence. The three ungifted members of the team completely misread her intentions and began to whoop and slap me on the shoulders. I grinned back at them even though I was pretty sure Willodean wasn't about to club me over the head and drag me to her cave.

With no notice at all, we were gone from New York and back in Ukraine. Willodean had teleported us to the front of the little Orthodox church the dragon used as his lair.

Two of the nonhumans saw us appear. They dropped what they were doing and rushed us. A hairy middle-aged guy that looked almost human, save for a six-pack of eyes that occupied the real estate between his nose and forehead, leveled his pitchfork at us. An ogre approached unarmed, but he was big and strong enough to seem a greater threat.

Willodean lifted both of them a few feet off the ground with a thought and spun them in the air like rag dolls. After a few revolutions around their own axis, she left them hanging upside down.

"Had enough?" she asked sweetly.

The bug-eyed guy, who had dropped his pitchfork, managed to nod. The ogre threw up, bile dripping down the side of his mouth and onto the ground beneath him. It wasn't a pretty sight.

Willodean released them and the two tumbled to the ground. The hairy guy rose to his knees while the troll lay there and retched.

"You," she addressed the hairy guy. "Fetch me Clarissa immediately." Her tone didn't brook an argument and whatever fight the dude had originally had in him was long gone. He nodded again and rushed off.

Willodean turned her attention to the church. She furled her brow, and the wide wooden doors literally flew off their hinges.

"I always wanted to make a grand entrance," she murmured as she marched inside. I rushed after her.

The dragon was there, attended by several residents of Monster Town. His three heads coiled and stared at us.

"I'm baaaack," Willodean half sang.

Without preamble, one of the heads spat a fireball at her. It came to a halt a mere two feet from her face, sizzling in the air. Willodean beamed and blew air at it, as though extinguishing a match. The fireball retraced its path backward and exploded on contact with the dragon's head that had launched it. The beast bellowed and the air smelled of singed snake.

"Everyone out except the reptile," Willodean ordered.

The poor monsters didn't have to be asked twice. They jostled each other to try and get out the doors first. They went to great lengths to avoid contact with Willodean, who still stood in the door. Some flattened themselves against the wall as they sidestepped around her on their way out.

Zmey Gorynych rose, its elephantine body bumping against the walls, tail flapping back and forth in the irritated-cat routine I recalled from our last visit, its vestigial wings spread uselessly and almost comically above his back.

The dragon unleashed a curse of ancient magic at us powerful enough that I could feel it deep in my bones. Unchecked, it would've exploded our hearts right inside our chests. But Willodean was able to neutralize it effortlessly, as she did several more arcane attacks that followed.

"What, not in a mood to bloviate this time?" she taunted the great serpent.

Without his followers to impress, the dragon didn't bother with conversation. When the magic attacks failed, he charged at us across the hall, crushing the pews with his flanks, each step a small earthquake.

Willodean extended her arms, and an invisible force pushed the dragon back. His enormous mass strained against this moving barrier. His claws left deep gashes in the floor planks.

The dragon cast another spell, and his wings began to transform from pathetic little vestigial growths to mighty leathery appendages that extended to and pressed against the walls. He reared up on his hind legs and, using both wings and his three heads, tried to dislodge the roof and climb outside.

"Oh, no you don't!" Willodean cut the air with her palm in a karate-chop motion. A similar force to the one that had been pushing the dragon back got hold of his right wing and ripped it off his back. Blood sprayed from the severed vessels and the dragon's roar changed from the sound of fury to that of anguish and pain.

Willodean focused on Zmey's three heads. She tangled and twisted them and started tying them in a big messy knot. The dragon coughed up bits of fire and gasped for air. Its body thrashed, pulping everything in its path.

"Do you think maybe he's learned his lesson?" I asked. "You're killing him."

She looked at me and there was no compassion in her eyes. "He deserves it. And I *am* the goddess of death."

I blanched, Mose's warnings playing in my mind.

"Step outside," she told me.

I didn't move. I'm not even sure if it was defiance or morbid fascination that kept me standing where I was at that moment.

Suddenly I was outside the church, teleported to where we had first appeared a few minutes earlier.

Other nonhumans stood around me, watching as the church building shook. None dared approach it. When they noticed me appear in their midst they scrambled out of the way, eyeing me warily and ready to run at the first sign of aggression.

"Damn it," I said to no one in particular and took a step toward the church.

The old building collapsed in on itself.

"Damn it," I said again. I rushed toward the heap of lumber and sheetrock that used to be a church. "Willodean!"

"Right behind you," she said, her voice filled with amusement. I whirled around. She stood there and watched the rubble settle, a satisfied expression on her face. She added, "You should probably not blaspheme, considering."

I made a face at the woman who'd just beaten a dragon to death and then dropped a building on him, Dorothy style. "Get over yourself."

She laughed at this.

"Seriously though, you didn't need to do that."

Willodean tilted her head. "He was an enormous asshole. He would've killed us a week ago if Dolus hadn't snatched our bacon out of the fire. Who knows how many others that three-headed monstrosity had snuffed out?"

She turned toward the assorted monsters, who glanced nervously at the collapsed church. None of them would meet her gaze. Her voice boomed as though she were using a megaphone. "Listen up, everyone. The idea behind the Sanctuary is a fine one. You deserve safety and security. You deserve a place where you can support each other, a real community. That evil snake"—she pointed at the church—"wanted only to control you. He got you to do things you shouldn't have done. You can't terrorize your neighbors just because they're human. That's no better than them doing the same to you. The only chance for long-term security is to make lasting peace with the communities around you." She walked toward a group of the Sanctuary's residents, and while they flinched and shrank away, none ran.

"You can certainly protect your territory against those who come with ill intentions. But you may no longer assault passersby whose only crime is being human. Behave, and you will have my protection should you ever need it. Disobey me, and I'll return to mete out punishment. I'll be watching." She dismissed them with a wave. "Go and spread the word to others. And bring me Clarissa!"

The menagerie of supernatural beings hustled off in different directions.

"That's how you act as a god," she said. "Instead of hiding in shadows and meekly pulling a string or two, which seems to be the way Dolus does things."

"You browbeat citizens into shaping their society according to your ideals? Pretty sure they've already failed that experiment in this corner of the world."

"You liberate them from the tyrants and nudge them in the right direction. Then you leave them alone to figure out how to build and run their own society."

"I think I liked the old Willodean better," I said.

She shrugged. "Same Willodean. But now I have the means to do something about my opinions."

Our debate was interrupted by the appearance of the goblin scientist. Clarissa walked over, doing her best to put on a brave face. The hairy guy Willodean had sent to fetch her, as well as several other beings, including the satyr we'd captured on our previous visit, stood a respectful distance away. They appeared afraid but still ready to come to their friend's defense against an overwhelmingly powerful foe; a fortitude none of them had displayed while Willodean had deposed their dragon leader. It made me feel predisposed toward these underdogs, despite my less-than-stellar experiences with them in the past.

Clarissa approached and stared at us defiantly. "I see you didn't bring the angry redhead this time."

Her statement confirmed that Moira had escaped her pursuers. I couldn't help but feel relieved to hear this. The rogue sorceress was a terrible person, but she was honest about it, and she'd fought alongside us when it would've been more prudent to cut and run. Having failed to secure something valuable enough to redeem her she was probably holed up deep, hiding from her Cabal ex-pals. Odds were we'd never cross paths again but somehow, I knew I wasn't that lucky.

"She wanted the weapon you created for herself," said Willodean. "We only want the means to stop it."

"I told you the truth the last time. I destroyed my notes, and I've never discovered any kind of antidote."

"Will you permit me to take the knowledge from your mind?" When Clarissa tensed, Willodean added gently, "I won't do it without your consent. And I will only use it to try and fix things."

Clarissa appeared dubious. "Can you comprehend the underlying science?"

"We'll find out together, if you're willing." Willodean extended her hand. "Late in life, Oppenheimer wished he could have stuffed the atomic genie back in its bottle. I'm offering you the chance remorseful scientists don't often get."

Her jaw clenched tight, Clarissa gave an imperceptible nod. Willodean laid her palm on the goblin's temple and closed her eyes. After about five seconds, she drew her hand back and whispered, "Whoa."

Clarissa's shoulders slumped. "You couldn't parse the information, could you?"

"I can do it, but it will take some time. There's so much .... You're a really smart lady."

Clarissa drew back, old hurts apparent in her face. "You mean, for a goblin?"

"I mean for a person," Willodean said in a soothing voice. "You must've been underestimated so often by so many over the years, both as a goblin and as a woman. I'm sorry about that. But my compliment was genuine."

Some tension drained from Clarissa. "I'm sorry I snapped at you."

"That's all right. May we go back to your house and sit? I'm afraid this may take several hours."

I doubted Willodean needed the rest, or even so much time. She was considerate of Clarissa, trying to be gentle with her. The vengeful dragon-fighting goddess had been replaced with the kind, compassionate woman I'd gotten to know in recent weeks. I liked this aspect of the new Willodean better, and its return filled me with hope.

Clarissa must've realized some of this too. She didn't know Willodean well, but she proved to be quite perceptive. "Certainly. Please follow me."

The goblin and the goddess walked away from the town center and toward the familiar house at the edge of the Sanctuary. Neither of them so much as looked at me. I made to follow them but thought better of it. Instead, I wandered the Sanctuary. The word had spread quickly, and its residents gave me a wide berth. I found a patch of thick grass with a view of a wheat field and lay down.

For the first time in what felt like ages I wasn't rushing off on a quest, battling monsters, or trying to escape some threat with my life. And although this respite was short, and I was painfully aware of the trouble that awaited us back home, I couldn't help but enjoy the warm sunshine and the gentle breeze caressing my face.

This whole time I'd taken charge and made difficult decisions, both for myself and others, but now it seemed I'd become a bit player in Willodean's story. She had the means and the will to set things right. She'd grown into her ascension as easily as putting on a comfortable pair of slippers. I thought back to how quickly she'd asserted herself when she'd woken in my apartment, how she'd accepted the realities of the supernatural world I'd revealed to her that afternoon, and realized that it wasn't some divine power that allowed her to assume her new role so completely; she'd had this ability to adapt all along.

Four hours later, Willodean and Clarissa reemerged and found me lounging on the grass.

"I've learned all I could of the gifted gene," said Willodean. "I think I can use my powers and this knowledge to reverse the effects of Hanson's bioweapon. I can cure Herc!"

I rose from the ground and stretched. "It's about time," I said. "A more experienced godling could've accomplished this twice as fast."

Willodean laughed. Whatever she had become, she still appreciated my snarky sense of humor.

"Let's not waste any more time then." She turned to Clarissa. "Thank you. Truly." She traced her palms along the sides of the goblin's head, performing some subtle magic.

"What was that?" Clarissa asked.

"A blessing," said Willodean. "If Hanson, or the Cabal, or anyone else come around, they won't be able to extract any information from your mind."

Clarissa smiled, and I realized it was the first time I'd seen her do that. She revealed a set of small, sharp teeth, which made her look far less human. But then, she seemed to have found a home where that didn't matter.

It had been morning when we left New York and late evening by the time we departed from the Sanctuary. Back in New York it was midafternoon and my body was utterly befuddled and not especially happy with these time-zone jumps. I wondered if one could develop jet lag while traveling via magical portals and divine teleportation.

My phone vibrated. A dozen missed calls and messages that had come in while we were out of the country popped up on my screen. I glanced at the first few and cursed. "Hanson's people are attacking the Watchtower!"

All signs of the congeniality Willodean had displayed when dealing with Clarissa were gone from her face and body language. She smiled in a way that made me afraid, and we teleported again.

CHAPTER 21

WE reappeared at the base of the massive Manhattan Municipal Building where Karl had confronted me a few days earlier. The building was on fire in several places, and many scorch marks from arcane blasts marred its façade.

The Watch and Herc's Irregulars fought together against a superior force of gifted mercenaries and monsters, and the good guys were thoroughly getting their asses kicked.

The attackers seemed well organized and well trained. They had submachine guns as well as various magical items, and all of them had their own magic to tap into. The defenders relied on their charms and amulets, which was perfectly fine in brief skirmishes, but not so effective in the case of a prolonged engagement.

A mercenary fired a barrage at an Irregular whom I didn't recognize. The bullets shredded the force barrier he'd put up. It only managed to slow them down, but marginally slower bullets were just as deadly at this range. The Irregular slumped on the sidewalk, clutching a wound in his side. He desperately clutched an amulet, attempting to put up another shield. The ammo had to have been enchanted with some top-grade sorcery to do that. I winced as it evoked the memory of recently getting shot point-blank.

Nearby, Gord was engaged in a melee against a pair of trolls. The trio of basketball player-sized combatants exchanged furious blows. Gord drove the butt of his shotgun into the jaw of one troll, blocked the blow from another's massive fist and drove an elbow into his belly. Despite not having time to reload, he was managing to hold his own against two larger opponents.

Willodean rushed into the fray. She dominated the battlefield like a comic book superhero showing up to toss mere mortals around like so many rag dolls. Enemy bullets, hexes, and fireballs bounced off her aura as though it were a force barrier—and it probably was.

My instinct was to join the fight, but Hanson wanted something inside the Watchtower, and I had to make sure he didn't get it. I rushed through the building's corroded front door and down the staircase into the basement level.

The Watchtower was deserted, save for Mose, who stood by the door into his office like a colossal statue of a sumo wrestler carved out of muscle. The sigil of the effulgent eye at Mose's feet shone bright enough to justify its name. The light emanating from it was so intense, I had to avert my eyes. Intricate incantations written in dead languages pulsed along the walls, floor, and ceiling of the Watchtower. They spread like a spiderweb with Mose and the sigil at its center. Beads of sweat pooled on Mose's bald head as he fed his power into this network of protective spells.

"Willodean is back," I told him. "She's kicking their asses outside."

A corner of Mose's lip lifted in what might've been the world's most ephemeral smile.

I stared out at the abandoned desks and offices. I'd never seen the Watchtower emptied out. "How are you holding up in here? What can I do to help?"

"You were right about Hanson," said Mose. "The carnage outside is only half the battle. He marshaled arcane forces beyond anything that has dared to attack the Watchtower directly in the past. The building still stands only thanks to the nexus of power underneath it, fueling the protections cast by generations of the best mages in the world."

I shuddered. I could imagine nothing short of a direct nuclear blast to be capable of bringing down the Watchtower.

"What's Hanson after?"

Mose sighed. "I can't tell you that."

"Come on, boss. After all this, you still don't trust me?"

"I trust you, Conrad. But you couldn't stop someone like Willodean from plucking the information from your mind."

"Fine," I said, irritated. "Can you take whatever it is and go? Maybe hide it at your cabin in Rochester until we get things under control?"

He sighed again. "Fleeing is riskier than fighting. I'm at my strongest here, at the nexus. I'm the final line of defense. Even if they somehow defeat the new goddess, I will hold them off here for as long as it takes."

"I just watched her take down an ancient dragon without breaking a sweat," I said. "But if you think there's a chance they can defeat her …" I walked over to the supply closet meaning to load up on extra charms, only to find it had been cleared of anything that could be used as an arcane weapon. I was far from the only one among the Watch staff who had to rely on such trinkets anymore.

"It's unlikely Hanson and his underlings could defeat a goddess of death," said Mose. "But the power of the dark magic they've brought to bear caught me by surprise once. I daren't underestimate them again."

"All right, then." I headed back out.

"Conrad," he called after me. "When this is over, you're welcome to return to the Watch, if that's what you want."

It was as close to an apology as I was going to get from Mose. He always did what was best for the Watch, and he wasn't going to get sentimental about it. Nor was he making platitudes; his invitation was genuine.

"I've been getting a lot of job offers lately," I said, thinking of Dolus and Chulsky. "What none of those folks realized is that I never truly stopped being a part of the Watch."

That was as much of an apology for deceiving him, or thanks for allowing me back, that Mose was going to get from me.

I headed upstairs, readied my weapons, and stepped outside the protective wards of the building and into the fight.

This was promising to be a long, grueling battle. Not a skirmish of magics as I'd been used to, but a true war with each side willing to throw lives into the meat grinder for as long as it took for them to win.

Willodean dominated the fight wherever she appeared, overwhelming anything the attackers tried to throw at her. Then she would blink away for minutes at a time, leaving us to struggle against the enemy's superior numbers and stronger magic.

Hanson's most powerful spellcasters thought they were safe as they rained hexes and incantations upon us remotely. Willodean methodically tracked the threads of dark sorcery, like a bloodhound on the scent of its prey, back to the source, and she killed them. Every time she returned, covered in blood and grime, her visage grew more terrible. She had become a true goddess of death, reaping souls on the battlefield.

Each time she was gone the enemy forces, who still outnumbered us, attempted to rally. Whereas our typical foes would cut and run once they realized they were facing anything more than easy prey, these men and monsters appeared to fear retreat far more than they feared us.

It was in the heat of the battle that I found Terrie Winter. She still had her powers and she still wielded her staff. I wanted to talk to her, to apologize for deceiving her over the years, to thank her for the note of support she'd left me when everyone else in the Watch had abandoned me outright, and to regale her with my tales of adventure. But we were surrounded by enemies and the best we could manage was to lock eyes for a fraction of a second. Some friendships are so strong that a meaningful look is enough. We fought side by side, watching each other's backs, just like old times.

Our victory wasn't glorious. We simply outlasted the bad guys, crushing the last remaining pockets of enemy mages, scattering to the four winds what monsters were willing to flee rather than fight and die. We paid a high price for repelling the attack. It wasn't expensive charms and rare enchanted weapons. It was the lives of our friends, those who'd volunteered to defend the Watchtower just as the Watch had defended the mundanes for generations.

Willodean appeared beside me, stinking of gore and sweat. She was breathing heavily. Droplets of somebody else's blood streaked down her left cheek like tears.

"Are you all right?" I asked her. "You look like you're running on fumes. You have to get some rest."

"It's sort of the opposite," she told me, her voice hoarse. "The magic keeps welling within me and I have to use it all up or I feel like I'm going to explode."

"That can't be good. We need to get you help. Can you use your powers to find Dolus?"

She shook her head. "I can sense tens of thousands of gifted, across many miles. Some are like the tiniest dots I have to squint to see, while others glow bright with power. But none of them are even remotely as powerful as I am. If Dolus or other gods are out there, they know how to hide."

"There must be another way. We can ask—"

"Later," she cut me off. "We can deal with this later. For now, we have a more pressing mission."

"Hanson?"

She nodded. "I was able to snatch the information from the mind of one of his lieutenants. I know where Hanson is hiding."

There was no rest for the gifted. Herc and John Smith marshaled what was left of the Watch and the Irregulars' forces for an assault on an industrial complex in Yonkers.

I had to use every bit of my persuasive powers to convince Willodean not to go in there on her own. Nascent Anodynes had proven to be rich in magic resources and full of surprises, and I worried that they might spring a trap that would be too much even for her. Instead, she focused on healing the middlings, one by one.

Willodean was able to combine the knowledge she'd gained from Clarissa with her divine power to reactivate the gifted gene inhibited by the bioweapon. I watched with equal parts relief and jealousy as she ministered to Herc first, then John, and then the rest of the gifted who were present. Anyone who'd come and fought on our side in this conflict won the prize of getting their powers back. Any of them who'd survived, that is. Even at the height of her powers, Willodean wasn't willing to risk trying to bring back to life any of those who'd fallen in battle, the way she had done with me. We couldn't afford her falling into a coma again.

Despite our terrible losses and despite battle fatigue, after witnessing or experiencing the rebirth of their powers, the morale among our people was at an all-time high.

The sun was setting over the Hudson as our forces surrounded the NAi compound. Since I was the only middling Willodean couldn't cure and she wanted to keep my secret safe, I had no choice but to keep out of the main action and instead was placed in charge of the backup team of two Irregulars who guarded one of several exits from the compound. We twiddled our thumbs and chewed our lips nervously as we listened to the sounds of the battle taking place at the main entrance.

The metal door we guarded at the side of the beige building squeaked as it opened and Vaughn stepped out.

Hanson's right-hand man looked haggard. There were bags under his eyes and sweat stains under the armpits of his tailored button-down shirt. His hands were trembling.

We leveled our weapons at him.

Vaughn raised his hands. "Please," he said. "Marko has gone insane. He's slaughtering his own lieutenants, killing anyone who might reveal his plans and disclose the location of his hideouts, willingly or otherwise. I may be the only one left alive who knows these things. Protect me, and I will tell you anything you want to know!"

"Search him," I told my two comrades. I turned my attention to Vaughn. "All right, prove yourself useful and you might live. Why did Hanson unleash the middling affliction?"

"I thought that might be obvious," said Vaughn. "He who controls whether someone else is a gifted or a middling is the most powerful gifted of all."

"Bullshit," I said. "You wanted chaos, and you wanted to take out members of the Watch, but without drawing attention to that fact. You attacked the Watchtower directly because Willodean showed up in New York flexing her powers and you knew that your window of opportunity was closing. What does Mose have that Hanson wants badly enough to do all this?"

Vaughn looked at me, stone-faced, as though evaluating how much truth he had to reveal or how many lies he could get away with.

"Something very powerful," he finally said. "More powerful than all the wizards and monsters running around this city. As to the specifics, Hanson didn't trust anyone enough to share those. Not even me."

"You're not being especially helpful," I said. "Perhaps we should send you back inside and feed you to Hanson." He blanched. "Speaking of that bastard, where is he? What nasty surprises does he have in there?"

"There aren't many of us left. Hanson is holed up in the warehouse where the supply of the gas is stored, and he's exceptionally well armed. He's going to try and kill your ascended friend. He might even succeed."

"Don't you think you should have led with that? What has he got in there?"

"He has an enchanted blade, and an armor made of Atlantean crystal."

I cursed under my breath. A single shard amplified one's powers tenfold. An armor made of the stuff might just be enough to kill a god.

"I have to warn Willodean," I told the Irregulars. "Keep a close eye on him!"

I ran toward the main entrance.

I caught up to Willodean deep in the bowels of the installation. True to what Vaughn had told me, they were encountering virtually no resistance. I warned her about Hanson.

"He's but an insignificant worm," she boomed. "If he thinks he can kill me, let him go ahead and try!"

"Whoa there, easy on the comic book villain talk." I had to move at an undignified pace to keep up with her. "You don't need to use that megaphone trick from Ukraine, either, I'm right here."

"Sorry," she said at a bearable volume. "It's hard for me to tone it down just now. I'll burn some of this energy when I tear that asshole Hanson's limbs off."

"Yeah, that's not really helping," I said.

"The warehouse is this way." John Smith pointed, having consulted the schematics loaded on his phone. Once Willodean had taken off in the direction he'd indicated, John told me, "You can't talk her down right now. Do you remember high school physics? She's got the magical equivalent of the potential energy of a bowstring stretched to its limit. Best thing we can do is point her at the bad guys and let loose."

I rushed after Willodean, and the others followed.

When we burst through the warehouse doors, Willodean was facing off against Marko Hanson, decked out in shimmering green samurai armor made of enormous chunks of Atlantean crystal. Any one of the individual pieces that comprised it was much larger—and many times more expensive—than the shard I had once liberated from the Crimson Prophet. The armor was translucent and glowing. Its own built-in nightlight illuminated the suit-and-tie getup Hanson wore underneath. An elaborate crystal kabuto helmet, complete with gilded horns and a faceplate, adorned his head.

In the dimly lit warehouse, Hanson's emerald glow and Willodean's ember aura made them resemble theater actors under stage lighting.

As we filed into the warehouse, the two of them studied each other warily.

"You're the one who fancies herself a god?" asked Hanson. The helmet muffled his voice, making him sound a little like Darth Vader. There was no fear in that voice. Instead, it was filled with cold fury.

"After all the evil you've done, do you still consider yourself a man?" she replied without missing a beat.

"Damn," I whispered to John. "Anyone who's seen *Ghostbusters* knows the proper response to when someone asks if you're a god, but her comeback was pretty good, too."

Hanson raised his armored hand and pointed at Willodean. "Regardless of how many layers of power you wrap yourself in, you're still nothing but a pathetic middling on the inside. And when I'm done with you, you'll be a dead middling."

I wanted him to keep talking, to spill his secrets and plans like a Bond villain, but Willodean was in no shape to wait. She screamed and unleashed a pair of lightning bolts from her hands at Hanson. Beams of energy powerful enough to deep-fry a dragon slammed

215

into Hanson and bounced off his armor. The squat samurai wannabe staggered back a step, but remained otherwise unhurt.

Energies ricocheted off the Atlantean crystal and put several holes in the walls and ceiling of the warehouse. One of the bolts skewered a steel cylinder. Gas hissed as it escaped from the punctured container.

"Bioweapon!" I shouted. "Everyone, fall back!"

None of us was certain if exposure to the gas for the second time would strip the gifted of their restored powers again, and none were willing to take that chance. Our troops filed out and retreated to a safe distance. I stayed behind, protected by my immunity to the stuff. For once, being a middling was an advantage—if you could call staying inside the boxing ring where the magical equivalent of Godzilla and Mechagodzilla were currently duking it out an advantage.

Willodean and Hanson hurled arcane energies at each other at a rate and intensity that would have both drained and killed even the most powerful among the gifted under any other circumstances. I don't know how many charms and amulets Hanson was using in addition to the armor that was amplifying his own magic, but it was definitely a whole lot if he was able to go toe-to-toe with a pissed off goddess. I may have fancied myself a magical Batman, but he was more of a Bruce Wayne—a rich jerk who could afford all the toys—and I mean *all* the toys.

But why would he make a stand in an enclosed space full of debilitating gas? I crept closer to get a better look at him as he stood there illuminated by the clashing magics. The gas would be a trap for any gifted who came after him, and perhaps he didn't know it was ineffective against an ascended middling, but wasn't he as vulnerable as his adversaries? I inched closer yet, aware that a moment's attention from Hanson souped-up in his battle armor might be enough to turn me into a very unattractive puddle on the concrete floor. One of the gas canisters to my far left exploded and I froze, but the two combatants had eyes only for each other.

It wasn't clear whether Hanson's armor made him more powerful than a god or whether Willodean was finally running out of juice after hour upon hour of fighting, but the bad guy seemed to have an advantage. He edged toward her, one step at a time, as though moving through a force shield made of molasses. She retreated one step, then another, then grunted like a pro tennis player on a serve, and fell to one knee.

I was only a few feet away when I saw it: a breathing mask under the translucent helmet, connected to a thin flask-like oxygen tank on his back via a short tube.

At least a dozen canisters were leaking Hanson's unholy concoction. The air was filling with gas and the reflected light emanating from the combatants made the warehouse look like the dance floor at a club that had its fog machine cranked up to eleven.

Hanson closed in on Willodean and unsheathed a wicked-looking kukri blade. Was this the enchanted weapon Vaughn had warned me about when he said Hanson might succeed at deicide? Willodean was on her knees now, desperately struggling to keep up her force shield. She strained as though she were pushing back against the weight of the Empire State Building.

Hanson raised the kukri.

I tried to tackle him from behind but he whirled, surprisingly agile for a guy in a suit of armor. He used my own momentum against me, shoving me forward. I grabbed hold of the plastic tube that was connected to his oxygen tank as I tumbled past him and pulled with all my might. The stretchy tube didn't rip and didn't disconnect from the tank, but the maneuver dislodged the breathing mask, stripping it off his mouth and nose and partially pulling it from under the emerald helmet.

Hanson dropped his blade and frantically tried to adjust the mask, but his helmet's faceplate was in the way. He held his breath as he struggled to take off the helmet, granting Willodean precious moments to recover her wits and her strength. She hit him with a renewed torrent of energy that knocked him onto his back.

I scrambled onto my feet and grabbed one of the leaking canisters. It was surprisingly light for its size. I carried it over to Hanson and shoved the cracked part from where the gas was escaping as close to his face as I could. This was probably pointless—the room was filled with the gas by then—but it was the best idea I could think of, in the heat of the moment.

Hanson finally managed to free himself from his helmet, and I tackled him again, keeping the breathing mask from his reach. Unable to hold his breath any longer, Hanson gasped and coughed as his evil creation filled his lungs.

I knew from past experience that the effect of the gas wasn't instantaneous, but it seemed to be working pretty quickly on Hanson. Either they'd adjusted the formula, or the concentration in the canisters was really high, or the psychological effects of what was happening to him was getting to the pharma douche faster than its physical effects ever could. In any case, the outcome took him out of the fight.

Once his gifted gene became suppressed, the tens of millions of dollars' worth of Atlantean crystal he wore became no more effective than a Halloween costume. Without his enhanced abilities, his artifacts alone were no threat to a goddess. Hanson thrashed on the ground while Willodean recovered and then used her magic to pull chunks of his armor away from him. She did this methodically, as though stripping bark from a tree trunk, until no piece of crystal remained within his reach.

"You wanted me to die like a middling," Willodean rasped, standing over her fallen foe. "Turnabout is a bitch."

"I'll never become like you!" Hanson stared at her with pure hate in his eyes. Then he bit hard on something and convulsed.

"Was that a suicide pill?" I asked Willodean, drawing from my shallow pool of knowledge about spy movies. "He doesn't strike me as the type."

But, apparently, he was. In moments, he was foaming at the mouth. Willodean grabbed his temples in her palms and I was briefly confused, thinking she was trying to save him. Then I thought back to what she'd done with Clarissa and realized that she was attempting to read what remained of his mind.

After a few more involuntary convulsions, Marko Hanson lay still, his pharmaceutical empire literally burning around him.

"A bad death for a bad man," I said, because the moment felt in need of an epitaph.

Willodean let go of his head and stared at me, her eyes wide. "We were wrong," she said.

I blinked in confusion, and also because the gas was irritating my eyes.

"Hanson was nothing but a figurehead, a straw man," she said. "It was Vaughn all along. Vaughn is behind all of this!"

I cursed.

"South-side entrance of the building. He's being held there! Can you—?"

Before I finished the sentence, Willodean teleported us to where I had been stationed when the assault on the NAi compound began.

The two Irregulars I'd left behind were dead, lying in a pool of their own blood, their throats cut with something jagged. Vaughn was gone.

CHAPTER 22

WE held a council of war at the Watchtower. Mose took up an entire side of the conference table. To his right sat John and Terrie and Karl—Father Mancini and Gord had both been injured in the battle. They'd survive, but they weren't in the condition to be there that day. Across from the luminaries of the Watch sat Hercules Mulligan and two of his lieutenants. I had the opposite side of the table from Mose all to myself.

I recounted the fight between Willodean and Hanson, and the grisly scene we'd teleported to at the end.

"When we found them dead, Willodean went berserk. She swore to track down Vaughn and disappeared on me. Didn't even bother to teleport me. I had to ride the company bus back here, like a mundane."

"We've been receiving reports about Willodean from all over the city," said John. "She's poking at every wasp's nest of bad guys she can find. She may be looking for Vaughn, but after tonight, all the monsters that migrated to New York because it was a fertile feeding ground will either be dead or packing their bags while counting their blessings."

"You were exposed to a huge dose of the middling gas, Conrad," said Karl. "Should you be here, in the room with us? Without, you know, going through decontamination or quarantine?"

Terrie and the Irregulars all gave him withering looks, but the ex-prospect didn't flinch. He maintained eye contact and waited for me to respond.

"Gee, Karl, I'm doing fine after that ordeal, thank you for asking." I channeled as much sarcasm as I could muster into my voice. "If I feel a sudden urge to cough, I'll make sure not to turn in your direction."

"There has never been any evidence that the middling affliction is contagious," said Herc. "Pretending otherwise was one of the tactics Hanson ... I mean Vaughn, used to spread chaos and instigate anti-middling tendencies." He zeroed in on Karl. "By repeating their nonsense you're continuing to play into Vaughn's hands."

Karl opened his mouth to respond but Mose raised his meaty hand, forcing the newbie to swallow his rebuttal.

"We don't have time to bicker," said Mose. "We must restore order to the city. Figure out patrol patterns and lines of communication between the Watch and the Irregulars. John, Hercules, I trust you can work this out?" The two men had known and liked each other for a long time. There would be no egos getting in the way of them working together, and everyone at the table knew it. "Excellent. I'll leave you to it. Conrad, may I see you in my office?"

I followed him.

"We have to do something about Willodean," Mose said once I shut his office door behind me. "What's happening to her is exactly what I feared, what I warned you about. She's drowning in her own magic, and she doesn't have much time left."

I was going to point out that she'd saved all of our asses, but Mose knew that. He wasn't blaming me for the decision I'd made. Ever the pragmatist, he was seeking to handle the problem.

"What's going to happen to her?" I asked.

"Her mind is still mostly human and unprepared to deal with the power flowing through her. She might hold out a few more hours, another day maybe. Then her mind will shatter, but her body will go on, animated by malevolent death magic. By this time tomorrow she might level half the city."

"Well," I said. "That's ominous. How do we help her stay in control and rein the magic in?"

Mose gave me a long, appraising look, then he reached into one of the drawers in his desk and retrieved a blade. He placed it on the table in front of me. It was Hanson's kukri, the god-killer weapon.

"No way!" I said.

"You're the only one who stands a chance." Mose pushed the kukri across the desk toward me. "The only one who can get close to her before it's too late. While there's enough of Willodean left to recognize you."

I shuddered and took a step back as though the kukri were a venomous snake. "There must be another solution."

Mose stared at me again in that evaluating manner. "There is." He sighed. "You may not like it any better."

I stepped closer to the table. "Try me."

"There is a way for a god to use their power to neutralize the power of another god. Once they lock in, they just keep bleeding each other's strength until one of them reverts to a middling. They survive, but to someone who has experienced godhood that may be a fate worse than death."

"It's not a fate worse than getting your brain fried by your own overflowing magic," I said. "But then, where do we find another god on short notice? Do you think Dolus will finally show himself once Willodean starts bringing down skyscrapers?"

"No chance," said Mose. "Gods keep a low profile for a very good reason. There are celestials out there so old and powerful that the likes of Dolus or Willodean are mere ants by comparison. Those beings don't like the universal order dickered around with. Dolus has stirred enough trouble by manipulating you two into stealing the ambrosia that he'll probably have to lie low for a few decades."

"Dolus claims to be a part of a group of protector gods, kind of like the Watch," I said. "Don't you think our situation is the sort of problem they might tackle?"

"No," said Mose. "For them, there's nothing to be gained in this. If they wait a day, the situation will … sort itself out. Besides, a freshly minted goddess of death might already be more powerful than someone like Dolus. Even if he won, his power would be greatly diminished and he'd need many years to recover. He doesn't strike me as the sort to risk that. I think he and his pals will sit back and accept the collateral damage. And no other sensible god would get involved, for fear of losing or diminishing their own power."

I drank in all this new information. Interesting as it was, it didn't sound too useful. "To summarize, we have to find a nonsensible god, powerful and stupid enough to engage in a magic-measuring contest with a goddess of death gone mad. I don't think I can find that on Craigslist."

"We'll have to make our own," said Mose. He retrieved another object from inside his desk. It was an ampule filled with viscous liquid, glowing with an unmistakable shade of amber.

My eyes grew wide. "You have ambrosia?"

"It might be the world's only remaining portion. Then again, I never suspected the Traveling Fair had one either, so who knows. Point is, you can ascend if you choose to. Your mind is far better prepared to handle it, though there's still some risk—"

"Right. If godhood lasts more than four hours I'll need to consult my physician," I said. "Dolus explained this to me already."

My eyes never left the ampule. Here was the treasure worth the trouble and the expense our enemies had incurred. Vaughn must've wanted the ambrosia. It must've been why he'd released the affliction, why he'd chosen to inflict all this chaos and pain upon the Watch and the city it guarded. His plan only made sense if he were a natural middling, rather than a victim of his own bioweapon. I recalled Vaughn's willingness to expose himself to the gas when he'd first dosed Herc and myself with it. Yes, that had to be it! If someone like Vaughn had learned about the vial of ambrosia in Mose's possession, he would to go any lengths to obtain such a prize.

In a single chess move, Mose was not only taking his best shot at neutralizing a dangerous goddess but also getting rid of an item that painted a huge target on his own back. For all its incredible value, the vial wasn't of much use to Mose and the Watch, not that I could see. There was only one flaw in his plan.

"Hang on," I said. "What makes you think I'll be able to take down Willodean when I ascend? Dolus made it clear trickster gods are less powerful than gods of death, and perhaps most other gods."

"Here's the rub," said Mose. "You definitely won't. If you exhaust all your power, you may reduce hers to the levels where her brain can manage things for a time. And, if we're lucky, by the time her powers gradually ramp up again she will have learned to control them. It's the longest of long shots, Conrad. This," he pointed at the kukri, "remains my preferred solution."

I stared at the ambrosia. The power to ascend, to finally have magic of my own—better than that, to become more powerful than any gifted—was within my reach. I knew I couldn't deny it. The remaining question was, once I had it, could I make myself sacrifice it for a remote chance at saving someone I'd only known for a few short weeks?

I shoved the traitorous thought under the floorboards of my mind. "All right," I told Mose. "Lay it on me."

"One condition," he replied. "You take the blade with you. If the other way doesn't work, you may yet find the courage to do the right thing."

"Sure, Mose. If I'm going to ascend, I probably don't want to leave a god-slaying butcher knife in mortal hands, anyhow."

Mose handed over the ampule. I held it to the light and watched the liquid slosh lazily inside, like thin honey. Even having witnessed firsthand what had happened to Willodean it was difficult to accept that ingesting this stuff would give me superpowers. Of course, there was still a small chance it could outright kill me. In my quest to become a full-fledged gifted I've taken far greater risks.

I popped the ampule open and toasted my boss with it. "Cheers."

I felt like Alice in Wonderland as I drank its contents.

Describing apotheosis in mortal terms is as difficult as explaining a rainbow to a blind person. I could say that the world came into focus, as though I'd always needed glasses and, for the first time in my life, put a pair of them on. I could go on and on about my heightened senses—about being able to smell the coffee brewing on the floor above and hear the pigeons beating their wings even higher up, outside the building. I could recount ways in which I became aware of my own body. Without expanding conscious thought on doing so,

I healed scars from old injuries, mended a once-broken bone that hadn't healed quite right, and extinguished a handful of rebellious cells that could, decades later, possibly grow into tumors. But none of those descriptions and anecdotes would suffice. None of them could describe how I felt. To try would be akin to writing an operations manual where only poetry should suffice.

"How are you feeling?" asked Mose.

The sound of his voice broke my reverie, and I realized that while I thought it had lasted only a few seconds, I'd been out of it for more than an hour. It seemed Willodean wasn't the only one whose brain needed time to adjust.

"Better than ever." I looked up at Mose, noticing subtle things about his aura that I could never perceive before. "Wait …. You're a god, too?"

Mose smiled at the astounded look on my face. "A very minor deity, but yes. I'm the god of this nexus."

I could feel the raw magical power bubbling deep in the earth under the foundation of the building. It was a lake of primal magic trapped by the building above it like sparkling wine by a cork. From the cornerstone on up, the building channeled and contained the naturally occurring magic and bent it to the will of its overseer.

In the old days, most deities had been localized: a god of the river, a god of the largest tree in the forest, a god of the mountain …. They were called *genii loci* in Latin, "spirits of the place." Had Mose manipulated the Watch into serving as the guard dogs for his treasure trove, or had he been raised to godhood and appointed to the task by some ultrapowerful celestial?

Another thought occurred to me. "You were a middling once, too. And yet, you cast me away."

"I'm the guardian of this place. It is a grave responsibility, and it comes with impossible choices, just like being the head of the Watch."

A presence at the edge of my awareness distracted me from replying. I could sense Willodean's essence. She was a miniscule dot drowning within a whirlpool of magic. Her presence kept blinking in and out of existence, like an irregular heartbeat.

"I think I'd better go to her," I said. "As soon as I get a better grasp of my powers."

"Don't waste too much energy test-driving your new abilities," cautioned Mose. "The stronger you are when you confront Willodean, the more of her energy you'll be able to leech off."

"I need to get the feel for what I'm doing."

Mose frowned. "Hurry. She's deteriorating fast. And Conrad?" He nudged the kukri toward me. "Remember your promise."

I picked up the kukri. It had a weird feel to it—not quite an aura, but a wicked vibe of a sort I found difficult to describe. I just knew I didn't want to accidentally nick myself on that blade. I sheathed it and teleported toward Willodean, finding the task as easy as stepping through a door.

Willodean was somewhere in the Bronx, standing in the center of a playground that was fenced off and surrounded by residential buildings. It was a strip of land where city planners had also planted half a dozen trees and then called it a park. She was deliberately and steadily demolishing a handball wall. There wasn't much of it left but she kept firing energy bolts at the pile of cinder-block rubble that remained. A cloud of smoke and dust rose from the rubble. She may have selected her target at random, but I had to believe it was a choice. She could have just as easily been attacking a nearby building. A shred of her humanity survived, and she was trying to minimize the damage. For now.

I took a few steps toward her, but before I could call out her name she turned and unleashed a psychic attack I barely managed to block. Fighting against it was akin to holding back a river with a rusty bucket. She ceased the attack and stared at me with blank eyes. The heartbeat light within her detectable by my newfound powers went off again. I felt her arcane energies focus on me, like storm clouds gathering overhead.

"Oh, crap," I said, and 'ported away before she unloaded on me again.

I emerged at the Brooklyn Heights Promenade. The scenic spot, usually packed with people in the evening, was deserted due to the recent crime wave as well as our battle for the Watchtower, which the news people had billed as another terrorist attack in lower

Manhattan. I needed time to sort things out, so I stretched out on a bench and gazed at the gorgeous Manhattan skyline.

Whatever warning Mose had had to offer about the difference in our power levels, he'd undersold it big time. I had about as much of a chance in a direct confrontation with Willodean as a toddler had at defeating Mike Tyson in a prize fight. My only advantage had been stealth. I'd seamlessly picked up the camouflage trick from Mose when I saw him do it; it kept me hidden from the other gods. Willodean either didn't know how to do the same, or wouldn't bother. I could sense her 'porting around and each time she arrived at a new location she lit up on my mental map of the city like a Rockefeller Center Christmas tree. She also kept getting stronger. She gathered magic onto herself the way a hurricane moving across the Atlantic gathered water. The longer I waited, the less likely I was to make a serious dent in her power levels.

I was sorely tempted to walk away. I had more power than I'd ever dreamed of, and I felt better than I ever had in my life, both physically and mentally. Willodean was inevitably going to destroy herself, spend herself like that Atlantic storm front when it reached the shore.

Except there was no telling how many people would die and what path of destruction she'd leave behind before it was over.

I wished that Dolus would show himself and use some clever trick to power Willodean down. Or perhaps one of the enormously powerful celestials that Mose had warned me about might take pity on us and hand out a little divine intervention. Unfortunately, there was no indication that either of those eventualities was anything more than wishful thinking.

In the end, it came down to who I was. Was I still the sort of person who ran toward danger, who shielded others from harm, no matter the personal cost? Or was the ascended version of me something else? Had gaining a shred of power changed me, forced me to become a lesser person because now I had something of value, something worth hanging onto?

I thought of the millions of souls who were as helpless as an ant colony in Willodean's path. I thought of Mordecai, and Herc, and Terrie. They were people who'd showed me kindness, helped me, cared about me, called me a friend. No amount of power was worth half as much to me as their safety.

I would protect them, and I would save Willodean—again—if I could. And if I failed .... I wrapped my hand around the handle of the kukri. Mose was right; sometimes you couldn't avoid having to make the really tough decisions. Whatever the cost.

Slowly, I rose from the bench and stretched. I only had one chance to use up my power as a divine fire extinguisher, so I had to pray to a better god than I that my half-ass plan would work. I had some preparing to do. Then I would run toward danger one more time.

It was half past midnight and Brooklyn was burning. Hurricane Willodean floated above Bensonhurst.

I teleported to within a block of Willodean and watched as she soared high above blocks of four- and six-story apartment buildings. The goddess appeared ablaze, like a small sun. Her eyes were filled with amber light so radiant I couldn't look at them straight on. Below her, my borough suffered. In her wake lay a swath of houses with caved-in roofs, obliterated trees, and larger buildings with scorched walls and scattered fires consuming some of the apartments on the top floors. Willodean could no longer control her magic and avoid collateral damage.

The oracle's prophecy came unbidden into my mind. *Your future is fire. I see difficult decisions and you'll make the wrong ones. A flame wave will burn the buildings, char the churches, scorch the schools, and strafe the streets* .... Was this the moment she'd seen? Was I making the wrong decision? I clenched the smooth hilt of the kukri.

Screw you, Agnes. I make my own destiny. I waited until I could detect the tiniest glimmer of Willodean's essence within the goddess and teleported directly into the path of the most powerful being I'd ever encountered.

I appeared suspended in the air in front of her, wearing the Atlantean armor of her sworn enemy. I wore no helmet, hoping she'd recognize my face, gambling she wasn't so far gone as to assume

I was Hanson. Even so, it was about the most suicidal among the laundry list of suicidal things I'd ever done.

All her senses focused on me. Once again, I felt the terrible energies of the gathering magical storm. Before she could strike I shouted her name. Her *real* name. And when that made her hesitate I held up a small paper rectangle.

"Please!" I shouted over the howling wind and crackling fire that surrounded her. "I'm not your enemy. I want to help you."

The magic welled within her. The air around us crackled with electricity. Gusts of wind whipped at me and threatened to rip my secret weapon from my hand. Willodean screamed and unleashed a torrent of energy capable of obliterating me on contact. She aimed high and the massive bolt blew past my shoulder. Moments later an explosion boomed behind me. Windows shattered in the nearby buildings.

Having spent a shred of her magic, Willodean held back. I didn't dare waste a moment. I floated toward her until we were within an arm's reach of each other. I said her name again. "You must remember who you were. Who you *are.*" I handed her the creased photo I was holding. "This should help."

Two hours and twenty minutes earlier, my first stop had been the Watch armory. They had already collected Hanson's priceless armor and painstakingly put it back together. I would have expected no less from the Watch. But I also knew they'd still be cataloging and studying it before it disappeared into the well-warded vault.

I didn't bother asking the lone gifted who was studying the pieces' permission to borrow the armor. I didn't bother to explain that, if I was to syphon off sufficient power from Willodean I would need the amplification qualities of the Atlantean crystal. Instead I thumbed my nose at him, said "*Yoink!*" and disappeared along with the suit of armor and the table it had been laid out on.

I heroically resisted the temptation to 'port back for a moment, just to see the look on the poor schlub's face.

In need of a private, well-protected place to work, I teleported into Mordecai's showroom. There I painstakingly fitted the suit over the clothes I wore. It was too small on me, since it had been designed for the much-shorter Hanson, but I made it work. I tried a minor spell or two and was satisfied that Atlantean armor amplified god magic, though not to the same ridiculous degree as it had for the gifted.

I hesitated when it came to the helmet. While I wanted every bit of power, my plan relied on Willodean not blasting me into Kingdom Come before I had a chance to try anything. I left the priceless helmet, carved out of a solid chunk of Atlantean crystal and easily worth more than everything else in the shop combined, on the table along with a note:

> *Mordecai,*
>
> *Thank you for everything. Don't spend this all in one place.*
>
> —CONRAD.

I teleported to South Carolina next.

I'd admonished Willodean to tell no one, not even me, who she really was. But she'd let enough information slip that, given sufficient need, I could and would uncover her identity. I knew she'd been a kindergarten teacher and that Willodean had been her grandmother's name. I knew she'd had a fiancé named Greg, who had been killed the day she was abducted by the Traveling Fair. I knew roughly when that had happened, and it was only a matter of using an internet search engine rather than magic to find a Greg who'd been murdered in a home invasion, with his fiancée tragically missing. I found their home through property records. A single glance at the photos still hanging on its walls was all the confirmation I needed.

I handed Willodean a photo from that wall. It was a picture of her and Greg holding hands. They were smiling the big innocent smiles of people who didn't know about gods and monsters. Of people I didn't usually encounter in my line of work. Of people who were happy.

"This is who you are," I told Willodean. "You're not the kind of person who hurts people. That"—I pointed at the devastation behind her—"is not who you want to be. It's not who Greg would have wanted you to be."

She clutched the photo with both hands. Its edges began to burn. She stopped the flames and cooled her hands through visible effort. Her eyes lost the white-hot glow and a sizzling tear rolled down her ash-covered cheek.

"There is a way to come back. I can help you, but I'm not strong enough. We can only do this together."

She licked her cracked lips as she stared at the photo and mouthed a single word.

"How?"

"I can help syphon off enough of your magic that you'll be able to put a lid on the rest. But I need you to use up, or burn off or whatever, as much energy as you possibly can while I do it. We have to empty your reservoir faster than it can fill back up. Do you understand?"

I could see that she was fighting with all her might to remain coherent, to stay in control. We had to begin soon, but I needed her willing help. That was our only chance to make this work.

Willodean looked up from the photo she was still clutching for the briefest moment.

"Ready," she whispered.

"There." I pointed at the playground below us. Nice and abandoned at this time of night. "The handball wall, like you did in the Bronx. Hit it with everything you've got, and don't stop for a moment, no matter what."

Willodean took a deep breath and flared up like the Human Torch. The photo disintegrated in her hands, but neither of us permitted ourselves to dwell on it. She unleashed holy hell on the poor concrete wall, and I used every bit of my armor-amplified magic to neutralize hers.

We hung there for what felt like an eternity, each using every ounce of our willpowers to keep going. Between the crystal suit of armor and Willodean's cooperation, we were almost equals. For a second there I entertained the insane hope that I might actually outlast her. I might remain Conrad Brent, the Trickster God of

Brooklyn, while Willodean would go back to being a middling for a decade or so, until we could find her another dose of ambrosia, and everything would be right with the world.

The chunk of crystal wrapped around my forearm broke with a loud *crack*.

I glanced down and saw a spider web of cracks spreading through the chunks of crystal I wore. My armor was shattering from within, succumbing to the overbearing magical forces I was channeling through it.

I was so close! Willodean's flame was sputtering and dying down. I knew that if I could last another ten, twenty seconds, her divine energy would be completely exhausted.

Three seconds. Five. Seven. Pieces of armor broke off and rained down in a shower of green shards. Ten seconds. I put every ounce of magic I had remaining into one final push.

And then the world reset to the finite, human version of itself I'd known before I'd tasted ambrosia, and I was falling.

They say your life flashes before your eyes in the final moments before you die, but I'd already died once before, so I'd seen that movie and it wasn't captivating enough to watch the second time. I stared at the clouded sky above as I fell, and I felt strangely at peace. I had to believe I had drained enough magic from Willodean to save her. My suicide mission appeared to have been a complete success, including the suicide part. Willodean was in no condition to bring me back again.

Something held me fast, suspending me less than ten feet from the ground. The force that yanked me back knocked the air out of me, but it was nothing compared to what gravity had been going to do. They say it's not the fall that kills you; it's the sudden stop at the end. I floated the rest of the way down, light as a feather.

Above me, a large shadow flew across the sky.

As I lay spent on my back spent, I squinted, cursing at my fallible human eyesight, to try and sort out what was happening seventy feet above ground.

I saw Mose, God of the Nexus, come to finish what I had started.

The huge man landed on the edge of the roof of the building nearest to Willodean. He couldn't afford to waste an iota of magic and it had probably taken more than that to float his William How-ard Taft-esque girth.

Mose was a *genius loci*, a spirit of a specific place, and the lion's share of his power was tied into staying as close to that place as pos-sible. Here he was miles away from his nexus, taking on a goddess who possessed power far greater than his own. If he wasn't both lucky and careful, the Watch would lose two gods that night. The pragmatic, logical Mose was making a desperate gamble with his very divinity.

But he wasn't merely a minor godling. He was Mose, the im-placable leader of the Watch who had seen worse things and faced greater odds than anything even my considerable imagination could serve up. So he stood there, and he matched the goddess of death's power until the flames in her eyes had gone out completely and she, too, came tumbling out of the sky.

Mose slowed her fall the way he had mine. After she landed in my arms I watched him stumble and collapse to his hands and knees. I wanted to get up there to help him, but I couldn't leave the uncon-scious Willodean alone. By the time others of the Watch reached us and I pointed them toward the rooftop, Mose was long gone.

CHAPTER 23

TERRIE and I stood outside the Manhattan Municipal Building. Its entire façade was covered in scaffolding. A dozen union workers milled about on the sidewalk while a single guy in a hard hat intermittently drilled a hole in the ground.

"At this rate they'll finish the renovations by the end of never," I said.

"We caused half of that damage," Terrie pointed out. "In my book that means they can take as long as they want." She paused as the mating song of the industrial drill filled the air. When the construction worker stopped again, she asked, "How's Willodean doing?"

"That's not her name anymore," I said. "She's back home, recovering in a hospital. She doesn't remember anything that happened in the last couple of months. None of the magic, gods, or monsters. As far as she's concerned, she got knocked hard on the head during the home invasion where her fiancé tragically perished."

Terrie made a face. "That's a little too convenient, isn't it?"

"The initial amnesia was a natural side effect of the trauma her brain suffered after the ascension. I had a very talented mage ensure some of that memory loss became permanent."

234

"That is a horrible thing to do, Conrad. Who are you to make that decision for her?"

"I'm her friend, Terrie," I said softly. "I'm the closest thing to family she has in the world, and I make no apologies for choosing to protect her like this."

Terrie considered this. "You want to protect her from what she did."

"She killed a lot of people. It wasn't really her fault, but do you think she'd be able to sleep at night knowing the truth? Do you think she could live with herself?"

The buzzing of the drill interrupted our verbal sparring.

I'd told Terrie the truth about being a middling. Besides Mose, she was the only one at the Watch who now knew everything. I'd been terrified of her reaction, but it went well, considering. Terrie had been more curious than put off. She asked loads of questions and listened sympathetically as I kvetched about the struggles of being a middling and pretending to be a real boy. It was the ascension and my brief stint as a higher being that fascinated her. I described the experience as best I could.

"Do you miss it?" Terrie had asked. "Is it worse for you now, having tasted near omnipotence?"

I'd had some time to ponder that. Of course, I missed the rush of raw power and the feeling that anything I could conceive of was within my reach. But, strangely, the experience had made me more at peace with my affliction. I felt I was better off understanding both the cause and the potential of my condition than raging at the senseless cruelty of the unfeeling world.

On the following day, and inspired by my success with Willodean, I'd told Herc the truth, too. He listened to my story stonefaced, his expression gradually souring. When I finished, he said, "I wouldn't have cared for one second that you were a middling. You should've known that. I thought we were like brothers, and all this time you lied to me." I told him I was sorry, but the damage had been done, the cut of betrayal deep. "I don't know if I can ever forgive you," he said. "I sure as hell can't forgive you now. You should go." I went. His words hurt me more than losing divine powers, and I wasn't at all surprised by that.

When the drilling ceased again, Terrie said, "If it were me, I'd want to know. Promise you'd never do anything like that to me, no matter the circumstances."

"After this, I'm done lying to my friends," I said.

Terrie heard the hurt in my voice, so she dropped the subject. "We should go inside," she said. "Everyone else is probably here already."

We descended into the Watchtower where Father Mancini, Gord, John Smith, and Karl Mercado waited for us in the conference room.

"Mose is gone," Gord said with no preamble. "Many years ago, he disappeared for several decades. No one knows if he's alive or how long he may be gone this time. We need to elect a leader who'll run the Watch until he returns."

"I should think it an obvious choice," said Father Mancini. "Conrad went above and beyond, risking his life many times in order to save the city and this very organization, even after we falsely accused him and treated him in a way that makes me deeply ashamed."

I was shocked to see most of them nodding in agreement. But I also knew the rift between us hadn't fully healed. They were offering me the position because they felt they owed me, not because they thought me the best man for the job.

"I'm no leader, and I sure as hell am no bureaucrat. But I do agree with you, Father, that the choice is obvious." I pointed at John, dressed in one of his perfectly fitted suits. "John Smith has been Mose's right-hand man for years. We all trust and respect him, and none of us should have any trouble accepting his authority."

This second nomination was accepted unanimously.

"I suppose you'll be wanting your borough back," Karl said to me. In my absence, he had been appointed a temporary guardian of Brooklyn by the Watch. This was an obvious if rare oversight by Mose, and had only happened because the Watch had been under attack, overworked and understaffed at the time. "We may not always see eye to eye," Karl went on, "but you're a better man than I gave you credit for, and for that I owe you an apology. I'll stand down whenever you're ready."

"That's big of you," I said. "Especially since an even cushier vacancy just opened in Manhattan." Karl may have genuinely been extending an olive branch, but it was under the false impression that

I was an early victim of Vaughn's bioweapon and not a natural middling. I wondered how he'd feel about me if he knew the truth, but there were only so many heart-to-heart chats I could handle in so short a time.

"I'm sure John has somebody more qualified in mind," Karl said with false modesty. "Perhaps Hercules could be persuaded to rejoin the ranks?"

"Not happening," said Terrie. "You know we've asked. Repeatedly."

"I'm willing to give it a shot, Karl," said John. "But you must learn to respect your colleagues. The Watch isn't an organization that encourages office politics."

"It's an honor." Karl nodded somberly. "I won't disappoint you, John."

"You'd better not or your old berth at the nuthouse can be made available again," I mumbled under my breath.

"Conrad," John said with some steel in his voice. "My statement about respect goes both ways."

I was already regretting pushing for him to be leader.

After the meeting, I drove back to Brooklyn. I'd liberated my '84 Oldsmobile from the garage where the Watch had kept it. The car purred like a loyal pet reunited with its master. I parked next to my Sheepshead Bay home and knocked on my landlord's door.

"*Seichas*," came the voice from the second floor, followed by footsteps. Sasha, a Russian man in his late sixties, dressed in an Adidas track suit, appeared in the doorway.

"Conrad!" He slapped me on the shoulder. "Is good to see you!"

"I came to apologize about the trouble earlier," I said. "About those people coming to take my stuff. I wanted to let you know that the misunderstanding got sorted out. I have my job back, and everything. I was hoping to move my things back in, but if you'd rather I found another place to live, I completely understand."

Sasha walked outside and beckoned for me to follow. He popped the garage open, revealing some of my furniture.

"I did not know if they will come back, so I hid for you," he said. "In communist country is dangerous to trust wrong person. You tell wrong person political joke or take bribe from him, he report on you. To survive, you must learn to tell right person from wrong person." Sasha looked me in the eye. "You are right person. You can live here again if you want."

"Thanks, Sasha. I really appreciate that."

"You get car and apartment back, but you lose something," said Sasha. He sounded earnest.

"What do you mean?"

"I mean, where is girl?"

Willodean. A pang of pain jolted through me whenever I thought of her.

"You're right, Sasha. I lost something important. She's not ever coming back."

"Is too bad," said Sasha. "She was right person, too. I liked her. Don't worry, you will find another girl sometime, yes?"

"For sure," I told him.

"I help you move furniture back in when you want." Sasha took a yard sign from the garage and used an old dumbbell to hammer it into the ground toward the front of his lawn.

"What's this?" I asked.

The sign read HOLCOMB in huge gold letters surrounded by blue stars and red stripes.

"You don't hear? Bradley Holcomb is running for mayor." Sasha tested the sign to make sure it was firmly planted into the dirt. "He is smart rich businessman, will make good mayor. He promise to stop criminals and clean down city. You vote for him, *da?*"

I mumbled something noncommittal, excused myself, and entered my apartment for the first time in weeks.

It was good to be home, yet it didn't feel quite right. I'd met gods and monsters, made new friends and lost old ones, ascended and died, but now I was a middling again, back within these familiar walls, restored to my old job and old life. It felt anticlimactic somehow. Having briefly been elevated from a pawn to a rook in the never-ending chess game of life, I was having a difficult time with the prospect of returning to obscurity.

My phone rang.

"This is Daniel Chulsky," a clipped, cultured voice spoke at the other end of the line. "I'm following up on our conversation back in my office. About some freelance work. Are you available next week?"

"I might be." I stared out the window at the peaceful, ordinary, boring block outside. A weekend's rest was probably all I could handle before rolling up my sleeves and getting my hands dirty again. "What would you like me to do?"

"If it isn't too much of an inconvenience," said the CEO of Abaddon, Inc., "I'd like you to save the world."

9 781647 100544